"The H...
history,...
—*RT Book R...*

Praise for Mary Wine's hot historical romances

"Sizzles with passion and romance...a notch above other Highlands historicals."

—*Publishers Weekly*

"Impossible to put down...one of the genre's finest Scottish-set romance writers."

—*RT Book Reviews*, 4.5 Stars, Top Pick

"As usual for Ms. Wine, historical facts are masterfully woven into her story, giving it authenticity seldom found in historical romances...a must-read."

—*Night Owl Reviews*, Top Pick

"An absolute delight! You will forever be astounded as well as gratified by reading Mary Wine's Highlander series. Scottish Medieval fans are sure to be in awe."

—*My Book Addiction and More*

"Entertaining and engrossing...Mary Wine weaves a tapestry of a tale with adrenaline-pumping action, sweet and spicy love scenes, a touch of humor, and a twist and turn here and there."

—*Long and Short Reviews*

ALSO BY MARY WINE

One

Gordon land

THEY WERE WAITING FOR HIM TO BLESS THE MEAL.

He was laird, and it was his place to begin the evening supper with a prayer. Somehow, in all the times his mother had spoken of that moment with longing in her eyes, she had never mentioned to him just how much it would remind him of facing down his enemies.

More than one man was giving him a glare that made it plain they felt they were as entitled to the position at the high table as Diocail was.

Diocail Gordon eyed the bread his staff delivered, and hesitated. It was misshapen, and when he did grasp it, his fingers sank in because it was wet, the top part soaked with water as though it had been sitting out in the rain. He cleared his throat and said the prayer before ripping the bread to indicate everyone might eat.

The hall was only half full, which surprised him. The laird provided supper for his retainers, yet it

appeared a good number of them were choosing to find their meals elsewhere. The clumps of wet bread glued to his fingertips might be one reason—if a man had a wife to turn him better bread—but that didn't account for the number of retainers missing.

Diocail sat down and watched, seeking more clues. Maids were entering the hall now, and they carried several large trays toward his table. While the bread might have been lacking, these platters were full of roasted meats that looked very good to his eyes. It was a bounty to be sure, and his predecessor's captains began to help themselves.

Along the table that sat on the high ground were men who had served Colum, the last laird of the Gordons. Diocail had given them all a chance to challenge him, and none had. Instead, they maintained their high positions. At the moment, that entitled them to a good supper, served in front of the rest of the clan to make their position clear. There wasn't an empty chair, and each man had a gilly behind him to take care of his needs. Some of the older captains had two young men standing at the ready, which made Diocail narrow his eyes. When a man was young, he often became a gilly to learn focus, but there was a gleam in these young men's eyes that didn't make sense.

Diocail didn't suffer in ignorance for long.

Supper began to make its way into the hall, but it was far from sufficient. Men fought over what was brought, elbowing each other as they grabbed it from maids, who tossed their trays down because of the fray, afraid to get too close to the tables. There were clear pockets of friends who clustered together to

defend whatever they had managed to grab from the frightened kitchen staff. Any man who tried to break into their ranks was tossed aside like a runt.

Diocail never started eating. He watched the squabbling and then realized exactly why his men were fighting when no more food came from the kitchen. Whatever a man had managed to grab was all there was, and the lucky ones devoured their fare quickly before someone else managed to rip it from their grasp.

"Colum was a miser," Muir told him. Diocail's newly appointed captain was making a face as he tried to chew the bread. "Dismissed the Head of House in favor of one who would be willing to serve less food without complaint. There is nary a rabbit within a mile of this keep because so many take to hunting to fill their bellies."

Muir was disgusted too, looking at the piece of meat in his hands as though the taste had gone sour. Diocail realized it was because a young boy was looking at it as well, his eyes glistening with hunger. Muir lifted the food toward the boy, and the lad scampered up the three steps to the high ground to snatch it.

"Even though I am no' in the habit of questioning the Lord's will," Muir growled out between them, "I confess, I wonder why that man was graced with such a long life when he sat at this table feasting while his own men starved."

"It makes me see why no one else was willing to defend him," Diocail answered. "Seems it was justice that saw him stabbed in his own bedchamber."

"A justice ye did yer best to shield him from." Muir sent him a hard look.

"He was me laird," Diocail answered. "A man I had sworn to protect. His lack of character did no' release me from the bonds of honor. Yet I confess, I am grateful I lost that battle, and I am no' sorry to say so. The bastard needed to die for what he's allowed the Gordons to become."

"Aye," Muir agreed, looking out at the hall once more. There was now a cluster of children in front of the high table, all silently begging for scraps. All of them were thin, telling him that they weren't just intent on being gluttons.

No, they were starving.

And that was a shame.

A shame on the Gordon name and Diocail's duty to rectify. He waved them forward. They came in a stumbling stampede, muttering words of gratitude as they reached for the platter sitting in front of him and Muir.

The platter was picked clean in moments.

Diocail stood up. The hall quieted as his men turned to listen to him. "I will address the shortage of food."

A cheer went up as Diocail made his way down the steps from the high ground and into the kitchen. Muir fell into step beside him. The kitchen was down a passageway and built alongside the hall. Inside, the kitchen was a smoke-filled hell that made Diocail's eyes smart and the back of his throat itch. He fought the urge to cough and hack. It was hardly the way to begin a conversation with his staff.

"The weather is fine and warm," he declared. "Open the shutters."

Instead of acting, all the women working at the long tables stood frozen, staring at him. Their faces were covered in soot from the conditions of the kitchen. Many of them had fabric wrapped around their heads, covering every last hair in an effort to keep the smoke from it. Muir opened a set of doors to try and clear the air. Diocail looked at the hearths and realized the smoke wasn't rising up the chimneys. No, it was pouring into the kitchen, and the closed shutters kept it there.

The staff suddenly scurried into a line to face him. They lined up shoulder to shoulder, looking at the ground, their hands worrying the folds of their stained skirts.

"Where is the Head of House?" he asked softly. It was God's truth that he'd rather face twenty men alone than the line of quivering females who clearly thought he was there to chastise them.

Colum had truly been a bastard of a laird. He'd made his people suffer when the true duty of the laird was to serve the clan.

One of the women lifted her hand and pointed. Diocail peered through the clearing gloom and spotted the Head of House. She was seventy years old if she was a day. Whoever she was, she was deep in her cups and sitting in a chair on the far side of the kitchen as she sang and swayed.

"Sweet Christ, little wonder the supper is a poor one," Muir remarked next to Diocail's ear.

"Who is her second in charge?"

The women continued to look at the floor. Two of them were beginning to whimper. Muir took a step

back, but Diocail reached out and grabbed the man's kilt. "Do nae ye dare leave me here alone," he muttered under his breath.

"Someone must be making decisions," Diocail said as gently as he could in an effort to coax one of the women forward. What did he know of speaking to frightened females? Two more started crying, proving his knowledge was extremely lacking. Their tears left smears down their cheeks.

"Mercy, Laird," a younger woman wailed. "I need me position. I swear, I will serve less, *please* do nae dismiss me."

The entire group suddenly dissolved into desperate pleading. They came toward him, backing him and Muir up against the wall as they begged him not to send them away.

Diocail had never been so terrified in his life.

"No one is being dismissed." Diocail raised his voice above the wailing.

It quieted them for the most part, which allowed him to see that a good number of his retainers had made their way into the kitchen after him. Those men were now glaring at him, making it plain that these were their wives or women and they didn't take kindly to him upsetting them.

Diocail looked at the woman who had spoken. "Mistress?"

"Eachna." She lowered herself but looked up at him, proving she had a solid spine, and while there was a worried glitter in her eyes, there was also a flash of temper that made it clear she thought his visit was long overdue.

Christ, he'd only been back at the castle for two days.

But he'd known that taking the lairdship meant his shoulders were going to feel the weight of the burden that went along with the position. He intended to rise to meet it.

He gestured for her to straighten, and the rest of the women suddenly lowered themselves.

"Enough of that." Diocail felt Muir hit him in the middle of his back because his voice had gained a frustrated edge. Diocail drew in a deep breath and regretted it as his lungs burned.

"I am here to resolve the issue of supper, no' have ye all quivering. So…" He resisted the urge to run his hand down his face in exasperation. "If ye might explain the lack of food? There was no' enough served, and I would see the men satisfied."

He looked to Eachna, and her companions seemed quite willing to allow her to be the target of his inquiry. They shifted away from her, proving Colum had dealt harshly with his staff.

Not that such was a surprise. The old laird had been a bitter man who died with hatred in his eyes while his blood drained out of his body from stab wounds inflicted by a man hungry to take the lairdship before time claimed Colum's life. Being killed by one of his own clansmen seemed to be something he'd earned through neglect.

"The last laird decreed it so," Eachna answered after she took a shaky breath. "The shutters are kept closed to reduce how much wood is needed to keep the hearth fire burning."

He gestured to the women watching him. "And this is the extent of the staff?"

"She dismissed half of us to save the coin." Eachna pointed at the besotted Head of House. The woman was still happily singing in a voice that lacked both tone and rhythm. So soaked in ale, she hadn't noticed anything happening around her.

Diocail lost the battle to keep from rubbing his forehead. Eachna's eyes widened, but she stiffened her back and remained facing him.

"Double the fare ye put forth. And hire ten more women to help ye here. Someone take that woman to her home." He pointed at the Head of House. "She'll be provided for."

Eachna's eyes widened. "But we have only one hearth because the chimney fell on the other, and the roof leaks." She pointed at the shimmer on one of the long tables from fresh rain that made the wet bread understandable. "And the wall fell off the back of the storerooms two winters past—"

"Ye're on yer own," Muir muttered.

Diocail sent the man a glare. "In that case, ye can look at the storerooms and decide what needs doing."

His captain tugged on the corner of his bonnet before all but running out of the kitchen as though he'd faced demons straight from hell.

At least the smoke was thinning thanks to the door being open. His eyes were still burning, but Eachna sent him a look that made it clear she wanted him to suffer the conditions she did. He cleared his throat. "I've no experience in running a kitchen, mistress. Perhaps ye might speak yer mind."

Something flashed through her eyes that impressed him because she was no meek maid. No, there was a sharp wit inside her head. He watched her fix him with a hard look before she began her questions.

"How much fare do ye want on the tables, and how much do I pay each new girl, and—"

His head was pounding. Diocail suddenly understood why the Head of House was in her cups. He needed a drink rather badly himself.

What bothered him was how none of the men clustered in the doorways seemed to be taking notes of the repairs needed. Instead, they simply looked to him to right matters.

"Whatever ye are paid…increase it a third…for all here…" There was a happy little murmur around him. "And hire whomever ye feel is fit. We'll begin there while I see to the repairs needed."

Eachna snapped her mouth shut and nodded. Diocail reached up and tugged on the corner of his bonnet out of habit before making a quick path toward the door.

Escaping the kitchen didn't offer him any relief. His captains were waiting for him in the passageway. Each had a list of needs that took until nearly midnight to be heard. It was Muir who finally appeared with a flask of whisky and a sack that Diocail truly hoped held something to fill his belly.

"Sweet Christ, I should have let Tyree have this lairdship," Diocail said as he took a second, longer swig. Tyree had been the man to try his hand at killing Colum, and in the end he'd succeeded in spite of Diocail's attempts to protect his laird.

"He was a murdering swine," Muir declared as he reached for the flask. "So I'm rather grateful ye did nae allow him his way in murdering Colum and laying the blame for the crime on ye."

"Grateful enough to help me bring order to this madness?" Diocail asked pointedly.

Muir offered him a chunk of bread from the sack. It was rough fare, but they were accustomed to it from the years they had lived in the far north. Muir was more than a captain; he was his friend. Diocail smiled as Muir withdrew a thick slice of cheese and broke it in half. They chewed in silence for a moment before Muir answered.

"When it comes to the retainers and stables, aye. As for the running of the kitchen…" Muir cast a hopeless look toward it. "What ye need is a wife…but no' just any woman will do."

"Aye." Diocail tipped the flask up again. "Eachna is a fine girl, but she has no' been taught how to run a large house."

They both fell silent again as they consumed more of the food and faced a topic neither had any experience with. Not many a man did. It was why men wed, and women too, because together a man and woman might combine their knowledge to make a successful home. He'd been taught the logistics of defense and negotiation needed to foster relationships with other lairds.

But how much fare to put on the tables?

He had no idea or even how to go about making sure there were ample hands to prepare the food. Diocail felt his brain throbbing as he contemplated all

the things needed to run a kitchen, and those were only what he knew about. What truly nauseated him was that he knew damned well how lacking his knowledge was. He knew how many men to ride out with, how many horses, and his education included how many blacksmiths it took to make sure those horses were shoed, how many stable lads it took to make certain those animals were fit to ride, how much feed and what sort was needed to maintain a horse's strength.

A hundred details, and a kitchen was no different. No wise man made the mistake of thinking it an easy thing to keep running smoothly. Their current circumstances were proof of that surely enough.

"Ye need a wife, one raised with the education to see this place set right. No' that any decent girl would have this house as it is," Muir added. "Try to contract one, and she'll run home to her father the moment she sees the condition this castle is in. But ye need one. A wife, that is."

"I hoped to have a bit of time before getting down to that part of being laird," Diocail groused.

"Best set yer secretary to sorting through the offers in Colum's study." Muir didn't offer him any respite.

"Do nae hold out any hope," Diocail replied. "There is a decade of letters sitting there. Any offers are long past their time of opportunity."

His new lairdship was proving to be far more challenging than he'd ever thought it might be. Somehow, in all the times his mother had spoken to him of the day he'd take over the Gordon clan as laird, she had never mentioned just how complicated the duty

was. There was building to consider, horses, men, training—and the list went on. All things he'd been taught as a man.

Now there was the kitchen, and God only knew what else went along with running one smoothly.

Well, not God.

He let out a grunt. Here was something he knew less about than the Lord above.

Women.

And, more precisely, a lady and the duties she would have been trained to do.

There were reasons a laird wed a woman from a highborn family, and one was that she would come with an education as diverse as any given to a laird's son. Running a kitchen was more than turning bread; it was knowing how much bread to set out to rise in the morning so that the supper table was full and how much grain was needed to make it through the winter and how many hands were needed to produce it all. His head began to ache. He didn't know what went into bread, much less how much was needed to see an entire castle through a day, but as laird, his duty was to make certain the tables were laid with fare.

Nor did he know anything at all about helping a lady settle into the place he hoped she'd make into a home. Muir was correct; she would run back to her father before sunup.

Diocail took another swig of the whisky, wishing it would dull his senses, but all it did was warm him enough to make him conscious of the draft coming through the holes in the roof. He tipped his head back and discovered stars peeking at him where tiles were

missing, likely from the winter storms. Colum was a bastard for leaving his people to such circumstances.

Laird of the Gordons. Diocail's mother's dream.

And his nightmare, it would seem.

&

It was cold.

Of course, she'd expected it to be so, standing in nothing but a shift in the street.

"Ye're contemplating yer options now." Gillanders chuckled at her plight and rocked back on his heels. "Ye keep thinking because it's going to take a bit of work on yer part to soothe me injured pride. Rejecting me offer so quick as ye did, now that was nae wise on yer part. No' with yer husband dead and ye without a single penny to yer name and the gambling debts he left as well to be accounting for. Lucky ye were that I made ye an offer at all instead of tossing ye into the gutter. Ye were quick to lift yer English nose, but that will nae keep ye from freezing, now will it? Aye, me pride is wounded. Deep. It will nae be soothed...easily."

The pudgy innkeeper leered at her. Expectation glittered in his eyes, and his meaning was clear to anyone watching. He wanted her to prostitute herself. His gaze swept her from head to toe as he all but licked his lips over the treat he intended to make of her.

She would not bend. Not now, not even if she died in a thicket from the Scottish chill.

So what if the villain had stripped her down to her chemise and left her standing in the street outside the Hawk's Head Tavern, where her husband had so

foolishly gambled the night before being killed by the men he'd been unable to pay and leaving her to face his debts? It wasn't as if there had been any affection between her and Henry.

She scoffed a bit as she caught sight of Gillanders's wife watching from inside the tavern with a pinched look on her face that revealed how little liking she had for her own spouse.

Marriage was a business, and that was simply that. Men sought brides who would bring them connections in business, and fathers looked for men who they felt would ensure their wives didn't starve.

Henry had failed rather completely when it came to his part of the marriage bargain. The truth was she'd loathed him and was going to enjoy telling her father every last detail.

At least that thought sparked a fire in her belly.

Temper is a sin.

Well, so was turning her out, so Jane decided to embrace the flicker of heat and sent the innkeeper a narrow-eyed look. "I wish you good luck in soothing your pride, sir." Jane held her head steady and ignored the way the wind cut easily through her smock. "For I will not invest any effort to please you. Pride is a sin after all, and as you have pointed out, my kin have already left you with enough burdens."

People were watching, and some even appeared moved by her plight, but her English accent proved to be a deterrent none of them seemed willing to challenge.

Gillanders's eyes narrowed. "Ye will change yer mind."

He was a very fat man.

Jane used the thought to brighten her spirits as she

turned her back on him and started to walk away from the boardinghouse he ran.

Although it would be more correct to say that he shouted at his wife and daughters and nieces while they performed all the work for not a single word of praise. He was fat on excess and laziness, and the man knew well how to feed those traits of his personality. Travelers were best to be wary of him, for he plied them with wine and then took them for every last coin they had.

Of course, he wanted something altogether different from her.

He wouldn't be getting it.

Even if her husband had promised it to him once his coin ran out and his need to gamble persisted with the aid of the drink Gillanders used to ply him.

No, she would not turn whore to settle her husband's gaming losses. There were limits to a wife's obedience, she had decided. By Christ there were, and she didn't care a bit for anyone who disagreed with her. And she wouldn't be sorry for the fact that Henry had been beaten to death by those he'd tried to cheat the night before.

All right, perhaps she was a bit…well…touched by the idea that he was dead, yet only so far as feeling remorse toward a wasted life. Henry had hidden his laziness from her father, convincing them all that he delivered wine to Scotland because the dangerous duty came with the promise of higher pay for the entire family business.

In truth, Henry had enjoyed being able to gamble and drink to excess while away from anyone who

might report his lapse in moral conduct. Henry had hidden his vices well, and her father would not be making another match for her so quickly once she made it back to England.

At least she hoped not, and she refused to allow herself to doubt because she needed her hope to keep moving as good wives going about their days stopped and stared at her indecent lack of clothing.

Well, that wasn't her shame, it was Gillanders's, and part of her enjoyed knowing that she'd had the strength to deny him the pleasure of breaking her.

Maybe later she'd regret it.

Not now.

No, she couldn't be weak.

So she walked on bare feet. Turned out in her shift, every last possession she owned taken because Gillanders considered it his right. She walked through the small village, refusing to look at the spot where her husband's blood stained the ground. Henry had never been a wise man, but she wondered what possessed him to wander outside the inn in the dead of night in Scotland. It had been a foolish action that he'd warned her against. Perhaps Gillanders might have interceded, in the interest of gaining what he believed was owed to him, but no one inside the inn had heard the fight.

That much she believed, because a dead man couldn't write to his father and beg coin to settle a debt.

She stepped on a sharp rock, and that was the end of her concern for her late husband. The only way she was going to survive was to use all of her wits for herself. Even then, she doubted she'd make it back to

her father's home in England before the weather took her life.

Well, she would bloody well try to best the odds. They had never been in her favor anyway. Born a fourth daughter as her mother tried to produce a son, her fortune had ever been a poor one. Which accounted for the choice of her husband. A third son of a wine merchant who was tasked with the duty of delivering orders into Scotland, Henry had seen her pretty face as a means to ease the costs of traveling. She'd seen him for the scheming lackwit he was.

Men might enjoy flirting, but when it came to business, they all wanted the most gain. Gillanders was certainly a fine example.

Well, she would not give him what he craved from her. Perhaps she might die in the wilds of Scotland, but she would not become a whore.

Even if she'd found marriage to be so very similar that she could barely tell the difference.

Well, now she was a widow.

✖

"Ye could send someone else to collect rent."

Diocail sent his captain a pleading look.

Muir chuckled as he checked the strap on his saddle. "Tired of playing laird already?"

"Another day of sitting at that high table, and I will be drooling like a daft man," Diocail confessed. He patted his stallion's neck. "It's a fine time to go out and meet me tenants. Once the snow flies, I will have ample time to deal with more troubles here. For the moment, repairs are beginning. A few months and

we'll have a better idea of what to focus on next, and I'd rather show me face and quell the gossip."

"Aye," Muir agreed. "There will be many who will enjoy ye making the rounds. News tends to get muddled as it travels. I'll no' be surprised to hear that it's being told ye had Colum drawn and quartered in the yard so as to take the lairdship."

"He'd have deserved it for the ruin he's allowed to befall this castle." Diocail cast a look at the twin keeps of Gordon Castle. His mother had raised him to be its laird, but she'd also run for the north country when someone had tried to poison her, taking him along with her as a babe on her breast.

Colum Gordon had held the lairdship with an iron fist, and his sister's bairn hadn't been a welcome rival to his own children. Fate had decided that Colum would outlive all of his sons. Diocail didn't think it was by chance either. No, men reaped what they sowed, and Colum had died knowing that his sister's child was his only heir. It was his due for the selfish way he'd ruled. Instead of applying himself to the duty of being laird, he'd taken the deference of his people and given nothing in return.

However, that left Diocail with the duty of being laird, a true laird, who improved his land and eased his people's burden. None of the Gordons expected it of him because they had never seen any better laird than Colum.

That fact filled him with determination. By Christ's nightshirt, there was a great deal to do, and he was going to rise to the challenge.

His uncle's senior captain looked down on him

from the top of the steps. Sorley had happily passed on the duty of riding with the new laird in favor of overseeing construction. The castle was in poor repair because Colum had focused all his energy into hatred after his son Lye Rob was killed, and the condition of the stronghold reflected his inattention. The roof in the kitchen was only the beginning. Walls were crumbling, the wells were insufficient for the needs of the castle, the stable was a damn drafty place that wasn't fit for man or beast, and the list went on. Under Colum's rule, riding out to raid had been a priority, not keeping up the castle.

One thing Colum had done was make certain there was money in the coffers. The old man had been a miser, hoarding all manner of things he demanded as tribute from his tenants.

The truth was Diocail just might face an angry mob when he left the castle due to the amount of coin Colum had squeezed from his tenants. The Gordon people felt oppressed, and that fact was supported by all the plunder amassed in the upper rooms of the keeps. Diocail checked the last of his gear and felt his determination tighten.

Perhaps it had been his mother's dream that he claim the Gordon lairdship, but he was planning to make it his legacy, so he'd be facing every tenant and making certain each one learned that he was a fair man.

He looked back at Sorley. Well, once the autumn had passed, Diocail would return to doing his best to right the conditions of the castle.

"I'll make good use of the time ye are away,"

Sorley claimed. "Going to finish the roof on the kitchen first."

"Dry bread on the table when we return," Muir declared. "We'll no' know what to do with that."

Diocail mounted, his horse shifting from side to side in excitement. Sorley offered him a solid nod. "Do nae worry, Laird, we'll be welcoming ye back when ye finish."

There was a glimmer of respect in Sorley's eyes that Diocail hadn't seen before. Considering there were still a few cousins who considered their own blood a claim to the lairdship, Diocail found it a welcome sight indeed. "Do nae spare the coin. Buy what ye need, pay enough men to see the kitchen in good order before the snow flies."

Sorley reached up and tugged on his bonnet, two other captains stepping behind him to show they supported Diocail's claim to the lairdship. The yard behind him was full of Gordons. They stood watching and listening while keeping their expressions tight.

Not that Diocail blamed them. Respect was earned. At least, that was the way he wanted to come by keeping the position of laird.

"When we get back, ye can get on with choosing a bride," Muir taunted from the back of his own horse.

Diocail shot Muir a sour look. "I bring a lass here as it is, and she'll run straight back to her father."

Yet the very real fact was that the clan expected him to wed.

And soon.

First the tenants. He raised his hand, and his men followed him out of the gates. It was just past first

light, and people were starting to bring in the harvest. They rode at a slow pace due to the wagons needed. More than one family paid its rent in goods. It was a time-honored tradition, one he wouldn't change. He shied away from thinking about the very real dilemma of putting those goods to use. There was another thing a true mistress of a large house was educated in: how to utilize the goods that came her way in order to gain what she needed to run the house.

Damned if he had any notion as to how to begin sorting the goods abovestairs or even who among his staff were due what for their loyalties. There were those among his retainers who likely harbored resentment because of what they had been denied in the way of comforts such as shoes or new shirts. He didn't have the knowledge, only the experience of having seen his aunt presiding over quarterly meetings where she handed out such things to her own household.

Yes, he needed a wife. A lady for the clan.

He might well have to resort to raiding to get one of quality though. It was enough to make his shoulders tighten until they ached.

One task at a time, boyo…

Men looked up and tugged on the corners of their bonnets when he passed. There was a gentler mood on Gordon land these days. Diocail enjoyed seeing more smiles and children. As Colum had descended deeper into his cups and hatred, mothers had started to hide their children when he passed, fearing he might lash out at them.

Now, they played openly, their mothers watching him from their windows. Diocail rode out of the

village and into the open, ready to prove himself worthy.

Very ready indeed. The challenges might be many, but he'd face them.

After all, he was laird of the Gordons, and he would not be shaming his mother's faith in him.

❧

Jane's belly rumbled.

She'd ignored it for a day, but by the next morning, she simply could not any longer. Not that it changed her mind. She wasn't returning to Gillanders and his offer to be his harlot in exchange for her keep.

Curse Henry for his gambling.

Jane regretted the thought. She knew it was unkind to think ill of the dead. Her body might ache, but she wasn't yet ready to regret the fact that she was still drawing breath. Life might be difficult, but it was still to be treasured. She stepped on a rock and winced as she moved toward the sound of water. It was only a temporary solution, but she cupped her hand and drank until she felt some measure of relief.

She straightened, looking at the water and seeking any sign of fish. Desperation was beginning to claw at her. The chill from the night lingered in her joints, and the water wasn't very satisfying.

No, I am not going back to the boardinghouse…

However, that meant she very well might die in the wilds of Scotland.

At least her situation made for a good tale. A hint of adventure—wasn't that what her stepmother had gleefully informed her would be her lot when

she'd decreed that Jane would wed Henry with his determination to travel into Scotland when it was so very risky?

Oh yes. How grand Jane's life had been with Alicia. Her stepmother had taken her husband's house in hand and made it plain that Jane and her sisters would obey her. Not that such an attitude was uncommon. Still, the happy home she'd enjoyed with her mother had vanished within months of her father taking a second wife. Of course, her father had never noticed because Alicia made certain her husband was very comfortable indeed. Complaints to her father had met with his confidence in his new wife's ability to raise his daughters into women who could run their own households.

Jane was bitter and not one bit interested in being repentant about it. What had all of her obedience to Christian values and duties gotten her? A husband who raised his hand to her, gambling away every coin and then going so far as to promise her favors to settle his unpaid debts.

Turned out in her shift.

Indeed I was.

And still, she preferred it.

Her belly rumbled again. It hurt now, the hunger.

Well, life had not been comfortable for her for many years, so there was no reason to think today would be different. There was, however, a very real satisfaction in rising to meet the challenges as they came her way. If that was pride, so be it.

She looked back at the water and moved a bit farther upstream as she watched for signs of life. The

water was tumbling out of a pool, and a fish slithered down the fall.

She blinked, thinking she'd imagined it. No, there was a plop as another fish swam too close to where the rocks gave way, and she realized someone had piled up rocks to make a dam of sorts.

Of course!

It made sense. She looked around, making sure no one was about before she pulled her smock over her head. Without a net or basket at hand, the cloth was all she had. Once wet, it would bring her even more suffering, but if sacrificing her comfort helped her fill her belly, she would take the shivers. She moved into the stream and held the ends of her garment under the water. Her belly twisted with hunger, her mouth beginning to water while she waited. Time seemed to slow down, tormenting her as she tried to maintain her confidence while ignoring how cold the water was around her bare feet.

At last there was another plop, and suddenly there was a fish flopping on the surface of her wet smock. She jumped with surprise, and the fish went sailing right out of her grasp. She whirled around, desperate to catch it. The sun shone off its body as it flailed and fought to buck itself back into the deeper part of the stream. Jane fought just as hard to reach the fish, skinning her knee as she landed next to it and clamped her hands around it.

Victory surged through her when she held it high. She carried it farther onto the bank and then struggled back into her wet smock. The fabric stuck to her body, but she smiled as she retreated into the forest in search of a way to cook her catch.

"Ye do nae have a knife."

Jane froze, looking up from her fish to see who her company was. She let out a sigh of relief when she realized it was a boy, a rather small one who looked up at her from where he was crouched next to a rabbit snare. His face reflected his disappointment over finding the snare empty. He looked at her fish, longing in his young eyes.

"The fish are too big for me to catch," he muttered. "Give me that one, and I'll let ye use me knife when ye get another for yerself."

He couldn't have been more than six or seven winters, but it was clear his life was as challenging as hers. He was thin, his face drawn with hunger. He held out his hands for the fish, aiming a smile at her as he tried to bargain.

"I know how to gut it and put it over a fire," he tempted her.

Fire...

"Can you start a fire?" she asked.

He was wearing only a shirt and a belt that held his knife. His feet were blackened from having no shoes.

"I can get a coal from the house," he assured her quickly. "But I can nae go home to me ma without something to eat. I am the man of the house now."

His eyes returned to the fish in her hands. "That's a fine, big fish, and there are plenty more."

Trusting him was a risk, but one she had to take unless she planned to eat her fish raw with her teeth. And a fire would warm her and help dry her shift. She hated that she was desperate enough to resort to such behavior. At least Fate was offering her another solution. Yet it would not come without a price. Handing

over the fish took a great deal of effort. She watched the way his face lit up.

"I'll be back," he promised. "I'm going to give this to me mother and bring back a coal from the hearth like I promised."

God, she hoped so.

He ran away from her, the fish in his hands, as she fought off tears to see it leaving.

Nonsense, she chided herself. *It will be a good bargain.*

At least it would be as soon as she caught another fish. Fate seemed to be in the mood to reward her because she watched another fat fish tumble down the rocks while she was getting out of her smock. This time, she was ready when a fish appeared on the fabric, clamping it against her chest and moving out of the water without tossing it into the air. Satisfaction filled her as she clothed herself once more and started to climb back up to where she'd met the boy. The truth was she wanted to catch more, but she had to quell that urge, for doing so would be a waste.

A thin taper of smoke beckoned to her. The sight of the boy leaning over a small pile of sticks made her tremble.

"Mother was very pleased." He reached out for the fish. "Asked me how I managed it without a fish basket." He started gutting the fish as he spoke, the fire popping as it caught. "I told her it was on the bank." He offered her the cleaned fish on a long stick. "I know it's wrong to lie."

"Well," Jane began as she placed the stick over the rocks the boy had used to ring the fire. "I was on the bank with the fish."

His lips twitched. "Ye are poorer than we are, I think. Ye do nae have even a knife."

"Yes," she agreed, warming her fingers over the fire. "My husband gambled while drinking and lost everything."

The boy watched her for a moment before he nodded. "We made a good bargain."

"Indeed," she answered.

He cocked his head to one side. "Are ye English?" Jane smiled. "Yes."

"Where are ye going?"

"Home," she said with less enthusiasm than she might have wished for.

He seemed confused by her response. "But… England is that way." He pointed behind her with a grubby finger.

Her victory over catching the fish died. "I see."

He opened his mouth to speak, showing off a gap in the front of his mouth where two teeth were missing. "I did nae think there was anyone with less than us."

He flashed her a grin before he turned and ran off. The scent of the fish cooking was a comfort but not enough to dispel the gloom from her thoughts. She tried to focus on the warmth from the fire. At last her fingers weren't frozen and the fish was cooking slowly, promising her relief from her hunger.

Perhaps she was only prolonging her agony.

Well, wasn't that life, after all? Each day a battle against all the things that might befall her? Perhaps she was in Scotland, in her shift, yet had that truly altered her circumstances?

Not by much.

Her stepmother's face kept her company as she ate the fish. Alicia was the mother of sons, so Jane's father had given her full run of the house and his daughters. Jane had thought her life hard then. She stretched out her foot and looked at her bare toes. At least she had had shoes.

It seemed she was being given a lesson in being grateful for what she had. Now, all that remained was to see if she survived the learning process. Alicia had often spoken of the way she managed the house as a kindness because she was making Jane and her sisters strong enough to face life as women. Perhaps there was truth in that sentiment, for somehow Jane had managed to reject Gillanders's offer. No one came into life with strength; it had to be earned, forged.

Perhaps Alicia was more of a friend than a miser. The very fact that her stepmother had not pampered her seemed to be some sort of gift that Jane had been too ignorant to understand the value of until today. Now when she needed her resolve, Jane discovered it firmly rooted in her because of the way Alicia had insisted she learn to make due and find her own solutions to life's demands.

Leaving the fire took effort, but the sun was climbing higher, and Jane had ground to cover. Her hands smelled of fish, and the scent gave her quite a bit of satisfaction.

Gillanders could choke on his offer.

And as for Alicia? Well, Jane would thank her just as soon as she made it back to England and her family. Love, it would seem, might be shown in many ways, teaching her to be strong among them. Her

stepmother had taught her to be a woman, which, it seemed, was far more important than years of bruised childhood feelings.

❧

"Laird."

Another tenant tugged on the corner of his bonnet as he placed his rent on the small table Lachie had brought. The man was a fine secretary, or at least he was learning. Diocail stood beside the table, greeting each tenant. He looked down and pushed two of the silver coins back toward the man.

"Laird?"

"I know what the MacPhersons pay, and Gordons will nae be giving more," Diocail responded loudly enough for the other men who were waiting to hear. "There will be fairness on Gordon land so long as I am yer laird."

The tenant was quick to take the coins back, reaching inside his jerkin to push them deep into a pocket. The man smiled and happily knelt to pledge himself to Diocail as laird of the Gordons. Diocail watched as the scowls eased from the faces of those waiting to see him. The level of resentment dissipated as his tenants offered him a grudging respect.

Well, their regard would take time to grow.

Later that night, once the business was finished, Diocail took a moment to sit. His men were roasting a few rabbits that had been given as rent, their conversation scarlet since they were well away from womenfolk.

He chuckled at one tale. The village they were visiting didn't have an inn, just a rather crude tavern.

Many tenants who had come to pay their rent were camped nearby. The scent of their fires mixed as the evening breeze blew through, hinting at winter.

"Get your hands off of me!"

His men went silent, their jovial mood changing in an instant.

There was a sound of flesh hitting flesh and the sharp intake of breath from a female.

"Damned English bitch," came a sharp reprimand. "Think ye're too good for the likes of me? We'll be seeing about that…"

A woman stumbled close enough to the light of the fire for Diocail to see her. Not that it was hard when all she wore was a linen smock splattered with dirt. The firelight shone right through the undergarment. In spite of her indecent condition, she faced off with the man bearing down on her, baring her teeth as she held up a thick stick.

"Try it and die," she snarled at her attacker.

Diocail watched the way she lifted the branch high, ready to wield it like a club. Her would-be companion stumbled from the thicket she'd been in, staggering just a bit to betray how much whisky he'd had.

"Would ye rather freeze?" he demanded of her as he eyed her stance and weapon. "Why? Ye're no virgin. A wee tumble is all I'm looking for. I'll share me supper and fire with ye once ye ease the stiffness of me cock."

"I am not a whore."

But she was English. Her accent was as clear as the moon in the sky.

"Ye're on Gordon land, English bitch."

"Which makes her my concern," Diocail interrupted.

The woman had been focused on the man chasing her. She jumped when Diocail spoke, whirling around to look at him. She masked her fear well, tightening her grip on her weapon as she tried to keep both him and her first attacker in her sights.

She had courage, he'd grant her that.

Even if it was foolish at the moment.

"Now why would ye be interfering in me fun?" the man demanded of Diocail. "Caught her sleeping on our land. That makes her a prize. Mine."

"Yet ye have no' caught her, and now she is mine."

Diocail slid between her and the man, glad to see his men had joined him. There was a sound from the woman, muffled as Muir clamped his hand over her mouth.

The man didn't care for Diocail's opinion on the matter. His eyes narrowed as he snarled. Diocail reached into his doublet and withdrew a silver piece.

"Let us be agreed." Diocail shook the coin so that the firelight caught on it. He watched as the man shifted his attention to the money, the glitter of lust in his eyes dying down. "Go find yerself more welcoming company, man." He tossed the coin toward him.

The man caught the coin, turning it over a few times before holding it in his hand and trying to judge the weight. There was another sound from behind Diocail and then a grunt as one of his men misjudged the tenacity of the female. Whoever he was, there was a squeak from the woman as he applied enough strength to keep her still.

"Aye," the man in front of Diocail said as he tucked

the coin into his sporran. "But I think ye might be regretting paying so much for her. Cold English bitch will nae thank ye."

He spat on the ground and sent a hard look toward the woman before he turned and left. Diocail waited until the sound of the man's feet crunching the undergrowth faded before he turned to consider their newest companion.

Niven had his arms wrapped around her, one of his huge hands clapped over her lips. She glared at Diocail as he looked at her.

"Forgive me, mistress," Diocail stated firmly. "Did ye wish me no' to interfere then? I rather thought the way ye were threatening to hit him with that branch suggested ye were no' very keen about accepting his offer. Of course, if I was wrong…"

Some of his men chuckled.

She blinked, clearly thinking the matter through. He watched her relax and shake her head.

"Let her go."

She stepped away from Niven, casting a nervous look at the other men. Some of them couldn't keep themselves from appraising her from head to toe. Diocail admitted fighting the urge himself. The fire cast enough light on her to make it plain she was a fetching female beneath her smock.

But she was not a whore, and he'd not gawk at her. No, her courage deserved more respect than that.

True to what he suspected of her, she drew herself up, set her chin, and looked him in the eye as though she stood there with a hundred men at her back to protect her. "You have my sincere gratitude, sir."

"What are ye doing on me land?" He made his voice as gentle as possible. Now that he was closer, he saw the evidence of Fate turning ugly against her. Her toes were bleeding along with her knee. Her fine porcelain skin and high cheekbones were crisscrossed with tiny scrapes and cuts from the thicket, and there were deep circles under her eyes from lack of sleep.

She was hungry too.

Starving.

He could see the way she fought to lick her lips now that she was close enough to smell the roasting rabbit from their fire.

And courage. She had an abundance of it, which Diocail respected because the only way to cultivate it was to face hardship.

"Who turned ye out in yer shift, lass?" Muir asked as she remained unwilling to share the details of her plight.

She cut Muir a quick glance but returned her attention to Diocail. "Does it truly matter how I came to be here?"

Perhaps asking a question wasn't very wise. Jane really didn't know the answer herself. Every inch of her body seemed to hurt, and she was once again so hungry her head was reeling. The scent of the fish was gone from her fingers now, yet she'd found herself sniffing them in some vain attempt to satisfy her empty belly.

Right then, the scent of roasting meat was the only thing she could concentrate on. In some corner of her mind, she realized being distracted was a grave error. The man in front of her was huge. She'd rarely seen his match. He was a mountain of pure muscle with

bulky shoulders and wrists she doubted she could close
her hand around. He was dressed in a kilt and doublet,
but he had the sleeves open and hooked behind his
back, his shirtsleeves pushed up to bare his forearms as
though he didn't feel the chill of the night air.

She, on the other hand, was shivering as the cold
licked her skin and cut through her smock.

"I suppose it does nae," he answered her, tilting
his head to one side as he contemplated her. He kept
his attention on her face, resisting the urge to look
down her body. Most of his men didn't afford her
the same respect.

What do you expect, Jane? You are nearly naked.

And starving. But Fate had delivered her here when
she least expected it, so she wouldn't allow herself to
crumble beneath the weight of her circumstances.

One dilemma at a time.

"Thank you for your assistance." She drew in a deep
breath and started to walk back toward the thicket.

"Stay where ye are, woman."

If she hadn't realized he was in command of the
men before, the tone of his voice would have driven
that fact home. He was accustomed to being obeyed.
When he turned his head slightly, she caught sight
of his bonnet. Three feathers were secured to the
side, all of them raised. She'd been in Scotland long
enough to know they were the mark of a laird.

"As you have noted, I have naught, so I cannot
repay you except with my gratitude." She spoke
evenly and with the poise that living beneath her
stepmother's iron rule had bred. "I have a great deal of
ground to cover and must be on my way."

"Where are ye going like that?" the man next to her demanded.

A quick look toward him, and she noticed that one of his feathers was raised. That made him a captain of some sort.

"Back to England and my father's house," she answered, trying not to sound as defeated by that prospect as she felt. There was no alternative, so no use dreading what had to be. "Since I am widowed."

The men ringing her suddenly nodded, some muttering that her situation made sense. Their stances eased now that they could understand her appearance. The harsh truth was that more than one woman had been turned out in her shift when her husband was no longer alive to protect her from his family. Such was the fate of many a bride who wed against the wishes of the groom's family. Without children or contract or powerful relatives, everything she had might be claimed as dowry and kept while she was discarded.

Tossed into the gutter…

She started to step around the man in front of her, and he shook his head. "I told ye to stay where ye are, lass."

He was tempering his tone now, making her feel much like a mare being gentled. His words set off a shiver down her spine. There was something so very strong about him. It was more than his muscle; it was the way he watched her, the set of his jaw as he contemplated her.

"And I have told you I must be on my way." A man such as he understood strength, so she would meet his determination measure for measure. "Excuse me."

She made it a few steps past him, just enough for her to feel a breath of relief moving through her, before he swept her right off her feet. She gasped and choked as he tossed her up and over his shoulder. But her face nearly caught fire with shame when he slapped one of his hands down on her bottom to keep her in place as he walked back toward their camp.

"You cannot—"

He was dumping her onto the ground before she finished protesting. At the last moment, he controlled her descent and she landed with only a jolt instead of the hard impact she'd been expecting. She ended up looking at him from where he'd deposited her on her backside.

"Ye'll be staying with us, mistress. Best set yer mind to it, for I've no wish to fight with ye."

"I will do no such thing." She stood but stepped back when one of her knees tried to collapse. She pushed her foot into the ground to steady herself and faced off with her tormentor. "You have no right to lay hands on me."

"I am Diocail Gordon." He didn't move back an inch, which meant they were a single step from one another, and she had to tip her head back to maintain eye contact. "And ye are on me land."

"Which I will be most happy to leave," she insisted firmly.

"The last thing I need is an Englishwoman raped on me land," he answered her. "I do nae know who yer husband was, but it's a good thing the man is dead because I'm of the mind to break his fool neck for wedding ye and leaving ye in such circumstances."

His words shamed her with how kind they truly were, although gallant was more fitting once she thought it through. He was rough and hardened and so completely suited to his environment that she found herself admiring him. However, the observation revealed how very far from home she was.

"Your intentions do you much credit, Sir Diocail," she said sweetly. "Yet I cannot stay in this company."

"I am no knight. Ye're in the Highlands, lass, and I am sorry to say I can nae afford ye any better circumstances than being in the company of me men. For the moment, it will be better than yon thicket and the men who have grudges against the English. Which they will have few reservations against settling at yer expense."

His captain slid up close to her, making her shift away. He offered her a harassed look before tossing something at her. She caught it, simply out of reflex, trembling when she realized it was a thick traveling cloak.

The scratchy wool was more dear than the finest silk. She was shaking with the anticipation of being wrapped inside it.

Diocail nodded in approval toward his man. "Put that on and sit down, mistress. I'll decide how to deal with ye in the morning. For now, me men and I are going to enjoy our supper. Kindly do nae make it necessary for one of us to hand-feed ye like a babe because we have to tie ye up so we can enjoy our meal."

"You would not dare," Jane exclaimed.

She realized her error immediately. This man lived for challenges.

Diocail Gordon's lips twitched, curling up on one side into what might have been a grin if there was

anything remotely attractive about the motion. No, it was menacing and too full of promise for her to dismiss. She wanted to think she might argue but knew without a doubt it was a useless fight that would cost her the advantage of being free.

And they were going to feed her and warm her.

Beggars simply couldn't be choosers.

Well, better a beggar than a whore.

She opened the cloak and swung it around her shoulders. Made for a man, it hung down to her ankles, and she had to gather it close to her body. Diocail watched her, daring her to defy him. There was something in his gaze that hinted that he enjoyed the way she hesitated before sitting down, but the hard set to his jaw confirmed just how good he'd make on his threat to restrain her if she tried him.

Of course, with his men watching, she couldn't really blame him. So she sat down and heard his men mutter with approval. The master of the house was never going to back down in front of his men, doubly so considering she was a woman and English. She would simply have to choose the time better if she wanted to prevail.

But she would be leaving, and Diocail Gordon would be the one adjusting to her way of thinking. By dawn, he'd agree with her anyway. It was simply the way life was. A person had to work hard to make sure their loved ones were provided for. That left little charity for strangers. Tonight, Diocail might be able to afford to be generous, and it was her good fortune, to be sure.

However, the men serving him wouldn't agree to

let her share their food when she brought nothing with her. No goods, money, or alliance. The meat they allowed her to eat had been brought to the fire through their effort, earned, and therefore their right to enjoy. They were loyal to Diocail because there was strength in numbers.

Tomorrow she'd leave. Return to her father's house where she had a family to help protect her. Alicia might insist she wed again, but even that prospect, however distasteful, paled against remaining in Scotland while England was ever willing to declare war against its neighbor.

An Englishwoman in Scotland. It would be a far better-sounding tale than the reality of it was proving to be.

❧

"Untie her without a dagger in hand to defend yerself, and ye're going to be meat for the hounds. That female is so angry, I think she might bash yer skull with a rock."

Diocail offered Muir a grin. "I gathered that all on me own."

Behind them, their guest was snarling through the gag Niven had reluctantly tied around her head.

"And I'm no' so sure binding her hands in front of her was wise," Muir continued. "She has more spirit than I thought to find in an Englishwoman."

Diocail sent Muir a deadly look. His captain wasn't a bit repentant, grinning back at him before he reached down and patted his crotch in sympathy for the knee their unhappy guest had shoved into Diocail's privates.

"A lucky shot," Diocail assured him. "She only landed it because I really did nae want to truss her up."

"Why did ye?" Muir asked, revealing what was really on his mind. "We certainly do nae need another unhappy woman in our midst. There is a kitchen full of them back at home, in case ye've forgotten."

Diocail sent him a glare. "Ye'd have me allow her to leave in her shift? Think me that sort of a monster? Simply to let her walk into a harsh fate brought on by her circumstances? Clearly her husband was a fool and a bastard for no' making sure she had a place."

Muir looked at the ground out of shame. "Aye, ye have the right of it, and offering her our protection— that's the honorable thing to do. But why tie her up?"

Diocail let out a stiff breath. It betrayed how frustrated he was. He didn't care a bit for how doing the right thing was making him feel. "Because she's a decent woman. Highborn, educated."

Muir nodded. "That's obvious in her bearing and speech."

"So, a woman such as that," Diocail explained, more than a little exasperated with the circumstances, "well, she can no' accept being in our company. It's no' proper to her way of thinking—a bunch of soldiers and no female chaperone. It's no' acceptable. But I can nae let her walk off into the thicket to be preyed upon and call meself an honorable man."

Muir was shaking his head by the time Diocail finished. "Aye, ye're right. I ken that now."

"Good, because I was no' jesting about no' need-ing a dead Englishwoman on our land. The Earl of Morton might be out of the regency now, but the

young king James is set to inherit England's crown. So me guess is he'll no' be wanting trouble between his two countries."

"Such as a nobleman's daughter found dead on Scottish soil," Muir finished.

"Aye."

"So what do ye plan to do with her?" Muir asked.

"I'll decide tomorrow," Diocail replied. "For now, let's get what sleep we might. She may be snarling, but she needs rest more than we do by the look of those circles beneath her eyes."

Although he doubted he was going to get very much sleep himself. Whoever their guest was, she was as foolish as she was spirited. Insisting on going on her way in nothing but a shift. Damned if he didn't enjoy knowing she was so brazen.

And color him foolish for enjoying what would surely get her rolled into a grave on the side of the road after some man with a grudge against her blood used her flesh to satisfy his vengeance. The world was a dark, harsh place at times.

But she knew that, or at least she'd tasted it recently. Her body bore the marks of her trials, and still she boldly refused to take his protection. It was admirable, stoking something in him that he'd not encountered in connection to a woman before.

He'd come across unbridled females before. His own mother had been one and proud of her ways. Whoever this lady was, she wasn't thumbing her nose at her place out of a need to rebel. No, it was far different from that. She had stiffened her spine and squared her shoulders to face what Fate had

thrust upon her. Perhaps she had brought it upon herself by running away to wed the man of her heart. Even still, he admired the way she took her due. And that only made him wish he'd never set eyes upon her.

He had enough people looking to him for solutions. Between his mother's dreams for him and the condition of his inheritance, the last thing he needed was a female who would have to be watched for her own good.

Diocail chuckled.

He and the woman had a great deal in common, it seemed, but he doubted she'd thank him for pointing it out to her. Which was exactly why he was enjoying the thought of doing just that.

❦

They were watching her.

Jane rubbed her wrists and tried to appear as though she was content in her circumstances, or at least submissive to their greater strength.

Well, your belly is full…

On that account, she could not harbor any ill thoughts against the Gordons surrounding her. Not even for the ache left behind from the rope they had bound her with. It hurt far less than her hunger had the night before.

"Take yer ease and return." Diocail surprised her by speaking to her. "If ye make me track ye down, I'll tie ye up again. That's a promise I do nae fancy making good on, lass."

"Why do you persist in this?" She climbed to her

feet and drew in a stiff breath as pain went shooting through her battered soles. With her hunger satisfied, it seemed the rest of her body was going to make its complaints known.

Loudly so.

"I've explained me reasoning." He aimed a hard look at her. In the light of day, she realized he had warm brown eyes. "I understand yer need to argue, mistress. Any decent woman would. We're a rough lot, no' suitable company without a companion for ye."

"And yet you deny me freedom when you know I must seek it?"

His expression remained unmoved. "I am laird of the Gordon. A dead Englishwoman of noble background—by yer speech and bearing—is the sort of trouble we do nae need. Protecting me clan will come before yer sensibilities. If an ill fate befalls ye, I will be called on to account for it to the king. Me men will no' harm ye. Best ye stay with us."

It was his solemn word on the matter. She didn't know very much about him, but he was an honorable man. Even if he was everything she'd been raised to think of as savage. The very sight of him was straight out of a winter fireside tale constructed to titillate with fear of the Highlanders. He'd pleated up his plaid and secured it around his waist with a thick leather belt. His doublet was of recognizable design, but it was also thick, rustic wool, and he had the sleeves tied back once again, making it plain that the chill of the morning wasn't something he considered cold.

He was a creature of strength who inspired awe

in her because of the sheer magnitude of his ability to survive in his climate. She was huddled inside the cloak, still feeling the bite of the morning air through its folds.

"Go on with ye, mistress." He'd lowered his voice, granting her some consideration for the delicate nature of the conversation. "Do nae test me, for I have no wish to put rough hands upon ye."

It was a warning, clear and firm. His expression made it plain that he wouldn't hesitate to make good on his words, and the memory of him tossing her over his shoulder was very fresh. She hobbled when she walked, her feet paining her more than she'd ever thought possible.

So much so that she sat on a rock once she'd seen to her more pressing needs and looked at the bottom of one foot. The sight was daunting. She had three large blisters, caked with dirt and red now. One was oozing, warning her infection was sure to set in if she didn't tend to the wound. As well as stay off the foot.

"How long have ye been turned out?"

"Jesus!" She jumped and muffled a curse when she landed on her feet and the blisters sent pain up her legs so acute, her knees threatened to buckle. "How do you walk so silently?"

"It keeps me breathing, lass," Diocail proclaimed with a touch of arrogance. "And makes hunting a bit more rewarding. Rabbits enjoy life as much as we do and tend to bolt if they hear me coming."

His pride was not bluster, but earned. For some reason, she decided that it enhanced his appeal.

Savage?

Yes, he was that. Yet there was more, far more than she'd ever stopped to consider might be beneath the label handed out to his kind.

"There's some water heating over the fire," he continued. "Do ye know anything of cleaning wounds?"

"Yes, of course."

He lifted one dark eyebrow. "No' many have the skill of a healer."

"I am not a physician," she explained. "I assure you, Laird Gordon, I was raised well."

"So why did yer family wed ye to a man who allowed ye to fall into such circumstances?" he demanded.

"I am a fourth daughter." She didn't owe him an explanation, but something in his tone made her answer him. She sensed a core of solid responsibility she realized had been lacking in her late husband.

Diocail frowned. "That's no reason."

"Henry was far better at acting the good suitor than he was at being a husband, and there was no finer offer."

"A father's duty is to make sure he does nae wed his daughter to a man who dupes him," Diocail responded. "Did ye nae suspect?"

It was a good question, and she had resisted thinking too long upon it during the few months of her marriage. No good would come of such thoughts, after all. The vows had been spoken and consummated, so wallowing in regrets seemed a poor choice when all it might do was make her miserable.

"Scotland's daughters decide whom they wed

then?" she inquired in a tone that made it clear she knew it wasn't so. "Do they boldly argue against their fathers' decisions?"

Diocail wasn't intimidated by her sarcasm. "I wonder if ye ran off with the man of yer choice." His eyes glittered with something that sent a shiver down her spine. "Ye're bold enough."

She shouldn't have enjoyed how much she liked knowing he thought of her that way.

Yet she did.

"See me as rebellious because I wanted to leave your company?" she asked.

He shook his head. "Nay. That proved to me ye are a quality woman."

He was a man who didn't hand out false flattery. His words warmed her and took her by surprise. She started to walk back toward the fire, simply because she felt far too much was on display beneath his keen stare. Every step hurt. She tried to keep her gait easy but winced when she stepped on a rock in just the wrong place. There was a snort behind her before she was once again swept up against Diocail Gordon's wide chest.

"Oh, do put me down." She detested the fact that it was necessary to plead with him. However, when it came to strength, he had an abundance of it. She wasn't used to feeling small. Her stepmother had often pointed out how unfashionably tall she was, and yet Diocail dwarfed her.

"Quiet, woman." He delivered her to a rock near the campfire. "I ken ye do nae have it in yer nature to whine, and I am grateful for that. But I

do nae need ye burning with fever while we're on the road. So ye'll stay off these feet until I can get ye some shoes."

"You may leave me right here, sir, and I assure you I will do very well."

Niven brought over a large bowl and placed it on the ground by her feet. The Gordon retainer sent her a look that made it clear he thought she was daft. Heat teased her cheeks because she knew he was very correct.

Yet it was only right to argue against being with them. She detested the fact that life was so very difficult at times.

Diocail walked to the wagon and pulled something from it. He returned and offered it to her. His expression was unreadable, and she caught glimpses of his men all slowing in their work to watch what she made of the parcel.

A test then…

What she held was a medical kit of sorts. She had to untie it. When she rolled it across her lap, there were pockets with bottles and all sorts of things needed for the treatment of wounds. She pulled some loose until she found what she needed.

Cleaning her own feet was another matter though. She might dip her feet into the bowl, but tending her own soles would be awkward. Diocail settled the matter by sitting down at her feet.

"Tell me what needs doing."

Her voice was a squeak, but she rattled off the instructions as his men found reasons to come closer. Controlling the urge to wince took precedence

though, as she gritted her teeth and wiped the few tears that escaped her eyes.

"Thank you."

"Ye can show yer gratitude by no' making a fuss." He scooped her off the rock and carried her toward the wagon. Someone had cleared a space, even spread out a thick sheepskin with the fleece facing down to cushion the ride. Diocail placed her on it and slid the tailgate of the wagon into place before securing it with a thick iron rod. "I've business to attend to, and it will be a difficulty if me tenants see ye trussed up like a pig on the way to market. So kindly do nae make it necessary. Ye'd be foolish to try to walk on those feet or in yer shift."

She would be.

And yet her pride stung almost as much as her feet while she sat there. Diocail Gordon let out a whistle, which called his men to order. They mounted in smooth motions that betrayed their strength and command of the beasts they rode.

Savages.

And yet the men had a majestic beauty. So adept in their environment. They neither appeared to be suffering hardships nor were burdened by their Highland home. They were jovial indeed as they set out. Diocail led them from the back of a black stallion. The wagon jolted down the road as the sun rose higher in the sky.

She'd really be a wretched creature to cause trouble today.

You are making excuses…

It was a solid truth, and yet she could not deny

that her feet were not as thick as her will. For the moment, she would have to accept the hospitality of the Gordons.

Yet again, she seemed to have no other choice.

Curse Fate. She was a true shrew.

Two

By NOON, JANE WAS READY TO WALK IN SPITE OF THE blisters on her feet. Never had she sat so many hours idle, simply wasting the daylight. It was a sin.

Sloth...

However, she was more concerned with the threat to her sanity, feeling sure she would go daft long before any true threat to her immortal soul took hold.

They'd reached a village, and Diocail was being greeted by his tenants. They lined up, some with goods and even livestock to offer as payment for their rent. They also took the time to swear their fealty to the new laird of the Gordons.

She sat through it all. Gratefully.

Still, by midday, she was ready to strike out and resume her journey. More than one person cast a curious look her way. Jane could hardly blame them. She could only imagine how she looked huddled beneath the cloak. Without a comb, her hair must be an unruly mop, and she doubted there was a clean patch of skin on her face after a week of walking through the wilds of Scotland. As the day warmed, the cloak became too

heavy. She shrugged it off and then regretted doing so when more than one woman's eyes rounded with alarm as she hurried her children away.

Diocail turned to discover the cause of the commotion. Heat teased her cheeks when she realized she'd interrupted him. It was his captain Muir who came over to deal with her.

"I didn't mean to draw attention to myself." Honestly, they had insisted she stay with them, so in truth, she didn't owe them an apology. Unless she was being realistic and honest about how much she needed their help.

Muir wasn't nearly as cross with her as she'd expected. The captain eyed her for a long moment before he ambled off. His sword was strapped to his back, his kilt swinging behind him as he went. He wore boots that had rows of antler-horn buttons running up the sides to his knees. Any Englishman would have called them rough, but she noted they were likely very warm and waterproof.

Something well suited to Scotland. Her own shoes had left her toes frozen for a good portion of the day, but she preferred them to bare feet, and that was a fact. Still, she admired the sturdy boots.

Muir disappeared and then came back into sight. He'd pulled something from the first wagon and offered it to her.

"It's a length of wool, naught more, mistress." He spoke in a voice kind enough if a bit uncertain. He had a dark beard kept better than she'd have expected, and he looked at her with a pair of blue eyes. "I thought ye might…" He made a

motion with his hand. "Fashion it around yerself somehow…"

He lowered his gaze to where her breasts were and turned red, looking away when he realized what he was doing. He cleared his throat. "Forgive me, lass…mistress. I've no' known many women of… yer station."

He seemed unable to stand still in his agitation. "Ye'll be needing a belt."

Muir latched onto that as a means of escape and nearly ran away. Jane took the time to consider the fabric he'd given her. It was a fine piece of wool in a light mulberry hue. She pulled it through her fingers and draped it around her shoulders so that it dropped down her front. Muir appeared again, relieved to discover her more clothed.

"Aye, no' too bad at that." He dropped a belt over the tailgate of the wagon. She pulled it around her waist and buckled it to hold the wool in place, working at the fabric to move it around her body and form a rather rough sort of skirt. Muir surprised her by remaining where he was and nodding when she finished.

"The cloak was too warm," she offered by way of explanation.

Understanding dawned on him, and he nodded again before cocking his head to one side and looking as though he was judging her. Something was on his mind, and she waited for him to decide whether to voice it.

"I was wondering—" He stopped, clearly waiting to see what she made of his comment.

"Yes?" The truth was her day had been so boring she couldn't curb her curiosity.

"Me laird thinks ye are a woman of some education. In womanly arts."

"I suppose so," she answered. "My stepmother insisted on devotion to my studies and the skills of housewifery."

The first hint of a glimmer entered his eyes. "Can ye sew shirts?"

The eagerness in his tone befitted a boy more than a huge, burly Highlander. It brought a smile to her lips and made her realize how long it had been since she'd been charmed by something simple.

"Mind ye," Muir was quick to add. "I know that, well, making shirts is a...private thing...between man and wife. But seeing as how ye are widowed—"

"I would be happy not to waste the daylight," Jane assured him.

Muir's lips curved into a wide smile. He held up a finger before disappearing once more. This time when he came back into view, he looked at his comrades before he turned to face her and pulled a bundle from the front of his doublet.

"Ye see, I'd nae ask, except for...I had a friend who promised me a new shirt. Her being a widow, it was no' a difficulty...and I always brought her some linen for her own use." Muir pushed a leather-covered bundle over the tailgate. It fell into her lap with a little plop. "However, seems she wed again this last year and, well, has her hands full with the two young lads her husband brought to the marriage for her to mother. Sorry she was to disappoint me, and I do nae wish to burden ye."

His face was flushed once more due to the nature of the topic. Shirts were an intimacy because they lay against the skin. Tailors made them only for the elite, and the rest of the population had to either wed or hope one of their female relations would gift them with one. Sewing was one of those refined skills that fathers often listed among their daughters' attributes when negotiating wedding contracts.

It was a skill she might trade for her supper and gladly so. "I sit here doing nothing," Jane told him, eager to have something of worth to offer.

Muir flashed her a smile before he reached up and tugged on the corner of his cap. "Just ask if ye need anything else."

He was gone in another moment. It was strange the way he wanted to be gone from her company as quickly as possible. Well, it wasn't as if she needed to understand her companions.

What mattered was letting her feet heal and regaining her strength and doing so without being kept, but by bartering her skill.

Sewing shirts, well, there was something she knew well how to do, and she wasn't being overly proud in acknowledging her skill in working the needle. She'd bloody well earned the right through hours and hours of practicing her stitches as a child. Unrolling the bundle, she felt a great deal of tension easing from her shoulders as she at last had a purpose.

Perhaps her companions would even take her farther down the road toward England. For the moment, though, she would simply have to be patient while her blisters closed. She opened the tie that held the leather

around the cut pieces of a man's shirt, a small needle book, and some thread.

She'd never made a shirt start to finish because sewing was something done when the rest of the day's work was complete. It would be mindless work and yet not so wit-numbing as doing nothing at all.

At last, her luck was changing for the better. At least that was what she would believe. The alternative was to think herself forever stuck in the Highlands of Scotland.

❧

"Ye have her making ye a shirt?"

Muir smirked at Diocail. "Ye are just jealous on account of the fact that ye did nae think of doing it yerself."

Diocail contemplated his captive as she plied a needle and grunted at his captain. "Have ye checked to make certain she is no' ruining yer cloth?"

Muir only continued to smirk as he nodded. "She's what ye thought. A decent woman who has been taught how to sew fine, even stitches. It's going to be a good shirt, and with her no' being able to walk and naught else to do, well, I'll have it before the week is out."

Muir was downright giddy.

"Bastard," Diocail grumbled. His captain's grin brightened.

Diocail was jealous. Shirt linen was expensive, and not many females knew how to handle it well. Sewing was a skill that required practice, the sort a well-tutored girl might receive. His captive was humming as she worked the needle with ease and confidence. A

wife made shirts for her husband as a sign of affection. It was an intimate thing.

The afternoon sun was teasing her hair, turning it into a glowing copper mass. In the morning light, she looked like a little brown bird. Nothing unique about her features. Ah, but when the sun kissed her hair, she became a flame. Even her eyes were a mixture of colors. Greens and browns and ambers.

She looked up and caught him staring. Perhaps he should have looked away, but the truth was, he just didn't want to. She still wasn't afraid of him or his men. Sat there in the wagon, using her delicate fingers to work thread into fabric as contently as if she were in the solar of her own home. Never mind that her circumstances were clear in her bedraggled condition. Not a whimper out of her, and she clung to her persistent need to leave them.

Of course she did. He was a Scot, a savage to her way of thinking.

Diocail chuckled as he turned back to his tenants. Little did she know how barbaric his home was and how much he longed for a woman like her to transform it into something more comfortable. Not that his idea of a home and hers were likely the same. Still, it was an amusing idea. He reckoned she'd take to running, blistered feet or not, if he made mention of it in her hearing.

❧

"I thought..." It was Niven who had ventured closer to her but stopped, tongue-tied, as he faced her. He was younger than Muir but still a man. He reached up

and hastily tugged on his bonnet. "I thought ye might enjoy some soap and water, mistress."

He set down a bowl and a bucket and flashed her an eager smile. "I'll fetch up some water from the river and then bring the kettle from the fire…" He was gone in a flash of bare knees and pleated wool.

"The lad is hoping to make friends with ye before the others beat him to it." Diocail came closer, stopping with one foot propped on a rock near her.

It was strange the way she felt when he was close, as though her breath was tightly lodged in her chest. She caught herself smiling and tried to force her face back into a neutral expression, but the corners of her lips simply refused to remain that way. When she looked into his brown eyes again, she was smiling once more.

"He wants a shirt as well."

"Oh." Understanding made her nod. "It seems a fair enough exchange. He need not worry about asking me."

Diocail contemplated her from behind the stern expression she'd come to expect on his face. It spoke of a harsh life in which he hid his feelings. She noted his sternness as Niven came back with a bucket, easily grinning at her without concern that his enthusiasm might make him appear weaker.

Well, weak was not a word that suited either man. Even the younger Niven. Perhaps approachable was better. She was looking at Diocail again and caught herself smiling at him.

Again.

She looked away as Niven poured some of the

water into the bowl. He was off again toward the fire and the promised kettle.

"It's a skill no' every woman has. Do nae speak of yerself so."

She drew the needle up, knowing the feel of just how tight to make the stitch without having to look. "A fair exchange for feeding me then."

"Aye, it is a fine barter, I'll agree."

Diocail spoke in that low tone that he used. She found it oddly enticing, like some sort of promise. He knew his strength was great and therefore held himself in check. Her husband had always shouted to gain his way.

Stop it. You cannot trust him…

Or any man, ever again.

A snap drew her attention back to Diocail. He'd shaken out a leather hide and laid it on the ground. He placed the bowl on it, making a clean place for her to stand while she made use of Niven's gift.

It was certainly that. She was itching just thinking about removing some of the grime from her skin.

"The men will go down by the horses." He spoke quietly as Niven returned with the kettle, steam trailing from it. "So do nae cry out unless ye fancy company."

"Of course." She was starting to shake with excitement.

She hadn't dared long for a way to clean herself. Muir suddenly appeared, two buckets in his hands. He nodded before placing them near the bowl. Niven had paused to consider his work, grinning at his accomplishment.

"Come on, ye puppy." Muir reached out and

tweaked the younger lad's ear. "Ye don't gawk at a decent woman like her."

The captain tugged on his bonnet before he turned and followed Niven. They passed the fire and went over a small rise before disappearing.

"None will peek at ye, lass. Yet we're close enough to defend ye. The horses will tell us if anyone comes near."

Diocail offered her another rolled length of canvas. He might have dropped it onto the leather, but she realized he wasn't going to allow her to be so timid. If she wanted it, she would have to reach for it.

"Thank you." She closed her hand around the canvas, but he held it for a long moment.

Their gazes were locked, and his went hard. "There is worse out there, lass. For all that I ken yer reasoning for wanting to leave, do nae do it. Me men will no' care for treating ye harshly."

But they would. The threat was clear. It was a promise that flashed in his eyes before he released the bundle and turned around to leave.

Jane realized she'd been holding her breath. It came out in a little sound that betrayed her. She thought she saw him hesitate between steps when he heard it, but he kept going until he'd disappeared from sight.

She should run.

But the moment she stood up, pain went through her feet, reminding her how little protection her pride was against the hard ground of the forest. What she wanted and what might be were, once again, two vastly different things.

So it had been for most of her life.

She laughed softly at herself and unrolled the newest canvas. It was a clever way to hold smaller items for traveling, and this one held lumps of soap and even a comb. She pulled a folded washcloth from one side and realized she as was giddy as a child who had just received a treasured toy.

She cast a last glance toward where the men had gone. They might be peeking, but the opportunity to clean herself was simply too enticing to hold up against her shredded modesty. Honestly, they had seen her nearly bare already. Better to make use of what she may while it was available. Who knew what tomorrow might bring?

That thought sobered her as she unlatched her belt and laid the wool off to the side. Her life had ever been one full of consequences and disappointments, her marriage the biggest of those. Henry had never made her giddy with excitement, not in word or deed, and if he were standing there, he would have declared loudly how superior he was to the Scots keeping her in their midst.

And yet Niven's thoughtfulness was a larger kindness than her own husband had ever thought to bestow upon her.

Stop it…

Lingering in the past was no use at all. If it were, she'd have cultivated a childhood of happiness from the memories of the time when her mother was still alive.

Instead she would concentrate on the present moment, which pleased her, restoring her humor. She took a last glance around before pulling her smock off. Fishing with it had cleaned it somewhat, but she still wrinkled her nose at the thought of putting it back on.

Well, there was nothing to help that.

So she grasped the linen cloth and plunged it into the bowl, carrying water up to wash the dirt from her limbs. The sun was a glowing ball on the horizon, making the experience a chilly one, but being cold paled in comparison to the exhilaration of being clean. The soap smelled slightly of rosemary, and she dug the remaining pins from her hair so she might wash it. There was even a longer length of linen to dry herself with. She ended up wrapping it around her head as she dressed again, grateful for the wool to put over her smock. Working the comb through her wet hair took patience, so much so she failed to notice when Diocail ventured back into sight. She noticed him walking toward her though, and there was no way she might have torn her eyes from him.

The man was impressive.

He was also dangerous, and she would be wise to remember it. His men might be trying to be kind to her, but they answered to him, and his command was absolute. Whatever he decided, it would be done.

"The sun is going down, lass."

She looked up at him, realizing no man save her husband had ever seen her with her hair flowing. It was a strangely intimate thing because her father had insisted on modesty caps. She suddenly felt as if she understood just why too. Diocail's attention was on her hair, his eyes narrowing just a bit as his face softened in a purely male manner. He liked what he saw—the appreciation was impossible to miss. It was not about being vain, no, more of an awareness that he found her attractive.

And you liked knowing it…

"I'll carry ye over to the fire."

He was already reaching for her when she shied away. He frowned, clearly taking it personally.

"I'm sorry," she offered. "It's just that my hair is down, and no one except my husband ever…well, I suppose I don't really have any choice in the matter."

Diocail's expression eased, and he stood with his hands crossed over his wide chest. The position made him appear even larger than he was. "What was yer husband doing in Scotland? To leave ye here with no one to look after ye?"

He'd tempered his tone, but a glint in his eye betrayed how little he thought of her husband. Many might have told her that she should refuse to answer, owing Henry some manner of respect, but the truth was, Jane felt no such loyalty.

"He was a wine merchant, delivering a large order of French wine, and no one else wanted to risk the journey so far into Scotland and—" Jane stopped and drew in a deep breath. "He drank too much while gambling, and…I was a widow by morning light. I really do not wish to speak of it at any great length."

Diocail made a sound in the back of his throat that made it clear he judged Henry harshly.

"Ye'd mourn for a man who left ye in such circumstances? Who brought ye along when he knew full well it was no' a safe place for him, much less a woman?" He shook his head. "Ye have too kind a heart. It's a man's duty to think ahead and make certain his wife is no' left in dire circumstances. The road may be lonely, but better to suffer lack of companionship and leave

yer wife at home where she is sheltered. That is the true duty of a husband."

"Your heart is soft too," she countered before she realized she was rising to his bait. It was difficult to be meek in his presence. "Others would have left me to my plight. Doubly so, since I am English."

One side of his mouth twitched. "Ye have a bold nature, mistress."

From him, it was a compliment. Jane realized she enjoyed it too. He wasn't a man easily impressed.

"Yet I believe I am bolder than ye are yerself." Diocail scooped her up, cradling her against his chest as he carried her toward the fire. "For I'll no' allow modesty to outweigh sensible thinking. Ye'll catch a chill if ye do nae dry yer hair. Ye'll have to content yerself with practicality tonight."

His men made way, clearing off a rock so their laird might settle her on it. The heat from the flames made her realize how cold she was. There was silence around her for long moments before one of the retainers cleared his throat and started to tell a story. He seemed to be searching his memory for the details of the tale, and Jane realized it was a childhood one. Something suitable for her company.

The effort they employed to cater to her gender charmed her. But it also made her realize how little happiness there had been in her father's house.

For the first time, she dreaded the need to return.

But yet again, she had no choice, for happiness was the stuff of stories told by firelight. The harsh light of day always defeated them. What was she to do? Stay in Scotland, where her blood was hated, and it had

already been proven that many would stand by while she was turned out to starve?

For the moment, she had landed among kind-hearted men, but she would be a fool to forget that they were in their country, and she was far from her own. While Alicia's house was stern and strict, it had made her strong, and there was family to protect her against men like Gillanders. Happiness had to surrender to logical thinking.

Tomorrow she would put the subject firmly to Diocail.

❧

Jane's feet healed slowly, keeping her in the wagon while Diocail kept to his duties.

She'd finished Muir's shirt by the time they were done with another village. Niven was quick to present her with a length of cloth, and in spite of her being behind him while she measured him, she was almost certain he was smirking at his comrades. They stood watching her, making her fight to keep her hands steady while she carefully noted the length of his arms, the width of his shoulders, the size of his wrists and collar. She used a bit of chalk from the sewing bundle to write the numbers on the board of the wagon so she would cut the fabric correctly. The length of creamy linen had likely cost a large chunk of the retainer's pay. He also entrusted her with a small leather pouch with buttons in it. They were well used but still very serviceable.

"Thank ye, mistress." He tugged on the corner of his cap and left her with a flash of a smile that made him appear very handsome, if still rather young.

He'd barely made it back to the fire before one of his fellow retainers launched himself at Niven, and they went rolling across the ground. The rest of the men decided to place wagers as the two wrestled, calling out encouragement to their man of choice.

Jane shook her head before considering just where she might cut the fabric. The table the secretary used suddenly moved. Jane gasped, turning about to discover Diocail behind her.

"Seems ye'll be needing this." He offered as he began to set it up.

The fight died down. Jane didn't look behind her because Diocail was far too mesmerizing. He set the table up and pulled the leather hide out to place on the ground. It was a welcome escape from the wagon, a chance to stand and stretch her legs. She hummed as she laid out the fabric, making sure it was neat and smooth without a single wrinkle to make the pieces less than perfect.

It would never do to waste fabric.

She heard a scraping sound and looked over to see Diocail using a sharpening stone on a pair of shears. He held them up, checking the edge before testing it gently with the tip of his finger. He caught her watching him, and once more she was smiling at him before she thought of it. A strange twist of sensation went through her belly, making her turn her attention back to the cloth, lest she appear witless before his keen stare.

She realized there was a space in the canvas sewing kit for those shears. Clearly, Muir had removed them. It was rather nice to know they considered her a

threat, even a small one. She decided she liked that far better than being nothing more than their foundling.

Jane looked at the numbers and measured the cloth twice before drawing careful lines on it with the chalk. The white lines were faint, and when she was finished, there was not a single bit of fabric unused. She marked the place where she'd open the neck and made sure she had two gussets to sew into the corners to round the opening before attaching the collar. There was even enough to put a box-pleated ruffle into the neck. She circled it, making sure she'd marked the fabric correctly before cutting into it.

She used the shears slowly, ensuring that no threads pulled while she was cutting. Her shoulders tightened as she concentrated, not allowing her thoughts to wander until she'd finished and neatly stacked the pieces in the bag she was using for her sewing.

She stood back, pleased with her efforts. But she also caught sight of the Gordon retainers. They'd come close during the time she'd been so intent on the fabric, watching her quietly.

"It is only a shirt," she muttered, quite unaccustomed to having her efforts so closely watched.

"Aye, but a fine shirt," Muir offered with a glint in his eyes. "I've never had a better one."

"You are being kind."

The captain shook his head and moved back toward the fire, his comrades following.

"Some men might take exception to ye questioning their word, lass." Diocail reached past her and took the shears. He noted her watching him as he tucked them into his belt. "Best I keep these for the now."

"Don't trust me, Laird Gordon?"

He offered her a grin. "Do ye trust me, lass? Perhaps ye might care to tell me yer name?"

His voice had an easygoing tone—he was toying with her, expecting her to refuse him.

"It seems to matter not at all." She sat down on the bed of the wagon once more. Her feet were healing, but she still felt the blisters, reminding her of her circumstances.

"And yet ye would return to the house of a man who wed ye unwisely."

Jane discovered herself scoffing at him. "And what would you have me do? Expect you to feed me? For naught? What choice is there except to return to my father's house since, as you noted so very correctly, my husband failed to ensure my well-being? Do you truly need another person looking to you for their bread?"

She'd given him pause. He considered her for a long moment, unable to form an argument against her words.

"Muir considers it a fair trade," Diocail replied after a moment. "Niven will likely join him now. They will no' quibble at sharing the supper with ye."

"Yet you are their master," she replied. "To you, I am a burden."

His expression tightened. "Is that the way ye were raised, lass? Thinking ye bring naught to those ye live with?"

She offered him only a raised shoulder. "I was a fourth daughter, quite the disappointment to both my parents. My stepmother made it clear I should be grateful for anything she chose to give me. I don't expect you to understand. You were born a son."

"Aye," he replied. "But to me uncle's brother's wife, and he did nae care to have a new branch of the family threatening his own bloodline. Burden, threat—both are challenges that test a person. Such circumstances can make a person stronger."

"Yes," she agreed. "I admit I learned to have finer stitches than my older sisters." Heat teased her cheeks when she realized she was boasting. "Prideful of me to say such."

"Honest too," he answered with a jerk of his head toward his men. "They may be rough, lass, but make no mistake, they know quality stitching when they see it. They'd no' be fighting over Niven's boldness if Muir's new shirt was no' something to be envious of."

"I never imagined they'd take to fighting." The skirmish was over now, Niven enjoying whisky as money changed hands over the wagers. "My apologies for disrupting your ranks."

"Disrupting me ranks?" He chuckled at her formal speech. "Christ, woman, ye know precious little about men. That"—he jerked his head toward the men behind him—"was good fun. Naught else."

"I doubt Niven would agree." In fact, the young retainer had blood running down one side of his face from a cut in his scalp.

"He'd be the first to do so," Diocail answered her confidently. "Because he knows the lads wouldn't bother if they were nae envious, and he knows he's stronger for being tested by his comrades. Fate knows what it's doing at times, placing us where she will. There is a reason ye are a fourth daughter. Me men

are grateful for it, for if ye were of higher station, ye would certainly no' be here."

Grateful. No one had ever described her in such a manner. "And you are laird, no matter what your uncle thought."

It surprised her, that they had something in common. It was a strange feeling, to say the least. One she enjoyed a great deal.

He choked out a bark of amusement. "Aye, Fate has a sense of humor, it would seem."

"Enjoy it. I have very recently seen the harsher side of Fate's workings." She was telling him what to do, offering her opinion when it had not been asked for. But he didn't bristle, didn't mutter "woman" at her as a reminder of her place.

"I know those as well." He nodded, once again appearing as though they had much in common. She savored the sensation because it made her feel less alone.

But that brought a prickle of guilt. She had no right to chastise her circumstances. Loneliness was certainly better than starvation or worse, and his men shouldn't have to sensor their conversation because she was near. They did enough for her.

"Good night, Laird Gordon."

She crawled back into the wagon and pulled the sewing bag into her lap. There was little light left, but she would make good use of it and earn her place. Diocail watched her for a long moment. She would have sworn she felt his gaze on her, which was impossible, of course.

And yet she was keenly aware of him.

She felt a teasing of heat on her cheeks as she

drew a length of thread off the wooden bobbin it was wrapped around.

Blushing…

She knew what it was and still couldn't recall ever having done so in response to a man before. Even if it was ill timed, she found it curious. Looking up, she found Diocail still standing there, watching her with his warm brown eyes, captivated by her.

She drew in a stiff breath and held it, feeling as though something had shifted between them. She must have annoyed him because his eyes narrowed before his expression tightened, and he granted her a half nod and turned his back on her.

Disappointment needled her.

You are being quite ridiculous…

There was a solid truth if ever she'd heard one. The man likely thought her a mouse, to be gasping just because she'd met his gaze. He was not a man to suffer timid females.

No, and she found that a pleasing trait in him.

Diocail Gordon was who he was because he had pitted himself against the odds and survived.

Likely it was better that she'd disgusted him.

So why did it bother her so greatly?

Because she longed to be something quite different than she'd been raised to be. Jane looked back at the fabric, drawing the thread through it in a careful stitch.

Careful…

Such was everything in her life. Years full of days dedicated to becoming the ideal set forth to her by the men around her. To deviate was unacceptable.

She spent hours on self-directed lectures. Had gone to sleep with her mind full of how many mistakes she'd made that day and the need to dedicate herself to doing much, much better the next day. Because men did not tolerate shrewish behavior. They craved submission and duty in their wives.

And her purpose was to please the men around her so greatly that one of them would honor her with a marriage proposal. Well, she'd accomplished that goal, and what did she have to show for it? An ill fate. Damned if she didn't feel cheated by God.

Diocail Gordon wouldn't be satisfied with a mouse for a spouse.

He hasn't asked you to marry him either…

It was a sinful thought, one that stirred up something in her belly. She allowed her mind to contemplate what manner of wife Diocail might enjoy. He chuckled when she argued with him, grinning when she expressed her opinion without being asked.

Men enjoyed brazen harlots too and let them die in the gutter. Discarded mistresses when the excitement faded. Scots also enjoyed ransoming women, a fate she didn't fancy.

Such were the lessons of her youth, repeated over and over, and still she sat there thinking about how all her proper behavior had yielded was a mean-hearted husband who had squandered her dowry and her dreams of love.

There was a bitter taste on her tongue, left there by the knowledge that she must return home. Decency demanded it. She wished she'd reaped the rewards of behaving. The truth was she was sorely tempted to

toss all of the rules out in favor of doing exactly what she pleased.

She smiled brightly as she thought about just what Diocail Gordon might make of such behavior. Very brightly indeed, even if she knew in her heart it was nothing but a fantasy.

❧

"Take me son."

Jane wasn't in the habit of watching Diocail while he was dealing with his tenants. She cringed, though, as the woman's voice reached her ears.

Another village and another line of tenants paying their due. The first wagon was almost full now after another week on the road.

"He's a fine, big lad who will grow into a retainer who will show no fear."

The woman was rushing and had to stop to drag in a breath.

"I do nae take children," Diocail replied in that soft tone of his. But his neck was corded. Jane could see his fingers gripping his shirt where he had his arms crossed over his chest.

"Ye must," the woman's voice came out in a thin whine. "Me man died a few weeks ago. I have naught."

And she was dying herself. Jane stared at the horrible truth as the woman began to cough. The effort shook her thin frame. She had a dirty piece of cloth in her hand that she pressed to her mouth. When she lowered it, the bright spots of fresh blood were clear.

A small face peeked around her tattered skirt. Jane felt tears sting her eyes as she recognized the boy who

had built her a fire. The woman reached down and gripped his hand. "Here…ye must…he'll starve… when I follow me husband…"

She changed places with her son, stepping back and leaving him standing in front of her in his dirty shift with his knife. "Show…the laird…how much… courage…ye have…"

The boy gripped the handle of his knife. He looked up at Diocail, blinking. There was a slight tearing sound as the fabric of Diocail's sleeve gave way under his grip. He grunted, releasing the sleeve and letting out a long breath.

"Aye," Diocail spoke.

He looked down at the boy as his mother dropped a kiss on the top of his matted blond hair and whispered something in his ear before hurrying away.

The boy did have courage, but he was still tender in his years. His eyes welled up with tears as he stood facing a man three times his size. The Gordon retainers were frozen, looking at the boy with confusion. Jane wasn't sure when she decided to move, but the mother was gone, the sound of her hacking cough drifting on the wind from behind some of the rough walls of the village homes. It grew fainter, and the boy's lower lip began to tremble.

Her feet were almost healed now. Jane walked over to where Diocail stood and lowered herself before him. There was still a line of tenants watching to see if he'd abandon the child. Jane held out her hand to the boy. He looked up, his lips curving as he recognized her.

Jane led the boy back to the wagon, and the laird

made no complaint. Muir sent her a relieved look before the business resumed.

"Are ye going to be me mother now?" the boy asked after Diocail went on collecting rent and oaths without a glance in their direction.

"For as long as we're together, I suppose."

He nodded. "Me name is Bari."

"And I am Jane."

And they were an oddly suited couple, both dependent on the will of Diocail Gordon.

❧

"So the lad gains yer name." Diocail stopped and placed his foot on a rock near her. "I suppose ye think me a monster for allowing him to be given to me."

Bari was sound asleep in the wagon. Jane could walk away from it now, providing she was careful where she stepped.

"You were being kind," she answered Diocail. "His mother won't last a month."

One of his eyebrows rose. "Think so?"

Jane nodded. "I've seen it. That disease of the lungs. You likely saved his young life, for it passes easily between members of a family. If he'd stayed near her and tried to help her, I doubt he would have escaped."

"Do ye think he has it?"

Jane saw the distaste in his eyes, but he asked anyway, clearly concerned for the welfare of all his men.

"I see no signs."

He sent her a hard look. "Ye must tell me if ye do, Jane. I can nae take him into the tower if he has it. I will ask ye again before we make it back."

Her name was oddly intimate on his lips. It felt as though they were becoming more and more familiar with each other. She had no idea why it unsettled her, and yet her belly was twisting once again.

"Surely you understand," she began. "I should be long away by now. However grateful I am, I cannot stay."

Diocail let out a long sigh. "And ye should clearly understand that I can nae leave ye in yer shift on the side of the road." He was back to gripping his shirt, tearing once more. He grunted and muttered a word beneath his breath. "Perhaps ye think because I'm Scottish, it makes it acceptable for me to see ye starving. How long will ye last before ye turn to prostituting yerself to avoid dying? Maybe I am no' English like yer husband, but—"

"I thank God for that," she exclaimed. "My English husband placed my favors on a gaming table and cheerfully rolled the dice and expected me to honor his loss. You are nothing like him."

She'd said too much. Far too much.

She'd known Diocail was a dangerous man; now she watched his expression turn deadly. "He did...*what*?"

She felt too much on display, her pride too torn and shredded, and tried to turn away. The only solace available was to keep her shame secret. Diocail reached out and locked his hands around her biceps, pulling her in front of him.

"Jane?" he demanded softly, but there was no missing the rage in his voice. "Explain yer words."

"There is no point." She looked him straight in the eye. "What's done is done, and he was beaten to death for his excess at the dice."

"He's damned lucky he was," Diocail exclaimed, "for I'd have broken his legs and left him alive."

Oh, but she liked the sound of that.

For a moment, they stared into one another's eyes, and he was absolutely everything wonderful in the world. A man of honor, one she might depend on to do all of the righteous things she'd been raised to believe good men did. She was so close she could smell him. Henry had never pleased her senses the way Diocail did. She liked the way he smelled and felt herself trembling as she watched his attention shift to her mouth. Everything else seemed to dissipate, leaving her with only the feeling of his hands on her and a tingle across the delicate surface of her lips while he contemplated them.

I would like his kiss…

"Is she yer strumpet, Laird?"

Diocail released her in a flash as young Bari's voice came from behind her. Jane fell back from him, realizing she had been nearly in his embrace and completely captivated by him.

"Is that why she wears no skirts?"

With the innocence of childhood, Bari asked what was on his mind. He rubbed his eyes and cocked his head to one side as he waited for an answer.

"No, lad." Muir was suddenly there, taking Bari up and back toward the wagon. "She's a decent woman. No' the sort ye say a word like strumpet to."

"But why has she no skirts?" Bari wasn't ready to let the matter go. "I heard the women in the village call her a strumpet and a doxy. I've never heard that word before, doxy."

Jane's cheeks heated as she heard Muir hushing the child.

"The next village is a larger one," Diocail explained. "There will be an inn with a proper bed, and I'll find ye something to wear or at least the cloth to be sewn."

"I really can't accept more from you."

He drew himself up and sent her a look she doubted many argued with. "As I have told ye before, mistress, ye best reconcile yerself to our company. For I'll bring ye back if ye are fool enough to try me."

A wise woman would have let the matter be. But wisdom had led her to where she was, and something inside her snapped. "I am quite done being told what to do by men."

Diocail had turned, meaning to leave her with those final words, but he snapped back around as her comment hit his ears. "Is that so, Jane?"

He was using her name on purpose now, trying to impress on her how little choice she had.

"And just what will ye be doing under yer father's roof?" he demanded as he stepped close enough to whisper. "But I am no' fool enough to send ye back to a man who has no sense when it comes to who he weds ye to."

"I refuse to allow you to pity me."

He liked that comment. Jane stared at him, confounded by the way his eyes lit with enjoyment. No man enjoyed a woman who was too free with her tongue.

Except for Diocail Gordon, it would seem, for he was grinning as though she was the most fetching female he'd ever set eyes upon.

She let out a huff. "You make no sense. Why do you let me tell you what I think? And speak when I have not been asked to?"

He slowly chuckled. "Because I like ye with the flames dancing in yer eyes, lass." He reached out and hooked her by her upper arms, pulling her toward him. His attention dropped to her mouth a moment before he pressed a kiss against her lips.

She recoiled, but not because it was unpleasant.

Quite the opposite, really.

For a moment, her belly twisted, and anticipation gripped her so tightly she was breathless. Never in her life had she realized her body might experience such a level of bliss. It overwhelmed her, making her yank away from him and the uncertainty he roused in her. She struggled to comprehend the way he'd made her breathless.

Was it right?

Wrong?

A sin?

A shame?

His lips curled, and he flashed his teeth at her while his eyes flickered with a satisfaction that made her cheeks burn. She was lifting her hand and laying it across his jaw before her thoughts cleared. The hard smack of flesh against flesh shattered the strange moment like a bubble that had landed on a thorn.

Diocail Gordon released her, backing away as he chuckled. "I deserved that, 'tis a fact I did." He opened his arms wide and offered her a slight lowering of his body in a courtesy. "And I enjoyed kissing ye full well." He straightened, and his expression tightened into one of promise. "Jane."

She snarled, stunning herself with how passionate the sound was.

What was happening to her? Was Scotland truly turning her savage?

It defied rational thought, and yet her heart was thumping so hard it felt as if it were hitting her breastbone, driving her blood through her veins so fast she felt light-headed and fought to stand in one place. It was exhilarating and unsettling on a scale she had never experienced.

Henry had never kissed her like that…

Disrespectful to the dead, perhaps, and yet it was a solid truth. One that left her wondering just what else she might discover if she embraced the heat licking at her insides.

⤳

"Now I'm jealous," Muir muttered as he nursed a flask of whisky. "I only asked her for a shirt, but ye get a kiss."

His captain had joined him on watch sometime after midnight and clearly had no reservations about discussing what he'd seen.

"I took a kiss," Diocail said, admitting to his sin. "And damn me for doing so when others might see. Jane deserves more respect than that sort of behavior."

"She's a decent woman," Muir agreed. "And knows a thing or two most females don't as well."

He offered the flask to Diocail, who shook his head.

"The lads are thinking it's a fine thing we have her to bring back home with us."

Diocail cast a narrow-eyed glare at his captain,

realizing Muir had been plotting to say his piece to him, no doubt with a bit of discussion among the rest of the men too. As laird, he would have to become accustomed to having every last detail of his life debated.

But that didn't mean he was going to accept the will of his clan when it came to personal matters. "Christ, man," Diocail exclaimed. "She'll no' be pleased by that idea." He opened his hand, and gestured toward the wagon. "She's English."

"Aye," Muir agreed. "Ye can nae miss that when she opens her mouth." He drew a long sip of whisky, clearly fortifying himself before he spoke his mind. "And yet she has a fire in her belly. Those feet of hers were torn up and no mistake. Yet she was nae giving in. Likely why ye stole that kiss. Heard the smack she gave ye all the way over by the horses."

"That's the part ye should be thinking more about," Diocail pointed at him. "I'm a savage to her way of thinking."

Muir slowly grinned. "Scores of Englishwomen live their lives without sampling passion. Now there is something ye might give her that she'll enjoy full well after tasting a cold English marriage."

"We are *no*'"—Diocail stressed the "no"—"talking about that."

"Glad to know ye're no' thinking about it, *Laird*."

Diocail grunted and left Muir to the duty of watch. He rolled himself in his plaid and closed his eyes, but sleep was still elusive. Jane invaded his thoughts, and her taste lingered on his lips.

He was a rogue to have kissed her. Yet he didn't truly regret it. Even if that thought shamed him.

And that was surprising because it had been a very long time since he'd been shamed. It made him chuckle, easing the tension that seemed to have been in his shoulders over the past year. Coming down from the north to Gordon land had always been in his mother's plans for him, but the reality had been damned difficult.

He slept lightly because there were plenty of Gordons who coveted the lairdship. His life had become one where he'd been forced to prioritize what he had time to worry about. Manners hadn't been high on the list. Not when he'd been focused on surviving.

Jane was a breath of fresh air. Or maybe he just understood how it felt to have Fate hurling more challenges at a person than it seemed possible to meet.

Indeed, he knew that path surely enough. Some might say that was why he refused to let Jane go, but the truth was he just couldn't stomach the idea of what would befall her on the road, and not because he pitied her.

No, it was far worse than that.

He wasn't going to let her go because if she was going to land in anyone's bed, it was most definitely going to be his.

He would be shamed by his thoughts if he wasn't so distracted by the idea of just how bright the flames would flicker in her eyes if he told her what was on his mind.

Rogue…

But at least it was better than letting her become a sad victim of harsh reality.

෯

Jane was turned about.

She realized she'd lost her way completely when she stood facing the inn where Gillanders had so cheerfully turned her out.

To be honest, she almost missed the sign because the rain was pouring down, the sky dark with black, swollen clouds. But she caught sight of the sign as she was encouraging Bari to hurry inside where Diocail and his men were setting up to receive the tenants who had come to pay their due.

Bari scampered inside as she stopped, oblivious to the downpour, blinking at the name of the inn.

Niven ran right into her and mumbled a word in Gaelic that needed no translation, and she went pitching forward through the open door, ending up sprawled on the tavern floor.

"What the devil?" Lachie asked from where he was setting up his paper and quill.

Another retainer reached down and hooked her by the arm, hoisting her up and off the floor while she was still trying to absorb the fact that she'd come full circle.

"She just stopped," Niven explained in bewilderment.

"Yes, I did," Jane stammered as she pulled at her meager coverings. "It was my fault. I'm sorry, Niven."

One of Gillanders's daughters was serving ale. She stood with eyes as round as full moons before she realized Niven was looking at her curiously and snapped her attention back to the mugs she was filling.

"Always happy to have the laird under me humble

roof." Gillanders said as he came down the stairs. He was laughing as he spoke to Diocail. "Ye'll not find a finer-laid table in three villages! Mark me words, me wife knows how to put the supper out!"

He caught sight of Jane then, freezing in place as his wife and daughters all drew back so that they were flat against the walls of the common room.

Gillanders was just as pompous as Jane recalled. He let out a snicker and slapped his thigh. "So ye found yerself a place with the laird's men." He sent a look at Diocail. "Right nice to have a bit of company along on the road when the wives are all back at home."

The tavern owner indulged in a round of snickers as his gaze swept her from head to toe.

Muir slid up to her side, moving in front of her as the tension in the room increased. Even Lachie looked disgruntled, rising from his bench.

Gillanders didn't miss it. He glanced around, taking in the disapproval being cast his way while his wife snapped her fingers at his daughters to send them scampering into the kitchen, the topic being too scarlet for their youth.

"Here now," Gillanders exclaimed. "What's the trouble? She's an English bitch, ye can nae mean to tell me ye'd argue with me over her?"

"Ye put her out?" Diocail asked. "In her shift?"

"Well, now, her husband left a debt that had to be settled, and since the man was dead, she was the only one to be doing it with. Can nae fault a man for taking what is owed to him. I'd have lost this tavern long ago if I failed to collect on what me family's hard work was worth."

Gillanders gripped his wide belt. He'd buckled it beneath his fat belly and looked ridiculous while attempting to be impressive.

"Besides, I made her an offer," Gillanders continued. "Thought herself too good to work for a Scot."

There was disgruntled muttering behind her from the men waiting to pay their rent and greet their new laird.

"You offered me a position as a whore." Jane likely should have kept her mouth tightly sealed, but wisdom seemed to be lacking in her at that moment. "I most certainly did decline."

There was a snort from the line behind her and a snicker. Diocail didn't miss it. He crossed his arms over his chest and eyed Gillanders. "The lady," he said, stressing the last word, "is under our protection now."

"Aye." Their host offered Diocail a wide smirk, which made Jane's cheeks burn scarlet. "I see that, Laird. No trouble at all."

"Good." Diocail looked past him to where his wife was wringing her apron. "Show the lady above stairs and produce her belongings."

"Here now," Gillanders argued, but his wife was already lifting her skirts and nearly running up the stairs. "There's the matter of the debt owed by her husband. I took her things in payment." He pointed at Jane.

"Well, now, as to that question," Lachie interrupted as he came closer with the large account book in his arms. "It would seem the Hawk's Head Tavern, owned by one Gillanders, has not paid rent in more than five seasons."

Gillanders opened his mouth and closed it several

times as he tried to formulate an argument. "There is the cost of burying her husband as well. Couldn't let him rot on the side of the road. I'm a Christian man."

"Of course ye are," Muir muttered. "Only allowed the man to be murdered."

"It was none of me doing." Gillanders exclaimed. "He wandered out, likely because of the cold bitch he had been saddled with for a wife. She turned him away, she did. More than one heard it."

"Because Henry brought his gaming companions up to our bed with the intention of having me settle the loss through the use of my body," she retorted. "Christian man that you are, you stood at the door intending to watch."

Niven growled. For all that she'd needed to stand up against the tavern owner's remarks, the anger on the faces of the Gordon retainers' faces made her regret her words. There was a fight brewing now, and she'd tossed on the fuel.

"Enough." Diocail's voice cracked like a whip. He looked over his shoulder at the men waiting, and they stopped their snickering. "He'd no' be the first man who discovered himself on the receiving end of violence after ill-placed bets, but that is a matter between men, and I'll no' stand for it being applied to his wife more than any of ye would have me taking me business to yer wives."

The inn was suddenly filled with the shuffling of feet against the floorboards and nothing else.

"Aye," Gillanders agreed. "Business between men. That's the way it should be."

Diocail nodded. He cut a quick glance toward Muir.

The captain nodded once before reaching over and grasping Jane by the upper arm. He tugged her gently toward the stairs. She cringed at the idea of going back to the place where she had last seen Henry, but staying behind wasn't appealing either. So she climbed the stairs and went through the door at the top.

"Stay in the room, mistress," Muir replied. "I think it will be best that way. Until the business is finished."

The captain tugged the door shut, leaving her listening to the heavy fall of rain on the roof. Despite the chill in the air, she turned and looked at the door, longing simply to run.

What made her quell the urge was the sight of young Bari. He sat cross-legged on the floor in front of a barrier of hot coals. The room was only a loft, and as such, didn't have a hearth. He was happily shoveling stew into his mouth with the aid of a chunk of bread and had to swallow before he spoke. "It's very fine of the laird to make certain we are nae sitting in the rain, is it no', mistress?"

A rap on the door saved her from having to answer. The door swung inward as Gillanders's wife pointed two of her daughters into the room. They carried two large bundles and stood for a long moment once they'd entered.

"It's all here," she muttered. "Except yer wedding ring. Me husband already sold it for the gold."

The Gordon retainer standing outside the door was named Aylin. He frowned as he listened, clearly taking note of the details. He turned and headed down the stairs.

"I've recently learned to appreciate more useful things over items that only feed vanity," Jane said.

Such as her clothing. The bundles were plump, hinting at a reunion with the things she'd taken for granted. She trembled with anticipation of being decent once again.

"Aye," Gillanders's wife said as she snapped her fingers. The two girls placed the bundles on the floor and left.

"Are ye nae going to dress, mistress?"

Bari stopped to ask her the question as he was crossing the room toward the door. The boy had taken to standing by Niven during the times when rent was being collected. The Gordon retainer would give him tasks to do, such as carrying smaller items to the wagon or helping to collect firewood. As much as she longed for company, seeing Bari finding a place made her happy.

His mother would have wept for joy.

"I'll be fine, Bari," Jane responded. "Go on and attend to your duties."

He flashed her a smile before he scampered toward the door. He stopped, turned around, and reached up to tug on the corner of his bonnet. "Mistress."

His manners attended to, he took off toward the door and it banged shut behind him, leaving Jane facing her past. She ended up laughing until tears rolled down her face. Sinking onto her knees, she tried to make sense of what Fate was doing to her.

Even after her amusement was spent, she sat there, contemplating the bundles that represented her past. She still couldn't make herself reach for them because she wanted nothing to do with any of her former belongings.

Of course, that left her sitting on the floor, defeated by circumstances. Which wouldn't do either.

The difficulty was she was held in the grip of some strange mood that refused to allow her to move as she sank deeper and deeper into her thoughts. She was neither happy nor sad, nor really anything else as she fought against the sheer amount of feelings trying to drown her.

What made her reach for the first of the bundles was the fact that Diocail was providing for her.

Oh yes, he was an honorable man, but some things were simply facts in life. No one received anything for nothing.

She didn't want to be a whore, but Diocail was buying her. The bundles represented too much to be afforded to Christian charity or kindness. Sewing a few shirts were fine payment for feeding her and taking her along while her feet healed. The bundles were an entirely different matter.

Diocail was exchanging rent due for them. He had people to provide for with that rent, men such as Muir and Niven and even young Bari.

The only choice Fate seemed to be allowing her was what she wanted to make of her circumstances. She might simply allow Diocail to shield her, but she would carry the shame of knowing that she was taking advantage of his honor.

That stung.

He deserved better. Had certainly treated her too well for her to use him. It was hardly his responsibility to see to her needs.

That is not the only reason you are looking to leave…

Her shame doubled because there in the loft room where she'd last seen her husband, she realized she had never enjoyed his kiss the way she had Diocail's.

Never longed for more of them…

The harshest truth was she needed to leave before she allowed herself to become his. Not because he insisted on it, but because she liked his touch and remaining was a simpler path than making her own way. Diocail would allow it because he was not a mean-spirited man.

She mustn't be weak.

She'd made herself that promise the day her mother had died. Her sisters had taken to holding her, and she knew when her father married again she couldn't allow them to coddle her. They were all at the mercy of their new stepmother's whims. They all had the same amount to worry about, and she would not add to any of their burdens. Such was the truest test of love among them.

At least her stepmother's frugality had a purpose. Jane began to pull her clothing from the first bundle and found it plain, yet serviceable and sturdy. She'd learned to sew a fine line because Alicia didn't waste her coin on tailors for her stepdaughters.

No, they were fortunate to receive cloth and needles. Jane's older sisters had sat her down and made her practice her stitches over and over and over again until she had them perfect. They'd traded time stitching for the tailor in exchange for learning how to cut the garments in the newest fashions.

So her clothing was nice, if serviceable. Considering her circumstances, it was a blessing. Knowing Diocail

had paid for it made her hesitate, but she realized her choice was clear.

Accept the gift of her clothing, which would allow her to be on her way, or stay, or reconcile herself to the fact that she was allowing the man to care for her with no recompense.

And wait for him to kiss you again…

What bothered her was not the fact that he'd kiss her again, but that she'd kiss him back.

Willingly…

Wantonly…

Whore or mistress, they were very similar indeed.

Jane stripped her smock away and washed with some water. She scrubbed her skin as best she might before turning back toward her clothing and lifting a clean shift from it. Two shifts. One of those things she'd taken for granted until now. One to wear and another to wash.

Stockings.

She smiled as she pulled them on and found relief from the chill that had been her companion for too long. Next came her shoes. She looked at them and happily slipped them on her feet. They weren't made of thick leather like the Gordon retainers' boots, but they were far better than bare feet.

Her hip roll was nestled in with her skirts. She tied it with a firm knot—she'd lost weight around her hips, and the knot was sitting in a different place on the tie.

Her underskirt was a nice wool. A cheerful green that made her smile when she saw it. The overskirt was a muted blue that wouldn't show the mud easily.

The bodice was a simple one that closed up the front so she needed no help with dressing. The feeling of the sleeves covering her arms made her smile.

Henry had railed against the lack of trousseau Alicia had provided her stepdaughters. The complaints had prompted the gift of a fine length of wool. Jane had thought to make the fabric into a surcoat, but Henry had kept her busy tending to his needs, and she had not found the time to make anything for herself.

Today she picked up the wool and draped it over her shoulders and head as the Scottish women did. They called it an arisaid, and Jane saw the function of it. By day it might serve as a cloak and shield from the rain, while at night it was bedding, since it was not sewn.

Today it would allow her to slip away.

Looking at the other things, she slipped her comb into a pocket sewn on the underskirt and made sure she tied it closed tightly. She was wiser now about what she would need to make her way back to England. She didn't dare take time to indulge the regret making her rethink her actions.

Instead, she turned her attention to the second bundle. Henry's things were inside it. If she were wise, she'd clip the buttons off the doublet and shirts and take them to sell, but she couldn't bring herself to do it. In fact, she wanted nothing of his, retying the bundle so she didn't have to look at it.

The belt Muir had given her was a fine one. It would be very useful on the journey, but she couldn't find it in herself to take it, so she folded the length of wool and laid the belt over it on the bed. She turned and wrapped her spare stockings and chemise together.

Somewhere, there was a chest with her second dress and the wine Henry had been delivering. Part of her would have enjoyed telling Diocail about it, but Gillanders would only claim Henry had owed enough to cover the value of it all.

Better to stick to her choice not to burden the Gordon laird with her keep any further. She ate the bowl of stew left for her and peeked out the door. The landing was clear, so she slipped through, cringing at how much noise her shoes made on the wood planks. She walked on her toes as she descended the stairs. Diocail was facing the line of tenants, Lachie poised over the account book as Muir looked on. The other retainers enjoyed sitting at benches and tables while they ate their fill. Gillanders's wife and daughters were hurrying in and out of the common room, bringing more bread and cheese to those waiting in line. Gillanders himself was off in the far corner, a gleam in his eyes as he collected money from the customers the laird's visit had brought him.

Jane turned and moved toward the kitchen. Gillanders's method of shouting at his staff ensured that no one took the time to look up from what they were doing to investigate her presence. They assumed she was a member of the family and stayed focused on their own tasks. As she passed, she took a fresh loaf of bread from the table without a moment's reservation. He'd taken plenty from her. She stopped in the doorway to push it into her bundle before she raised the wool up to cover her head and ventured out into the rain.

They were the hardest steps she'd ever taken.

Which was ridiculous. She chided herself as she

moved away from the tavern, sternly lecturing herself on the correctness of her plan. Her options were clear, and she didn't have the right to place Diocail in the position of conducting himself in an honorable way because Fate had dropped her in his path.

The best solution was to leave. So why did she feel so very torn?

The gray sky offered her no answer. At least the gloomy weather meant the window shutters were closed on the houses she passed. It was a good-size village, with shops and two-story buildings, and the road she traveled was brick. She noted the little splashing sounds her feet made as she went, enjoying the fact that she had shoes on despite their thinness.

But Fate wasn't finished with her yet, it seemed. She'd made it only a few blocks from the Hawk's Head Tavern before she ran into a camp at the edge of the village. Men who had come to pay rent to Diocail had been filtering into the village for days awaiting his arrival. Some had finished their business and returned. Two of them recognized her, emerging from beneath their tents as she passed by.

"Where are ye going, mistress?" one questioned her.

"Back to my father's house." It seemed a simple reply that wouldn't needle the man.

His comrade frowned. "After traveling with me laird?"

"He was simply being kind, offering me safe passage." She started walking again, but more men appeared, standing in her path, so she turned and faced the first man.

"As I am widowed, I must return to my father's house."

"No' after ye have been traveling with our laird," the man replied. "Hearing Gordon business."

She felt the tension tightening all around her. "I am no one of any importance."

"Ye're English," one man declared. "Of good family. Heard yer husband bragging about yer blue blood and how he was going to use his marriage to ye as a way of gaining an office from the nobles."

Henry would have done something that foolish, she didn't doubt it. And he'd left her to face even more of his unwise choices.

"Ye'll no' be spying on us," one declared.

His comrades agreed with a round of growling that sent a chill down her spine. She started to back up, but the man in front of her only frowned.

"And ye'll no' be going back to spy more on me laird," he declared. "Toss her in the cell we'll hang her once the laird has gone."

"Are ye sure?" one man questioned. "The laird seemed rather protective of her."

"Aye, he's a right honorable man. About time we had a laird worthy of our rent and loyalty," the first man declared to those surrounding her. "Which is why we're no' going to let some English spy prey on his nature."

Three

A HANGING WAS GOOD ENTERTAINMENT TO MOST people's thinking.

Jane heard the celebration starting up long before first light. The cell they'd shoved her into was dank and tiny. There wasn't room to lie down, and the stink coming from the corners made her resist doing more than leaning against the hard stone of the back wall.

At least she didn't suffer from the cold. No, she knew how much more cutting it might be. The fact that there was no door on the cell, just a collection of bars that kept her locked in, didn't bother her too greatly.

But the conversation coming from the camp chilled her blood.

"I say she kicks eighteen times…"

"Nae, it will be twelve…"

There was no one to act as her hanger-on in the event her neck didn't snap immediately. No one to hug her legs and pull her down so she died faster instead of kicking for long moments of agony.

It would, however, be faster than starving to death

or freezing. So perhaps Fate was being kinder to her after all. Diocail had certainly given her a fine last kiss.

She was losing her grip on sanity, but she didn't fight it. Far better to allow herself to float away on her own whimsy than to listen to the growing enthusiasm for her death.

Diocail Gordon was a fine man to do so over, too. He was a fine, burly subject for impure thoughts. Strange how at the end of her life she was indulging in behavior she had always resisted.

Lust...

As a descendant of Eve, she'd grown up listening to lectures in church about how important it was to avoid allowing herself to think of men. But now?

Well, she indulged herself for a long time contemplating Diocail Gordon. He was hard, and his gaze was piercing. She found his eyes strangely fascinating. They were confirmation of how determined he was when it came to matters that he'd set his mind to.

Or better yet, to those things he'd devoted himself to maintaining. So many men spoke about honor, and so often they abandoned those ideas when it suited their whim.

Henry certainly had.

The thought of her husband sobered her. Daydreams had never gained her anything. Only facing facts had granted her any measure of happiness. She tried to convince herself that love would grow in their marriage as so many told her it would. Henry himself had been pleasing enough the few times he'd come to negotiate with her father.

Things had certainly changed once their vows were

spoken and he'd taken her home. All of the mystery of the wedding bed had been ripped from her in an act that had taken only a few moments to accomplish. The physical pain was nothing compared to how alone she'd felt once he'd rolled aside and started snoring next to her.

No love could come from such callousness…

Jane looked through the bars, noting the faint lightening of the sky. A ribbon of pink began to widen. She waited for the first bird song and smiled when it broke through the sound of those anticipating her death.

Hangings were done at dawn. She heard the men coming for her, and in a way, it was a relief.

That didn't stop her from lamenting how short her years had been or thinking Henry might be waiting for her on the other side of death.

If there was any mercy in heaven, God would grant her freedom from that ill-fated match.

The village was large enough to boast a proper gallows. It was a raised platform in the middle of the town. There was also a post for whippings and stocks for public shaming, but the men who came for her pushed her toward the edge of the platform. A noose was already dangling over a beam.

"Do ye confess yer sins?"

A priest stood there, and the men behind her gripped a handful of her dress to turn her to face the man. Jane blinked, stunned by his presence.

"No need to confess, we know she's a spy," one of her captors growled.

"I am no such thing," Jane argued.

"Get on with it!" someone yelled from the gathered crowd.

Jane turned her attention to the people waiting to watch her die. They'd made sure the children had a good spot up front to watch the entertainment and the lesson to be learned.

"English bitch!"

The priest was pushed back as the two men shoved her forward. She was oddly aware of the way the rope felt as it came over her head. It caught several of her hairs, tugging on them before it lay against her bare collarbone.

Prickly…

"Hold!"

The crowd turned on whoever shouted, but the sound of hooves followed. Only a fool stood in the street when horses were running. The crowd split, pressing up against the walls of the homes.

Diocail had impressed her before. Today he was every bit the man she'd first thought him to be.

Dangerous.

His people saw it too, looking at their laird as he came into the square, his stallion's shoes making a loud clopping sound against the brick. He pulled up, Muir by his side as he raised his hand to stop his men. But he didn't stop—he rode straight toward her. There was a flash of sunlight off the bare blade of his sword as he pulled it from the scabbard in a graceful motion and swung it in a wide arc above her head. It sliced neatly through the rope, sending the two men behind her stumbling back to avoid being sliced along with it.

His horse danced in a wide circle, taking him away

from her. She watched the way he controlled the beast, clinging to its back with the strength in his legs.

"Here now…" One of the men behind her had recovered. "We caught her spying."

A few members of the crowd added a jeer, but they were in the minority, as many of them kept their mouths closed and waited to see what their new laird would do. The children who had been near the front all scattered, and with good reason.

Diocail Gordon was furious.

"A spy, man?" Diocail demanded. "Are ye daft?"

"She was leaving," he persisted. "On her way back to her noble house with everything she's heard on Gordon land."

"Aye," the second man behind her joined his comrade. "Her husband said plenty about how he was going to use her blue blood to gain himself a position."

"So ye hang a lass because her fool of a husband wed her for gain?" Diocail demanded. "What man does nae marry for such reasons?"

Agreement rippled through the crowd.

"Why else would she be slipping away from ye?" her would-be executioner demanded. "If no' to carry secrets back to England and maybe keep our king from inheriting the throne from Elizabeth Tudor!"

The crowd was jeering once more. Their fear had been touched upon by the name of the English queen.

"The Protestants will march up and burn our homes…"

"They want to murder us!"

"Kill our children…"

James Stuart the Sixth of Scotland might have been

reared as a Protestant, but a great many of his subjects were still followers of the Catholic faith.

"She ran because she overheard us plotting to wed her to the laird," Muir tossed out nonchalantly.

Jane recoiled, stepping back into the men who had just fitted her with a noose. Diocail snapped his head around to glare at his captain.

"Aye," Aylin added as he appeared behind her. The noose suddenly went flying as he pulled it up and over her head and sent it onto the bricks. "Besides, she's Catholic. All the older English titles are."

That appeased many in the crowd. They nodded and looked on as the leather binding her hands was sliced.

Her tormentors weren't willing to see all of their fun ended just yet. "Well then," one said. "Best get on with wedding her quick, Laird, before she slips away again."

It was a public stab at Diocail's ability to control her and the Gordons. The crowd seemed quite eager to test their new laird's mettle.

Diocail didn't show any signs of weakness.

"Aye, can nae be undoing a consummated union," his fellow hangman added with a vulgar thrust of his hips.

She was shaking her head, but Aylin tugged her over to the edge of the scaffold as another of Diocail's men offered her a hand. Between the two, she was put on the horse with one of the retainers without any effort of her own. Diocail had his hands full dealing with the men of the village, and Muir was watching his back. Having been denied a hanging, they were pressing him for a wedding.

"Best to get the lass inside, Kory," Aylin said to the retainer behind her.

The crowd didn't intend to be denied. They clustered around Diocail, which allowed Kory to break away by guiding his horse around the other side of the gallows. When they arrived, the common room of the Hawk's Head Tavern was empty.

Kory didn't trust her to make her way inside though. He grasped her upper arm and took her through the door as people came up the street behind them. Diocail came in behind her, cursing in Gaelic.

"Why did ye tell them I want to wed her?" He turned on Muir as he pointed at the window. "Listen to them."

The crowd had taken up position outside the tavern. They were calling for a wedding, some of them already playing music in celebration.

"The world has gone completely mad." She meant to think the words, but they crossed her lips as she stumbled back and landed on a bench.

Niven was suddenly there, pressing a horn mug into her hand. He actually lifted it toward her lips as she sat there frozen.

"Drink up, there, mistress," Aylin encouraged her. "Ye need to collect yerself."

She drank deeply and gasped as the liquid burned a path down her throat. "Christ, what was that?"

"Gillanders claimed it was his finest whisky. Maybe I poured ye the wrong one. Try this…"

The mug was swapped for another one, and once more Niven lifted her hand up to her mouth. She thought to argue but was distracted by Diocail stepping up and jabbing his finger in the center of Muir's chest.

"The woman tried to run the second she could. Does that sound like someone I need as a wife?" he demanded.

"The lass just needs to settle in," Muir responded as he pressed Diocail back. It was part wrestling, part argument.

"Ye're insane, man," Diocail ground out. "I'll no' be wedding her."

"Listen." Muir turned his laird toward the window. "Does that sound like a village that will be forgetting ye did nae make good on yer word?"

Niven tipped the mug against her lips, and she opened her mouth because she was absorbed with the way Muir was fighting with Diocail. Lachie joined in with the captain.

"Normally I would support ye, Laird," the secretary declared in a soft voice. "But it does seem that in this matter, a wedding would solve a great many dilemmas. There is the state of the kitchen to consider, and with winter closing in, another bride will not be simple to obtain, much less with the conditions at the castle and, of course, how unstable yer own position is as laird. No' many fathers will agree to a union with a suitably educated lady. Yet we have one here, and her father is no' close enough to raise an objection."

Niven was swapping out her mug again when Jane felt the first wave of whisky hit her brain. Somehow, she'd downed two mugs already, and her empty belly was making certain she felt the alcohol quickly.

But Niven was pressing yet another mug to her lips.

"What are you doing?" she demanded, slipping down the bench and getting to her feet before Niven and Kory managed to surround her. Aylin joined them, creating a solid wall.

"Drink up, lass," Aylin encouraged her in a tone Jane was fairly sure he'd use on a chicken right before he wrung its neck.

"Aye, it will settle yer nerves," Kory added with a smile too bright to be sincere. "So we can get on with what needs doing. It's a good match, and we'll be happy to have ye on Gordon land."

"Better than yer father's house, for certain. Judging by what I've heard of yer last husband, best no' let yer father choose ye a second one," Aylin added.

"I am not getting married to anyone," she insisted, but Niven wasn't relenting in his attempts to get her to drink more. He tipped some of the contents of the mug into her open mouth as she spoke.

Jane recoiled and fell on the bench, which just made the three retainers bigger and more imposing. They leaned down, clearly intending to keep pouring whisky into her. Desperation made her slip to her knees and crawl past them.

She ended up facing Diocail as he tried to dodge around Muir and Lachie. They both jerked to a stop a single pace from one another. What Jane didn't expect was to see Diocail in nearly the same condition as she was. His eyes were wide, his face flushed from arguing.

She doubted he felt trapped like she did, but his men didn't appear to be finished with their attempts to convince him of their plans. Now that Jane and Diocail were facing each other, Lachie tried to take command of the situation.

"I can draw up a contract of marriage quickly."

Jane shook her head, but the crowd outside the window was growing. Someone opened the door, giving

them a glimpse of Diocail and Jane facing each other, and a cheer went up. Diocail flinched, but he drew himself up stiffly and wiped the emotion from his expression.

"I will await ye both in the church."

Jane turned her head, realizing the priest had come inside to discover whether his services would be needed. While she was struggling with her horror, he opened the door and raised his hands.

"The wedding will be in a bit." The crowd quieted to listen. "After the contract has been drawn up."

The door shut behind him as a cheer went up. Jane was shaking her head, closer to fainting than she'd ever been in her life and equally near to screaming in rage.

"I refuse to wed again." Her head was starting to spin, but that single thought was solid.

"Ye'd leave our laird to face his people as a man who did nae keep his word?" Lachie asked.

"There's a fine way to be after he kept ye from being raped and fed ye when ye were starving," Muir added as he sent her a stern look from next to Diocail's shoulder.

"He'll be called a liar and worse," Niven added.

"Aye, he'll be known as a man who was taken to his knees by a woman," Kory spoke up.

"No' fit to be laird," Aylin said solemnly.

"Enough," Diocail growled at them all. He grasped her wrist and tugged her toward him, sheltering her with his huge body as he shifted to one side so that he was facing all of his men.

How had she never noticed how much larger he was than herself? She was reduced to peeking around his arm.

"Listen to the lot of ye," he chastised them. "Sounding like a pack of orphans needing a mother."

None denied the charge. Lachie and Muir grinned back at their laird unashamedly.

"Sorley will have the kitchen fixed by the time we return, but that will be for naught if there is no' a mistress to see to the running of it," Lachie exclaimed, looking like a hungry child. "Mistress Jane is an educated woman, and as a fourth daughter, she can nae be complaining too much about having to take her new house in hand."

"She's got the spirit for it too," Muir added. "Most females would have taken Gillanders's offer over being turned out in their shift."

"You cannot simply decide to take me to your home," Jane declared.

Her outburst caused a round of confident smirks that made her step away from them. Somehow, her refusal struck them as a challenge, and they were a determined bunch.

"Christ," Diocail muttered. He reached back and grasped her wrist, tugging her toward the stairs. His men took his move as an agreement. Their smiles brightened, and they muttered congratulations to one another as Niven and Kory quickly fetched Lachie his traveling writing desk.

She gasped, her feet sliding against the floor, locked in frozen horror. Diocail turned on her. "Ye prefer to oversee the writing of the contract?"

There was a crinkle of paper as the secretary laid a new sheet out. Jane grabbed her skirts and lifted them. She dashed around Diocail, which was a task

considering his size and the narrowness of the stairs. But once she reached the loft bedroom, he came in behind her and kicked the door shut.

It slammed, and he grunted at it before fixing her with a hard look. "If ye had stayed in this room, mistress, that crowd would no' be out there."

It was the truth. Still, she faced off with him, confident in her choice. "How was I to know your people would be so bloody suspicious?"

"So a Scottish woman would be welcome in the village near yer father's house?" he cut back. "No one would question a stranger's appearance?"

Jane let out a huff in defeat. "Yes, they would."

It was the truth. Strangers were always noted. No one could afford to lock all their doors and windows, what with the price of locks, so the village relied upon the eyes of its citizens to prevent thieves from making their way into their homes.

"So why did ye leave?" he pressed her. "Ye've been treated kindly, Jane."

"I know," she answered back, shamed by the truth of his words.

"I asked naught of ye."

"Which is why I had to go," she exclaimed, frustrated by Fate's desire to see her at the mercy of everything around her. Including her own values.

"Ye do nae make any sense, woman." He turned and paced to the other end of the room.

The reference to her gender needled her. "As a woman, I should just expect to be kept? Well, I won't be weak."

He stopped and turned to face her, his eyes

narrowing as he contemplated her. "No, I suppose ye would be opposed to taking something ye do nae consider yer due."

She nodded, relieved he understood. "I truly meant to honor your kindness by leaving."

He let out a snort and moved closer, pointing toward the street where the muffled sounds of the crowd could still be heard. "The world does nae always respond well to kindness, Jane."

She tipped her head back and scoffed at the ceiling. "Oh, I know that very well, Diocail Gordon. Fate has never had anything but sharp edges for me."

He'd intended to lecture her more on the topic but stood still as she agreed. He let out a long breath. "I know that side of Fate meself."

She believed him. For a moment, their gazes met, and she realized once again how alike they were. Both were trying to survive on their own terms. Perhaps she did not know the details of his life, but clearly he had been shaped by circumstances hard enough to make him strong. His forearms were cut with hard muscle, which only came from practicing with the sword currently strapped to his back. His demeanor declared it as well—the way he masked his emotions, carefully guarding his feelings. Sometimes, it was best to take the pain of the flesh and console yourself with the knowledge that your emotions would be spared because you had kept them buried deep inside yourself.

"Is your home truly in such dire straits?"

She likely shouldn't have asked him. It wasn't the sort of thing any man would like to admit, much less a laird who was trying to establish himself.

He grunted and crossed his arms over his chest. "It is. The last laird was a miser who let the place fall to ruin while squeezing his staff nearly to death in his attempts to hold onto what he perceived as his."

"That's why you give some of the rent back." She'd seen him do it quite often.

"Aye," he nodded. "I expect loyalty, but give due consideration in return."

"And now I've given the villagers cause to doubt you." She breathed out a low sigh. "I am sorry for it."

He contemplated her for a long minute. She felt the muscles along her neck tightening as his gaze sharpened.

"Ye'll just have to be facing what yer actions have brought upon us both," he said with a nod.

"I don't understand…"

One of his eyebrows rose. "Do nae ye, lass?"

Her breath froze in her chest, her belly twisting with a very strange sort of sensation. She might have labeled it excitement, except for her absolute abhorrence for marriage. No matter how attractive the groom might seem.

She was shaking her head, her lips moving, but no sound made its way out of her mouth.

Diocail only cocked his head to one side in the face of her blunt refusal. He pressed his lips into a hard line before he turned and walked across the chamber to the table. A bottle of whisky sat there; he pulled the rope stopper from it and poured a generous amount into two mugs. He tossed one serving down his own throat before he looked back at her.

"I do nae believe either of us has much of a choice in the matter. I can take ye back out there

and declare ye a spy or stand firm with what Muir said about ye fleeing a match with me. If I try to tell them ye ran because ye have reservations about being kept, they will declare ye unnatural and burn ye as a witch."

"You and your men can ride away," she argued, "and drop me on the road. These are villagers, not trained retainers such as your men. For all that they might yell at us, their horses are not trained as yours are. They will be left behind."

"True," he agreed. "But I do that, lass, and word will spread far and wide that I am no' a man of me word. That I consort with English spies and set them free." He answered her in a tone that made it clear he had no doubt he spoke the truth.

An ugly truth at that.

"In case ye do nae understand just what that means to a clan such as the Gordons, allow me to explain." He refilled his mug and drank its contents in one swallow again. The bite of the whisky made his lips tight when he lowered the mug. "The clan will split, and there will be fighting over who is to take the lairdship. After me, there are at least five men with equal claims. Blood will flow in the spring until one faction takes enough lives to silence the others."

More than an ugly truth—a horrific one, it would seem. It left them staring at one another. Jane felt the weight of the burden and witnessed it in his brown eyes. He might easily have left her to the justice of his people, but he stood there, willing to share circumstances with her.

"So." His voice was low, and she realized it

indicated he was trying to hide his emotions. "What do ye want to do?"

She looked away and heard him close the distance between them. He reached out and tipped her chin up with two fingers. The connection made her shudder.

"Do nae look away, Jane." Her name came across his lips like a caress. "Answer me."

"I don't understand." She shifted away from him, feeling his presence so intensely it was impossible to remain close and maintain her wits.

"Ye ken well what is happening," he corrected her.

"No, I mean to say"—she lifted her gaze to his—"I do not understand why you are sharing my fate. Only my sisters were ever my compatriots against harsh circumstances."

"Ye do nae mention yer husband."

She stiffened. "No, I did not."

Jane turned around, determined to maintain her composure, or at least renew her grip on it before she turned back to face Diocail. She'd laid enough on his shoulders.

But she ended up facing the bed. She stiffened, looking at the place where Henry had taken her as his rights allowed him and then she had woken to him informing her she had a customer to satisfy in exchange for his gaming debts.

"Here now, just a tumble that you will hardly remember come morning…Lord knows I never earned so much coin for so little work as you will on your back…"

Diocail cupped her shoulder and turned her back to face him. "He's dead." There was a note in his voice that hinted that he wasn't sorry either. "And ye bled last week, so his grip on ye is broken. For good."

Heat teased her cheeks at the mention of her courses. Yet it shouldn't have surprised her—the man had the keenest senses.

There was a thump on the door before it was pushed open. Muir peeked in, looking at the bed before he spied Diocail and tugged on his cap. The captain stepped to the side, showing that Gillanders's wife was behind him with her arms piled high.

"The tailor has seen fit to send over his wife's best dress for the occasion," Muir declared jovially.

There was a rustle of silk as the woman bustled into the chamber and her daughters followed with hot kettles of steaming water. There was a bump on the stairs and a muffled word of profanity in Gaelic, and then Niven and his comrades were carrying a tub through the door. They had to raise it up and tip it so it fit sideways through the doorway, but they beamed with victory as they succeeded and set it down.

More of Diocail's men followed with buckets of cold water that they poured into the tub with bright grins. They all reached up and tugged on the corners of their bonnets before they left. Muir was the last one, supervising the work until the last Gordon left.

"The tailor is waiting below to get a look at ye so he can find ye a fine doublet to wear to church," Muir said to Diocail.

Diocail reached down and plucked the second mug he'd filled off the table and chuffed it. Muir's lips twitched with amusement even as the captain maintained his respectful expression. Diocail shifted his attention to Jane for a moment. "What is yer name, lass?"

It wasn't what she'd expected him to say.

"Yer full name, for the contract."

The loft room was so silent she'd have heard a mouse sighing. All eyes were upon her as she hesitated. Gillanders's wife looked as though she pitied her, while her daughters blinked in curiosity to see if she would bend and take the man everyone agreed was the best match for her.

But it was the way Diocail, laird of the Gordons, stood and waited for her answer. He didn't growl or narrow his eyes, but waited.

"Jane Katherine Stanley."

❧

Diocail felt something strange.

It was moving through his gut, leaving him, well, he'd say giddy, except that sort of emotion was suited only to young lads such as Bari.

Diocail made it three steps down the stairs before he heard the rise of conversation in the common room.

"She'll have the kitchen running smoothly inside a month…"

"No more fighting for our fare at supper…"

"Likely knows a thing or two about healing…"

"And the stench in the passageways, she'll banish that as well…"

His men were desperate. Diocail cursed Colum again for the ruin in which he'd left the Gordons. Muir was in front of him. When they reached the bottom floor of the common room, his captain smiled.

"I should smash yer balls with me knee," Diocail growled as he passed Muir.

All he gained from the captain was a snort, a very

unrepentant sound that left Diocail's pride smarting while his men turned hopeful looks his way.

Damned bunch of orphans.

And yet they looked to him. It sobered him, tempering his wounded pride, leaving him with the trust they seemed to have in his ability to bring them a better life. For all that his mother had believed he was due the position because of his blood, he had always wanted to be more in life than a birthright.

He wanted to earn his place, not simply take it.

Well, they were waiting for him to take to wife a woman who would serve them as dutifully as they would protect her and her children.

He swept the room and found Gillanders. "Fetch up that load of wine her last husband brought ye." Diocail tossed some gold onto the tabletop. "We'll be needing it for the celebration."

His men cheered, and Lachie smiled as he dipped his quill into his inkwell for Diocail to sign the newly written marriage contract. The sound of the quill scratching against the paper filled the common room, and everyone looked on until it was done.

"I need a bath."

His men hooted with amusement, the jesting at his expense beginning.

And may God have mercy on them all.

❧

"How lucky to have just finished yer courses."

Gillanders's wife had no reservations against frank speaking. Her youngest daughter blushed, but not the older ones.

"Yer last husband was a poor one to be sure," she continued. "Better to know for certain ye will nae have the trouble of raising up his child and worrying it will be too much like its sire."

She turned and clapped her hands. Her daughters seemed to be used to such commands. They surrounded Jane, plucking laces from where they were tucked and popping open the knots while she twisted and tried to evade them.

And where will you go? Back to the gallows?

The feeling of the noose was once again as strong as if it were still resting against her collarbone.

So close...

She truly had come as close as one might to being hung, and she had survived. The faces of those jeering at her were burned into her memory, and it nauseated her to think that those same villagers were all looking forward to watching her wedding.

It made no sense...

Her clothing fell away, puddling at her feet as Gillanders's wife supervised with her hands on her ample hips. She snapped her fingers, and two of the girls lifted the kettles to add the hot water to the tub.

"In with ye now," she decreed. "Wedding the laird, ye're fortunate indeed. Make sure ye thank God in yer prayers for the parents who saw ye educated in the running of a house."

There was a splash and then another as the girls began to wash her. Jane shied away from their hands, but they had her surrounded, so she gave up and let them bathe her. The soap was sweetly scented with

lavender, and they scrubbed her from head to toe, rinsing out her hair twice before there was a double clap from their mother and she was allowed to rise.

Her skin stung, but in a pleasant way because she knew she was clean. Bathing was an indulgence for which she admitted to having a fondness. Let the church preach that it was a vanity; she honestly couldn't see how having feet that stank brought her closer to Christ.

So she'd washed her toes every night in the privacy of her room and taken turns watching at the mill door while her sisters had snuck down to bathe with the aid of the waterwheel that also drove the grinding stone.

"The dress is made of silk." Gillanders's wife was petting it lovingly. "Ye will look like an angel with the candlelight on it."

An angel. Better than being one in reality.

That thought kept her still as they dressed her in a robe so her hair might be brushed out and dried in front of the fire. One of them produced the chest from the wagon she and Henry had traveled in that contained her hairpins and other personal items.

They braided and rolled her hair, weaving ribbons into it. After that came a delicate chemise that was nearly transparent and floated down to cover her skin like a sprinkling of flower petals.

"Lace stockings…" There was another sigh. "I hear the English queen wears naught else."

The stockings were threaded onto her legs carefully and secured with more ribbons. A pair of red heeled shoes was next, just a trifle too small for her feet.

"Ye'll no' be in them long enough to care."

They pulled her to her feet and laced a corset into place before they tied a hip bolster around her hips, and then a farthingale was lifted high over her head so that she had to raise her arms before it was lowered. It was a slip with stiff hoops sewn into it to keep the skirts out wide.

The underskirt had a front panel decorated with thin strips of velvet. Jane couldn't resist petting one.

"Aye, it's no' often any of us has any reason for such finery." Gillanders's wife herself was bringing the overskirt, with more of the same velvet. "The tailor, he goes down to the lowlands every now and again, to the court, to keep his skills sharp on what is in fashion. This dress was for his daughter when he took her the last time. Showed her off, he did. Maybe by next year, she'll have herself a grand match."

The girls made little sounds of envy as the skirt was secured and the farthingale held it out. The bodice was cut low, showing off the plump swells of Jane's breasts. The girls eased the sleeves up her arms and used ribbons to secure them in place.

When it was all done, Jane didn't have the heart to do anything but smile. They all appeared to be enjoying the moment in that way women found pleasure in helping one another. She wasn't English in their eyes; she was a bride, and they were part of the celebration.

Life had too many harsh moments to squander the happy ones. Except that marriage had only been another bitter disappointment. She held that knowledge close to her heart, hiding it with a soft smile she had learned to maintain even when she had misgivings.

You will not be weak…

But it did appear she would be Diocail Gordon's wife. God help her.

❦

"Get in there!"

The door to the loft room was kicked in, and right after it hit the wall, Diocail stumbled across the threshold, Muir and Kory grinning at Jane before they yanked the door shut.

"I've a bloody good memory, ye pair of swine!" Diocail growled at the door.

"As do I." She hadn't meant to agree with him, but Diocail turned to look at her and slowly grinned.

"Good, because they are doing this to keep ye, and I'll warn ye now, lass, it will not be a simple thing to take the house in hand." He growled in a very menacing way before he shrugged and righted his doublet. The garment was half down his arms, trapping them against his body. It too was made of fine velvet and really too small for Diocail's shoulders because the men in the village didn't practice sword fighting as much as he did. It stuck, earning a snort from him as he struggled.

"Here now," she said, moving toward him. "You don't want to tear it. I imagine the tailor will charge you more than it's worth because you will have no honorable recourse but to pay if it is damaged."

"Waste of coin," he groused as he flicked open the tiny buttons that ran down the front of it. He shrugged, and she caught the garment as it slid down his arms. "I've never worn something so frivolous in me life."

Jane set the doublet on a chair and sat down to tug at one of the shoes. "I know exactly how you feel."

She held it up, showing off the two-inch heel with a narrow foundation that had kept her teetering throughout their wedding. The leather was worked in a lace pattern that must have taken days of labor to create. "Good for nothing except standing about and being admired. One little sneeze would have sent me stumbling."

Diocail took the shoe from her and contemplated it. When he looked back, she was pulling the other one off her foot with a sigh.

"Well, that is a relief."

She looked up at him as she rubbed her ankle.

"I thought ye were wobbling about near to fainting."

She sent him a narrow-eyed look. "I have a stiffer backbone than that."

He rolled his arms, and she heard his back pop. "It served a purpose though." He jerked his head toward the door. "The villagers are quite convinced that ye fled me."

Jane decided to hold her tongue and rubbed her other foot. They were left in an uneasy silence, while she was far too conscious of the reason they had been sent abovestairs.

To consummate the union, of course.

Below them, music was being played as wine flowed. Laughter came in bursts as people started dancing. None of them would leave until they knew the vows were sealed.

God help her, she simply didn't think she could lie in the same bed with Diocail as she had with Henry. And yet it was his right.

"Ye truly care naught for such things?"

Lost in her own thoughts, she was startled by his question and had to look at him for a long moment before she realized he was still holding the shoe.

"Not one bit." She pointed at his boots. "I'd rather have footwear like yours that keeps my toes from turning numb."

His lips twitched. "Well, ye'll no' have any trouble getting a pair on Gordon land. No' if ye truly have the education yer skill with the needle hints at."

With the velvet doublet discarded, he was wearing only his shirt and kilt. The moment was far more intimate than she was accustomed to seeing him. The reason they were both there was suddenly foremost in her thoughts, bringing heat to her cheeks.

He noticed her color, his gaze going to the stain spreading across her face. There was a glitter of victory in his eyes that struck her as very personal.

"In fact," he muttered as he came closer, reaching out to stroke one side of her face. "I might just have more than a few things ye will find to yer liking in me home, Jane."

There was a promise in his tone, and it sent a shiver down her spine that curled her toes. She was warm, overly so, and envious of his lack of attire. The dress felt too constricting as he drew his fingertips along her cheeks, stunning her with how much she enjoyed his touch.

There was a thump on the door before it was pushed in. Gillanders's wife and daughters were already moving into the room before they realized Diocail was there. They froze and lowered themselves.

"Yer pardon, Laird," Gillanders's wife hurried forward. "I did nae think ye'd be up so soon. We'll have her out of that dress and inspected in just a wee bit. Best ye go below."

Several older women were making their way into the room, clearly there to witness her health and lack of witch marks. It might be distasteful, but the idea of being accused of being the devil's harlot was far more so. The feeling of that noose was too fresh in her mind; she would not even consider refusing.

Diocail didn't want to move. She watched his eyes narrow with frustration and felt a prickle of it herself for being parted from him.

But the women were not going to give way. They gently slipped between him and her, pushing him back with their numbers until she heard him grunt and watched him turn toward the door.

Whatever the odd sensations had been, they dissipated as the women began to strip her and inspect her body. She recalled the cold detachment needed to stand still through the process very well from her first wedding.

❧

"There ye are." Muir reached out and grabbed Diocail by the shoulder. "I've someone for ye to meet."

A mug was offered up by Lachie as the secretary shooed the other men away from a table in the far corner of the common room. The woman sitting at the table was pretty; as Diocail took a second look, he realized she was wearing face paint. A distinct scent of rose water clung to her, and she noticed him taking a

second look, leaning slightly forward so he could catch a glimpse down her bodice.

He stiffened, frowning when he realized he was backing away. He'd never been a man to squander an opportunity to enjoy a fair lass when she was in the mood to offer him a look. Tonight, though, her loose moral standards didn't interest him the least bit.

Muir slapped him on the shoulder, pushing him close to the woman. "Here now, Janet here is just the sort of…ah…"

"Woman," Lachie supplied with a slight squeak in his tone.

Muir nodded. "Woman to help ye make certain yer new wife is…well…content."

"I would suggest satisfied," Janet purred as she swept a fan in front of her face in a lazy motion to make sure they all smelled how sweet she was. There was a little curve to her lips that suggested she was very conscious of her effect on the opposite sex.

"Ye brought her." Diocail glared at Muir. "A woman of…" He ended up making a gesture toward her while he struggled to find a word that wasn't offensive.

"Experience and knowledge." Janet spoke the pair of words with a touch of heat that wasn't lost on any of them.

"Aye," Muir crowed with victory. "Maybe the castle is rough, but ye can make sure the lass finds yer bed very nice to be in."

"Precisely," Lachie added as he flattened his hands on the table. "Janet knows what a woman desires and is bold enough to tell ye."

Janet's eyes slanted in a purely sensual way. Her

experience and ease with the topic were plain, and it pissed him the hell off because Jane didn't belong in a conversation of that sort.

"I admit, me patience is worn near thread bare," Diocail growled. "To suggest I need guidance in how to please me wife!"

"Every man does." Janet delivered her opinion with a delicate, knowing smile.

Muir was nodding, Lachie grinning from ear to ear when Diocail sent his fist into Muir's jaw.

Fight, well, he knew how to do that very well.

~~~

"Mistress… Mistress!"

Young Bari was halfway into the room before he heard the other women hissing at him. He looked up with the innocent, wide eyes of youth, blinking as he failed to comprehend that Jane was in nothing but her chemise and corset.

The women clustered around her as she crossed her arms over her breasts. "Out!" One of them pointed him back the way he'd come.

Bari pulled his thoughts together. "I need the mistress… below…there is blood. The laird needs…stitching."

With the door open, Jane was suddenly aware of the lack of music and laughter. The common room had gone silent far too early in the evening. It could mean only one thing.

A fight.

"Men," Gillanders's wife groused.

"Never content," another woman agreed, echoing the same disgusted tone.

"Best get dressed." One of the women tossed Jane her skirt as Gillanders's wife's heels made pounding sounds on the stairs.

"*Sweet mercy!*" floated up from the ground floor as Jane struggled to tie the waistband closed and pull her bodice on.

She looked rather off with her hair still braided with ribbons while wearing common wool, but the moment she caught sight of the men, she realized her appearance was of no concern.

The common room was a disaster. Tables overturned, benches tossed everywhere, including one that had landed too near the hearth and caught fire during the fight. Ale and wine were splattered everywhere, the scent of the liquor mixing with those of fresh blood and smoke.

There was profanity in the air as Jane swept the room, trying to decide who was the most injured.

"Here, mistress." Young Bari was back, pressing the roll of canvas that held the medical supplies into her hands. "I brought yer sewing one too in case ye need the needles."

"Good job." She praised him as she tugged on a table and turned it upright with the help of one of Gillanders's daughters.

"Someone will have to pay for all this damage…" Gillanders was sprawled on his backside, his huge kilt spread around him while his pudgy ankles and knees were on display. His wife and daughters flocked to him when he took to complaining. Jane decided he was making too much fuss to be dying.

Her new husband, on the other hand, had bright

red blood staining his shirtsleeve, and was enough to have her scurry over to him.

"It's just a cut," he informed her.

"One that is deep," she argued as she tried to pull the torn fabric away from the wound to see it better.

Diocail made a sound in the back of his throat that made it clear he didn't think he needed attention. He tried to rise off the bench he was sitting on, but Muir was suddenly there pushing him down by his shoulders. Diocail growled something at him in Gaelic.

"Ye damned swine," Muir replied. "I was only trying to help."

"I've had enough of yer ideas for one day," Diocail declared ominously.

His meaning was clear, and his tone slapped her across the face with how little he cared for their forced union. No one in the room missed it either. The rest of the Gordon retainers looked away from her as they stood around waiting their turn for her attention. The fight had included them all, by the look of them. Diocail realized he'd publicly insulted her, his eyes narrowing as he groaned.

"I need a chest from the wagon I arrived in," she said softly. Better to tend to them than dwell on her circumstances. "It has more supplies than you brought with you."

Muir nodded once before he was off and through the door, looking relieved to have a reason to escape.

"Here now, that chest does nae belong to ye," Gillanders argued. His family had him off the floor and sitting in a chair. "Yer husband lost it to me playing at dice."

The landlord had made a fatal error in judgment. The Gordons were all looking for anything to soothe the guilt they felt over her treatment, and Gillanders had just made a very large target of himself.

"Ye are a blood-sucking leach!" Diocail declared with a growl. "I'm ashamed to call ye a fellow Scot!"

Niven and Kory were moving toward the landlord, their fingers opening and closing into fists.

"Fleecing an Englishman is one thing," Niven declared. "A woman is another matter."

"Aye," Kory echoed the sentiment. "Ye've been unchristian toward the lady, and that's a fact."

"She's English," Gillanders said in his own defense.

"She's me mistress, man," Kory exclaimed.

"And a woman," Niven added. "Ye turned her out to starve when ye're the size of me horse!"

"She refused to work for her keep." Gillanders snorted, indignant.

"I declined to earn my way in your bed." She likely should have keep her mouth shut, but the day had been too long and far too draining.

Gillanders made the mistake of lowering his gaze to her cleavage, on display because she was leaning over to get a closer look at the cut on Diocail's head.

Diocail let out a snarl and lunged across the space between him and the landlord. There were squeals as the women recoiled, and some of the male members of the staff made an effort to protect their employer.

There was a thump at her feet as Muir dropped the chest. He looked at Bari. "Get yer mistress out of the way, lad!"

A moment later the captain was part of the fray.

The sound of flesh hitting flesh was harsh as men grunted and tried to beat one another senseless.

"Mistress," Bari implored her as he tugged on her skirts with a surprising amount of strength.

The fight ended as abruptly as it had begun. Gillanders was flat on his back again, his head lolling to the side as his eyes closed. The Gordon retainers all had rather satisfied looks on their faces even as they hunched over and cradled injured parts of their bodies.

"We're leaving," Diocail declared as he wiped the blood off his face with his sleeve and nodded at the unconscious form of Gillanders.

"Aye," Muir agreed. "And none too soon, to my way of thinking."

Kory and Niven were already heading toward the door to fetch the horses.

"And tell yer father," Diocail pointed at Gillanders's eldest son, who had blood running out of his nose. "If I hear even a whisper about me owing this family even a copper penny, I'll be back to settle accounts, and he will no' like it one bit. I promise ye that."

Diocail turned to Jane. "Fetch yer things."

Diocail had tempered his tone, making it even and respectful, but there was a core of solid authority that made it clear he was the laird. She nodded to him out of habit before she turned and ran up the stairs to the loft room. It took only moments to collect her meager belongings. Their wedding finery caught her eye as did the turned-down bedding.

At last, Fate was offering her hope. With no consummation, the union might be annulled. Diocail's tone suddenly struck her as a ray of sunshine instead

of an insult. The man clearly didn't want to be saddled with her for a wife.

Good.

She refused to consider the tiny prickling of disappointment attempting to dissuade her from being happy about them parting ways.

Clinging to him would be weak, and her resolve to remain strong was still the only thing she had left to call her own. She wouldn't be giving it up in order to force Diocail to keep her.

No, she would not be weak or take enough leave of her senses to do something so rash as stay in a marriage that saw no contract signed with her family. Diocail might cast her out at any time if he didn't fear her family. For all that Alicia ran a stern house, she'd never allow Jane to be treated in such a manner.

No, the only true security lay in returning to her family. No matter the temptation to stay.

Four

"It's a good thing ye are accomplished at making shirts."

Muir spoke to her sometime late the next day. The captain's eye was swollen shut, but he'd only allowed her to clean it once before waving her away, dismissing it as "naught."

"Yer husband is rather hard on his." Muir held up the tattered remains of Diocail's shirt. The blood had dried dark brown. Washing it would be a waste of time because the lower sleeve was shredded, as was a good portion of the front of the garment.

"So it would seem." Jane took the shirt, earning a grin from the captain.

She looked across the camp and found Diocail. He'd pressed them on to the next village and seen to the tenants waiting for him before riding out again. There was little light left when he called a halt to their day, and the lack of sleep the night before had everyone anticipating a good night's rest. Bari was already sleeping in the wagon.

Diocail was avoiding her.

It shouldn't bother her. Or at least she had to accept that she had no right to be wounded, since she felt an annulment would be the best for both of them.

However, she would need his agreement for that to happen. Her belly tightened as she moved toward him. Honestly, she should have had a better grip on her poise now that she had clothing. But it seemed being properly covered didn't affect the way she felt when Diocail looked at her, as if he could strip her bare with his brown eyes. There was a boldness in him that lurked like a promise in his warm gaze. He'd taken the slap she'd delivered like a prize, and she would be a liar if she didn't admit to wanting to know just what manner of husband he might have made.

But following foolish whims was likely to get her nothing more than dire circumstances, so she pushed herself forward, intent on securing his agreement to an annulment.

It was sound, logical thinking.

And ever so disappointing.

Lachie was sitting next to Diocail, but the secretary flashed her a grin before leaving as she approached.

"My apologies if I am interrupting."

Diocail offered her an unreadable expression. "Ye're me wife."

His tone was firm, which gave her a moment of pause. Jane drew herself up straight. "Yes, it was a necessary action, as you said."

He nodded.

"However, now that we are well away, I thought we should discuss the future." Her tone came across as congenial, which should have pleased her, since she

was battling to maintain her poise. It was frustrating the way her heart was accelerating, her voice trying to rise higher as though the discussion was somehow alarming to her.

"We've two more weeks on the road before we return home," he informed her.

"I see." She bit her lower lip. "I would think it would be best to leave me at the next crossroads so I can make my way back to England."

His eyes narrowed slightly. "And I think ye're daft for suggesting such a thing."

She didn't care for how easily he dismissed her opinion, even as she realized it was exactly what she expected from him. Negotiation wasn't part of his persona. He was a leader and took to the position more naturally than anyone she had ever encountered.

Which made it all the more important for her not to take shelter beneath his wing. He deserved respect for the honorable man he was.

"You needn't insult my intelligence," she countered. "I know very well you did not wish to wed me. I do not intend to exploit your kindness."

Something she'd said gave him pause. She watched him contemplate her for a long moment as though he was weighing his response.

"It's understandable ye did nae wish to wed," he agreed. "Yer last husband was a bastard."

Jane looked away, for some reason feeling exposed. Diocail reached out and cupped the side of her face, gently turning her back toward his keen stare. The simple touch sent a pleasurable shiver down her spine.

"It's his shame, and no mistake about it."

God but she enjoyed hearing him say that. How often had she heard it was her place to toil and please her husband? That the man was master of home and spouse? Happiness was merely a selfish desire she was expected to discard in favor of duty. Her temper strained against such dictates, and yet she'd kept it tightly leashed because the law favored Henry in every way.

"He's dead, and I'll say plainly it's a blessing," Diocail continued.

The temptation to take solace in his tone was growing. She drew back, severing the connection between their flesh as she drew in a breath far too shaky for her pride.

How could she respond to him? To any man? It was true she had a favorable opinion of Diocail, however, he was still very much a stranger. Better the devil she knew.

Which was Alicia.

"On to the matter of deciding when I will make my way back to my father's house." Her words came out in a rush, as though she was trying to convince herself of what she said.

"Yer father wed ye to a bastard," Diocail declared in a voice so low, she had to strain to hear it clearly. "I will nae be sending ye back to his house so he can do it a second time."

"As I told you, I will not be weak enough to take solace in your kindness."

There. At last her poise had proven solid. She stared straight at him, unwavering in her choice.

Diocail was just as solid in the way he stared back at

her. "As to that, lass, I'll be giving ye the time to get accustomed to me."

He stood and offered her a hand. She laid her hand into his before she thought about what she was doing. The connection sent another tremor through her, this one making her belly flutter.

"Perhaps I owe Gillanders a small debt for compelling us to leave. We were not forced to spend the night together."

She tried to pull back, but he slipped his hand down to her wrist and held her in place. She'd realized he was strong, just not the extent. At that moment, she was so keenly aware of him it frightened her. It felt as if she were drowning.

He moved closer, looming over her as she struggled to make sense of his words, her brain fighting off a rush of impulses. "I confess, I am no' certain I'd have made it through the night and kept me hands off ye when I knew I had the church's blessing to touch ye."

"But you did not want to wed me." She jerked against his hold. For a moment, he held her, letting her feel his determination through the grip, but then he released her, his expression tightening as she stumbled back and sent him a hard glare.

"So," she continued. "You can just forget about touching me."

Heat teased her cheeks as she spoke the words out loud. Why? She honestly didn't know. Part of her refused to ignore the fact that she liked it when his skin connected with hers.

He stepped toward her, catching a handful of her

skirt to keep her close. "And ye have some time to settle into yer circumstances."

He released her skirt, and she stumbled back again. The urge to step closer toward him and argue was strong. She bit it back, counseling herself to maintaining a calm demeanor.

He liked it when she flamed at him.

So she turned and began to walk away.

"I will be waiting, Jane."

Her breath caught with anticipation. She looked back, unable to stop herself. His lips twitched, rising into an arrogant grin of victory.

"Stubborn man," she accused. "Why me? You are a fine-looking man. I cannot believe you have difficulty...filling your bed."

Now he'd pushed her past being polite. She felt the sting of heat in her cheeks as she faced off with him. It increased as his lips twitched, declaring how much he enjoyed her distemper.

"Why are you smiling?" she demanded. "No man desires a shrew who doesn't keep to her place or hold her tongue."

The man laughed at her display of temper.

Diocail Gordon tipped his head back and roared with amusement while she stared at him in confusion. The truth was her mouth was open, but her tongue was frozen as he leaned forward, slapped his thigh, and opened his eyes to display the unmistakable glitter of satisfaction.

"Ye'll be filling me bed," he assured her as she caught sight of his men boldly listening to their conversation. "And ye can let yer spirit loose, lass. I

can nae wait to warm me hands on the flames I see in yer eyes."

"You will wait," she declared boldly. "Until… well…until…" Why had she never learned to curse? It was bloody unfair considering how Fate was determined to toy with her.

"Until we reach home," Diocail finished for her.

"I am not going with you."

His amusement died a little as determination filled his eyes. "Oh yes, ye are, Jane. That's a promise."

One of his men stepped closer to ensure she knew they agreed with their laird.

"To…take your kitchen in hand?" she tossed her hand into the air, so flustered she'd lost control of her actions as well. "For Christ's sake, find a large, round woman, and hire her as your Head of House."

"But why?" Niven spoke as he was thinking. "A round woman, I mean?"

Muir reached over and pushed him. "Do nae interrupt the mistress."

The title made her want to bare her teeth. She fought the urge, and Diocail crossed his arms over his wide chest, tucking his chin low and stroking his beard to hide the smirk curving his lips.

"Do not ever trust a skinny cook," Jane tossed out, completely frustrated with the lot of them.

Understanding brightened Niven's face along with those of his companions. Then their gazes swept her from head to toe, and they frowned.

"Her husband and father were both misers." Diocail seemed to know what his men were thinking. The worried looks in their eyes faded as her temper boiled over.

"I am *not*…going with you."

A moment later, she was hanging over Diocail's shoulder. His men hooted with mirth as she was carried back toward the wagon. Diocail tossed her into it with all the ease of moving a bag of grain.

"Diocail—"

He smothered the rest of her retort beneath his lips. The man reached around and cupped her nape before tilting his head and fitting his mouth against hers.

The kiss wasn't as brutal as she expected. No, it was hard with promise and sent a twist of anticipation through her insides. She shivered as he opened her lips with his, kissing her thoroughly and leaving her breathless. Her very skin felt more sensitive, her clothing tight as though it was holding her back from enjoying his embrace even more.

"Leave that wagon, and I will be happy to give ye me full attention." He reached up and tugged on the corner of his bonnet.

The light was fading, the last of the day departing. The evening breeze held the touch of cooler weather, but her temper kept her plenty warm as she fought the urge to test him. Diocail waited for a long moment, watching her as she curled her fingers into fists and settled for punching her puddled skirts.

A hint of disappointment entered his eyes before he turned and walked back to join his men. Young Bari was watching her as well, his eyes huge in his young face. Muir reached out and took him by the shoulder, steering him toward where the Gordon retainers were settling down for the night. Bari flashed them a grin, enjoying being allowed among

them instead of being sent to sleep in the wagon with a woman.

Diocail didn't lie down all the way. He settled back against his saddle to keep his shoulders propped up so he might open his eyes and see anyone approaching. He'd tugged the longer pleats that formed the back of his kilt up and around his shoulders before he settled down and pulled the fabric around himself. But his hand returned to the hilt of his dagger before he sent Jane a last look and closed his eyes.

Muir was sitting on a rock, slowly working a stone over the blade of his sword. The fire had been allowed to die down to just a single log, and the light illuminated his face as he took the first watch. They all knew their place and were devoted to one another. It was admirable, but that didn't mean she was going to agree to being taken along like some prize they had encountered on the road. Even if Diocail had decided she would be.

Tomorrow. Tomorrow she'd find a way to change his mind.

Diocail wasn't the only stubborn one among them, after all.

※

The harvest was finished.

They saw the effect on the faces of those they encountered. The labor of the spring had paid off in full root cellars and enough grain to put food on the table for their families. It was time for celebration and feasting.

Jane noticed the increase in people on the road as

they neared the next village. They moved toward the outer edge of the village, the scent of roasting boar floating on the wind as they heard music in the distance. They were happy faces too, eager for celebration before the winter shut everyone inside.

"No work today, lads," Diocail announced as he contemplated what was in front of them. "Harvest festival."

People were eagerly leaving their homes, the younger girls wearing wreaths made of autumn leaves and nuts. They wore their best clothing—many of the skirts looked new. Their steps echoed on the road as they all but danced toward the festival and what would likely be the last entertainment until after winter had passed.

"There are Grants here," Muir cautioned.

"Aye," Diocail nodded. "But we're on the edge of our land, so it's to be expected."

"Are you fighting with them?" Jane asked.

Muir sent her a grin as Diocail offered her a shrug. "The last laird was no' very good at making friends with his neighbors."

"Well, we can no' be leaving," Muir stated. "No' when it's our land."

"Symon Grant is likely here to get a look at me," Diocail answered. He shifted and raised his hand. "Let's no' waste the light, lads."

Their arrival was noted. Men raised their tankards as they sat drinking beneath the trees. Merchants looked up, hope of more sales glittering in their eyes. More than one young girl looked toward the retainers with wicked enjoyment in her eyes. A market fair was the perfect opportunity to indulge in a bit of flirtation that on a normal day would be considered improper.

Jane discovered herself smiling. It seemed a very
long time since she'd indulged in simple whimsy. So
very long since there had been anything except duty
foremost in her thoughts.

"There's something I'd like to see more often."

Diocail's tone was different. She turned and discovered an easygoing grin on his lips and a flicker of
relaxation in his brown eyes.

"Ye should smile more often, lass," he said softly.

He was waiting, offering her his hand to help her
out of the wagon. She could manage the task on her
own and almost said so.

Yet there was a grin on his lips and a sparkle in his
eyes she couldn't bear to squash beneath the weight of
reality. The music and scent of celebration were too
tempting, as was the gallant manner in which he was
waiting to play her escort.

She placed her hand into his before she realized
he was making a show of his favor. The move didn't
go unnoticed either. She watched several onlookers
turn to whisper to those next to them. Diocail shifted
her hand to his arm and turned so they were strolling
together. His men closed in around them as he took
her toward the festival.

Henry had never escorted her so gallantly.

Jane!

She truly meant to chide herself, but the truth was
she had never enjoyed Henry's touch so very much.
Being on Diocail's arm was, well, it was all the things
she'd once daydreamed about.

The moment was short-lived. She felt his forearm
tighten as a group of men started toward them. They

wore similar clothing, meaning they'd clearly dressed for function instead of fashion. Their kilts were formed with a slightly different coloration of plaid wool, but their doublets and jerkins were leather and thick wool, most of the oversleeves tied behind their backs. Just like Diocail, there was one man who was clearly the laird.

"Someone you know?"

She likely shouldn't have voiced the question. Women were expected to hold their tongues, and yet part of her seemed to be indulging in the fact that he claimed to like her unbridled.

"Symon Grant," Diocail replied. "His land borders me own."

The man in question was every bit as large as Diocail. He moved up to them and stopped with his feet braced apart as he looked directly at Diocail. It was clear Symon had come to see the new laird of the Gordons.

"Niven," Diocail called out.

The retainer was quick to answer his laird's summons. Diocail nodded to Niven before he released Jane's hand and stepped in front of her. Niven tugged her back as the new group came closer.

"Laird Symon Grant," Diocail offered first.

"Laird"—Symon drew out the title—"Diocail Gordon."

Around them, people aimed curious looks their way. Jane watched as a few of them began to wager. Niven was still trying to ease her backward, which sent a twist of apprehension through her.

Apparently, fighting wasn't out of the question.

"So this is Diocail Gordon..."

A woman was suddenly sweeping in front of Symon Grant, her eyes flickering with mirth. She stopped, and her skirts swished before she boldly settled a hand onto her hip and contemplated Diocail from head to toe. Whoever she was, she was a beauty and brazen.

"I must say," she informed them all with a voice as sweet as honey. "Me disappointment is nearly impossible to bear."

"Is that a fact, mistress?" Diocail asked in a guarded tone.

"It most certainly is," she continued. "For I have heard that ye—" She pointed a slim finger at him. "Are a consort of the devil, that ye slayed Tyree Gordon with spells from Satan himself, and that old laird Colum was the one who first made the pact with the unholy fallen angel, which accounts for how long he lived."

"Well, now," Diocail replied as he crossed his arms over his chest. "That is a great deal to live up to."

She pursed her lips and swept her gaze up and down Diocail once more. "Ye fall short, sir."

Diocail let out a bark of amusement. "In this case, I believe I will be content no' to measure up to the idea of a demon."

"Brenda." There was a soft warning in Symon Grant's voice. The man had amazing topaz eyes that Jane stared at for a moment before Brenda shifted her attention, looking at Jane.

"Oh yes." Brenda swept Diocail a deep courtesy. "On to the business, it would seem."

Symon nodded at her. Brenda wasn't repentant or

in any fashion submissive to his authority. No, there was a twinkle in her eye and a smile on her lips. She reached out for Jane.

"It would seem the men desire the women to be gone." She crossed over without a care for the fact that she was among the Gordons and clasped Jane's hand. "We should take ourselves off as the obedient creatures they desire us to be..."

Symon let out a scoffing sound, but the look he sent Brenda was amused. Brenda winked at Jane. "We'll simply have to content ourselves with spending as much of their money as possible."

Brenda's brazen attitude was infectious—or at least amusing. Jane laughed as Brenda tugged her forward. They ended up nearly skipping away from the men. There was a whistle from behind her that Jane recognized as Diocail's. She turned to glance back at him. He'd used it with his men before, and today was no different. Niven and Aylin nodded, one of them catching a purse their laird tossed into the air before setting a determined pace to catch up with her. A couple of Symon's men were already on their way to join Brenda.

"We'll have much more fun without them anyway," Brenda informed her as though the two women were compatriots.

In fact, Brenda had hooked her arm through Jane's and was strolling along as though the two were long-lost friends. "So tell me true," Brenda continued. "Are ye newly wed to Diocail?"

Jane worried her lower lip, which only served to confirm Brenda's suspicions.

"Hmmm…" Brenda made a soft sound beneath her breath. "I admit I am most curious now. There is a wild tale of ye being rescued from the hangman's noose and wed by demand of the crowd."

Jane let out a sigh. "All true. Laird Gordon has shouldered much for his kindness toward me."

Brenda made a scoffing sound in her throat. "This is Scotland." The woman turned to face her. "That level of meekness must be discarded at once." She leaned close. "I beg ye, else me cousin is like to expect the same from me."

Jane laughed. She tried to seal the sound inside her mouth and ended up choking. "I'm sorry, but—" She looked at Brenda, with her flashing eyes and perfect features. "I simply cannot see you needing to be so reserved."

"There was a time when I was." For a moment, darkness shadowed in her eyes, but she shook it off. "My first husband was a bastard as well. I was his chattel, and even if he did nae wager me favors against a roll of the dice, it was only because he hadn't yet thought to do so."

"You really have heard everything there is to know of my circumstances." And it was more than a bit unsettling.

Brenda merely shrugged and pulled her toward a merchant who was offering two mugs of fresh-pressed cider. Jane hesitated, but Niven placed a coin down on the counter before Jane could tell him no.

"Enjoy," Brenda encouraged her. "If what I've heard of Gordon land is true…" Brenda sent her a confident smirk. "And me sources are very reliable…"

She took a sip of the cider and nodded approval. "Ye'll be earning every treat Diocail pays for today tenfold."

"It sounds more like the man needs a competent Head of House."

Brenda nodded after lowering her mug. "Indeed. Yet this is the Highlands. Such a woman is not easily found, and more than one man has wed for such a woman."

Jane was distracted by the look on Niven's face. He had a gleam of satisfaction in his eyes and firm confidence on his face. He looked at her as though she were the answer to something, and surprisingly, she enjoyed it. She felt needed and more valued than she ever had before.

"Come on, then." Brenda took her by the hand and tugged her toward the waiting merchants. "Let's find ye something pretty. Yer dress is drab, no' at all what a bride should be wearing."

"I couldn't spend—"

Brenda turned on her in a swirl of skirts and flashing eyes that promised mayhem. "Ye most certainly can."

"We are planning to annul—"

There was a grunt from Aylin that made it clear the retainer wasn't pleased by her words. She glanced at her chaperones and found both eyeing her with disapproval. But it was Brenda's soft little "hmm" that claimed Jane's full attention. Brenda stepped in close so her words wouldn't carry.

"If Diocail is going to send ye back to England, why is he taking ye further north?" she asked bluntly.

Jane's eyes widened, but Brenda reached between them and clasped her wrist to keep her from recoiling. "Is he terrible to ye?"

It was a frank question. Looking into Brenda's eyes, Jane realized that for all her poise and brazen confidence, Brenda had tasted harshness. The sort a wife was forced to swallow at the hands of a man who believed himself the master.

She couldn't allow Diocail to be thought of in such a way. "In truth, he rescued me."

Brenda's eyes narrowed. "So it was the wedding night that turned ye against him?"

Jane shook her head. "He hasn't touched me. There was a fight at the inn, and we left…"

Brenda pressed her lips into a firm line. "Well then, I suppose ye might have a right to the annulment ye speak of, and yet ye are heading north. So, I do nae think Diocail shares yer mind-set."

Two solid truths.

"He has a mind to keep me." Jane enjoyed being able to voice her frustration. "Thinks we will suit in spite of the circumstances."

Brenda made a little amused noise in the back of her throat. "In true Highlander fashion."

"To his way of thinking, I am a challenge."

"Do ye have better to return to in England?"

Brenda watched her for a long moment, observing the way her question struck Jane. Brenda might play the carefree lady enjoying her day at festival, but there was a great deal of knowledge in her eyes. For a moment, they were bound together by that shared awareness of just how unholy the state of matrimony could be. "Of course, since ye are widowed, ye might try him and see if he is to yer liking without fear that anyone would ever know.

If ye have naught better in England, best to think on the matter a bit."

Brenda's eyes glittered with anticipation. She turned and cast a glance to where Symon and Diocail were talking. They'd acquired mugs of ale now, proving they were getting on well.

"You cannot mean that," Jane remarked far too breathlessly for her comfort.

"Why not? Men sample what they will quite often. He is a fine-looking man," Brenda remarked under her breath. "If ye had nae wed him, I might have given him the chance to impress me." She fluttered her eyelashes. "I'm curious to see if he can please a woman."

"Please?" Jane wished she didn't sound so completely ignorant, but she was simply too curious not to ask the question.

Brenda let out a breathless sigh and hooked her arm through Jane's before the two turned and resumed strolling slowly among the merchants.

"Ecstasy," Brenda muttered.

"That is a fable."

Brenda paused, making it look as though she were contemplating a table full of fabric. "When I was wed, I would have agreed with ye."

The merchant was quick to snap his fingers at his daughter, who hurried forward to display a length of green wool. It looked as though the man would have liked to do it himself, but the burly retainers with them kept him behind his table.

Brenda trailed a finger across the surface of the cloth. "This suits ye," she said to Jane. Niven was quick to move toward the merchant and begin to

haggle. Brenda made a little sound of victory under her breath before she tugged Jane further away from their escort and audience.

"Ecstasy is no' a fable." She sent Jane a look full of confidence.

Jane discovered her mouth going dry. Brenda smiled and winked. "The trick is to find the right man. One who is interested in being yer lover."

Brenda cast another look back toward Diocail. "He might do." Brenda grinned at Jane. "And no one need know yer private affairs."

"What of God?"

Brenda's eyes narrowed. "I have suffered enough at the hands of me lawful husband to appease the sin of taking fifty lovers." She looked straight at Jane. "From what I hear, ye have already done a fair amount of yer own penance as well."

Do you dare?

Jane settled her attention on Diocail for a long moment. She didn't look away, didn't shy away from the way he made her insides tighten. In truth, it was a thrilling sensation, sending heat into her cheeks and making her breath catch.

He caught her looking at him. He turned to glance her way, as though he felt her gaze on him. Such a thing was impossible, and yet she would have sworn there was a connection between them. Looking away took far more effort than it should have.

Niven was grinning at her with the length of fabric over his arm. He patted it in victory. "A fine dress it will make for ye, mistress."

Aylin was nodding his agreement. Brenda refused

to allow Jane to linger over the matter, tugging her toward another merchant to make good on her promise to spend as much money as possible. Brenda's joy in living was infectious, pulling Jane into the moment and away from her doubts. Happiness had always been such an unreachable thing, something that existed in stories along with the fae folk.

For that moment, though, Jane was laughing with Brenda, and her feet were lighter than they had ever been as the morning gave way to afternoon. There were food and sweets, late harvest fruit, and what seemed like endless cider. As the light begin to fade, the music started up. Jane sat on a straw bale, sipping at a new mug of cider that Muir had brought her when he traded duty with Aylin. It was spiced with cloves, cinnamon, and nutmeg, making it a potent mixture that hit all of her senses at once. Sweet and spicy and warm, it made her giddy.

"Come," Brenda announced after she finished her own mug. "Let's dance."

There was a long line of people forming for a new dance. The musicians were strumming out the first notes to signal they were about to launch into the song. Brenda pulled Jane into the mass of skirts and kilts. Someone took her hand as the music began. It was a country dance that had them changing partners over and over as they laughed.

Jane was no exception. She turned and clapped and then dove under a pair of clasped hands before reaching out to grasp her partner's hand so they might provide an arch for the couple behind them, and then she turned again to face a new partner.

Only this time it was Diocail. There was only a moment to absorb his arrival before they were swept along in the motion of the dance. He kept time with her, pulling her around and off her feet as they moved through the figure.

She was breathless in his embrace as the music came to a stop.

"Hmmm." He leaned close, his hands on her lower back. "Ye smell delicious."

She liked the way he felt. That seemed to be the only thought her mind cared to hold as she relaxed against him, laying her hands against his chest with a little contented sigh. "Muir brought me spiced cider."

Diocail's eyes narrowed slightly. "Did he now?"

She nodded, captivated by the way Diocail smelled. It was better than cinnamon, and she drew in a deep breath, letting out a little hum of approval.

"Come." He turned and captured her hand in his.

His grip fascinated her. It was so strong, so full of life, yet it didn't bite.

Henry had often bruised her.

Diocail didn't. He led her away from the dance as the evening breeze teased her with cool air. She needed the relief, for the dance had left her overheated. Even with dusk falling, she felt like kicking her boots off and trailing her bare feet through the stream.

Diocail took her toward the water. The sound of it was soothing, and the grass was still green along the riverbank.

"Now let me see if ye taste as sweet as ye smell."

He captured her in his embrace as he spoke, folding his arms around her as she made another little

breathless sound before he tilted his head, cupped her nape, and pressed his mouth against hers.

It felt perfect.

Far better than anything she had ever done. Brenda's words rose from Jane's memory as she kissed Diocail back. That made it all feel even better.

So she kissed him more firmly, slipping her hands along his chest, delighting in the feeling of his hard body beneath the fabric of his doublet. It wasn't enough, and when she found the open buttons near his neck, she slipped a hand inside and settled it against his skin.

"Touch me, lass."

In all honesty, she could not stop. The connection between them was enchanting. She stroked him, pressing her hands against his nape the same way he did to her and stretching on her toes as she gently pulled his head toward hers.

He let her complete the kiss, following her lead as she shyly moved her mouth against his. There was a tenderness in their connection that she had never encountered before nor expected to find. All that mattered was kissing Diocail back, and she discovered that boldness suited her very well. She loved reaching for him instead of being dutiful and submitting.

But his doublet frustrated her. She pulled on one of the buttons, breaking away from their kiss as she struggled to pay enough attention to the task to accomplish pushing it through its hole.

"Aye," he growled. His tone was a low rumble.

She trembled in response, but not out of fear. No, she wasn't afraid of him, at least not in the way she

had been of Henry. What she feared was the idea that he would come to his senses and not touch her again. She was certain she would writhe in agony if he abandoned her.

Diocail didn't disappoint her. He tossed his doublet aside, and in another moment, he unbuckled his belt and spread his kilt on the grass.

"Come, lass." He scooped her up and lowered her onto the wool. "And lay with me."

The light was only a memory in the sky, a faint scarlet glow that turned him ruby as he settled down beside her. Somehow, darkness suited the moment, enhancing the way she was so very keenly aware of him. The way he smelled intoxicated her, making her head spin and scattering her thoughts. Which left her with only sensation.

So much of it, and she was eager for more. Reaching for him, smoothing her hands over his body. Only his shirt remained as he kissed her again, this time parting her lips and teasing her tongue with his own.

It shocked her.

Anticipation was a living, breathing thing inside her, like a fire that crackled and popped as it caught. She discovered herself as needy as the flames licking along a new log added to the hearth, hungry for more fuel.

Diocail didn't disappoint her. He pulled at her laces, freeing her breasts and boldly cupping one. He was looking at the way he handled the soft globe. For a moment, cruel memory intruded, but there was no leer on Diocail's face.

His expression was pure enjoyment. "Ye're

beautiful, Jane. Christ forgive me, but I've thought about baring ye nearly without end for the past two days. Now…" He brushed his thumb gently over the tip of her nipple, sending a shiver across her skin. "Now, I can nae resist the opportunity to taste one of these…"

He leaned over and did just that, licking her nipple before opening his mouth and sucking it.

She gasped, arching beneath him. Was she rising up to offer it to him? She honestly didn't know because she couldn't think, couldn't do anything except twist as it felt as if there were too much sensation inside her to contain. A sound escaped her. So breathless, so passionate, she opened her eyes in surprise.

Diocail laughed softly and lifted his head, locking gazes with her. "I like that. The way ye sound when I touch ye."

There was a smugness in his tone. It should have needled her, but instead all she felt was a very strange surge of shyness, as though he was seeing a part of her she had always kept tightly concealed.

He released her breast and stroked the side of her face. "Do nae hide from me, lass. I promise ye, I will nae wound ye."

"I don't know you…" She was struggling to form thoughts. She needed to recall why she couldn't lay there, with the rising moon casting its white light across her bared breasts.

He was so close she felt his breath against her wet lips. "So tonight I'll give ye a glimpse at what I bring to ye as a husband."

The word *husband* was too restricting, but he

pressed a kiss on her mouth, cradling the side of her
face to keep her from turning aside. That was as much
resistance as she had left in her. His kiss pulled her
back into the heat where she felt like one of the flames
dancing along the wood.

He cupped her breasts again, increasing the amount
of delight in the moment. She was twisting again,
pressing herself against him. One of his legs came over
hers, slipping between her thighs and pulling them
apart. He was rucking up the fabric of her skirts, stroking her thigh as she gasped and arched.

It was pagan.

Or savage.

Or something sinful.

She couldn't form the thought, only respond to the
way he touched her. There was a throbbing at the top
of her sex far stronger than she had ever experienced.
It made opening her legs feel correct, as though she
needed to spread for him.

"Aye, that's the way, Jane."

His voice was a mere rasp, one she barely heard as
he smoothed a path from her thigh to her mons. She
shivered, feeling as though she couldn't survive being
touched on her mons and yet certain she would perish
if he didn't stroke that throbbing spot.

"Diocail..." Her voice was strained.

In fact, there was perspiration on her forehead, the
bare skin of her chest a blessed relief from the heat
coursing through her.

"Trust me."

"I do," she muttered, forcing her heavy eyelids up.
"I shouldn't."

And yet there was something about him that drew her to him. Perhaps it was that thing she'd been lectured on so often in her youth.

Lust...

Yet for all the stern warnings she'd heard, tonight the word only drove her closer to the edge of unbridled abandonment. She reached for him, slipping her hand along his neck, rejoicing in the feeling of his skin. A little hum of enjoyment escaped her lips as she pulled him down for another kiss, opening her mouth as she kissed him back.

He groaned low and deep, his chest rumbling with it. This time the sound was one of male enjoyment. She liked hearing it, deep inside herself, past all the layers of rules and expectation. In that place where she was only herself and faced with the realities of what she truly desired.

Which was him.

It was a craving. They weren't close enough. He felt it too, leaning further over her, and she shivered as she felt his weight. His kiss was harder now, and she answered him by kissing him back just as hard.

Brazen.

Fine, so be it. She'd never felt so alive, and she wanted more. Diocail didn't disappoint her. He teased the curls on the top of her mons before boldly cupping her sex. She gasped, opening her eyes to find him watching her from a mere inch above her face. There was a glitter of challenge in his gaze as he rubbed her, one of his fingertips slipping between the folds of her sex to find the spot that throbbed.

The touch sent a bolt of sensation through her. It

was white-hot and searing. She arched, but he held her down, rubbing.

"Diocail—" Her voice came out as a strangled sound.

"Let me show ye, lass." He was applying more pressure, increasing the need building in her belly for…for something.

"Show…me what?" She couldn't seem to draw in enough breath. Her heart was working at a frantic pace inside her chest.

"What yer last husband was too selfish to do…"

There was an edge of determination in his voice. His face was drawn taunt, and she couldn't keep her eyes open any longer. In fact, staying still was impossible; she wanted to twist, but he held her down, kissing her hard as everything seemed to center under his hand. She was nearly frantic for release, lifting her hips in the final moments to press herself against his hand harder as she clamped his hand between her thighs.

She cried out when it hit her. The pleasure ripped along her insides and slammed into her head. It sent her reeling, making it fortunate she was on the ground, for there was no way she would have remained standing. For endless moments, she was caught in a burst of pleasure so intense she writhed. It stole her breath, wringing her like a length of wet cloth before dropping her back down into reality in a heap of quivering limbs, more spent and more sated than she had ever been in her life. As well as more pleasured than she'd ever experienced.

She shifted, trying to make sense of everything. Diocail smoothed her cheek and gathered her close.

The scent of his body was so welcoming, the way he cradled her more tender than anything she'd ever experienced. It was bliss, and there was nothing more important than drifting off into the soft waves of it while Diocail rolled onto his back and held her.

❦

Brenda Grant knew more than she should.

It was a condition that came with being at court, among those who peddled everything they had—including their souls—for power. What should have been private was not, and to survive, she'd learned to read men very well while maintaining perfect poise to ensure they didn't know her own feelings.

"Ye're watching me."

Brenda didn't care for how hard she struggled to control herself as a man stepped into her path. He'd been shadowing her for several hours now, and she'd done her best to ignore him.

However, her best was not as solid as it should have been. Her gaze had strayed to his too many times, and now he thought it was some sort of invitation.

"I watch where I go, sir," she replied firmly. "Do ye know me cousin, Laird Symon Grant?"

"Scared of me, are ye?" He cocked his head to one side as he peered down from his greater height.

Brenda looked up to meet his eyes. "I said no such thing." There was a touch of heat in her voice. She chided herself for responding so dramatically.

"And yet ye feel the need to make sure I know who yer relatives are." He had midnight-black hair but blue eyes.

Brenda offered him a flutter of her eyelashes. "I find it distressing to see foolish men being…dealt with by me kin. It's more of a Christian duty to warn ye how hot Grant tempers run."

It was a double warning, one not lost on her company. His lips twitched as he grinned.

"Christian duty?" he asked slowly as he ventured closer.

Brenda offered him a confident nod as she fought the urge to step back. She forbade herself to show such weakness. All around her people were enjoying the early evening, so there was no reason to think she was in any danger. And yet her insides felt unsettled.

"Well then," the man muttered. "Would it be wrong to admit I find yer description of yer blood to be more of an enticement than deterrent?"

"It would be arrogant."

He offered her a shrug from his massive shoulders. "I can nae admit to being too distressed."

No, he wasn't. She was caught in the grip of a sensation. One that she'd rarely felt in her life. It made her pause as she took a moment to enjoy it but forbade herself to linger in the memory. Or in his company.

Brenda made to step around him.

"Ye've no' allowed me to introduce meself."

He'd stepped into her path. What made her stiffen was the fact that she spotted other men wearing his colors. They hung back, making sure no one interrupted their conversation.

"Ye are a Gunn."

His expression became serious. "And ye are Brenda

Grant, widow of a Campbell, who took a lover before ye landed in the keeping of the Earl of Morton."

"I'm no' flattered by how much ye know."

He contemplated her for a moment. "Ye should be. I do nae waste me time, Mistress Grant."

"If that is so, why do ye listen to so much gossip?" she asked pointedly.

"Clearly ye do nae know what a sensation ye cause when ye pass by." He offered her a soft chuckle. "There I was this morning, set to enjoy a mug of fine cider, no' even looking at the lasses."

He put on a mock innocent expression that made her clamp her lips tightly together lest she laugh.

"Ye strike me as the sort of innocent to be doing such a thing on harvest festival morning." Her voice was dripping sarcasm, but it was also husky, betraying how much she was enjoying the encounter. He made her feel strangely alive, as though she'd been half asleep.

His lips thinned in a purely sensual fashion. One that sent a touch of heat into her cheeks.

"Aye, as I said, ye passed by…" He made a walking motion with his fingers. "And the good wives began to chatter about ye."

"And, of course, their word is so very reliable." Brenda bit her lip because she realized she was jumping to defend herself. She shouldn't care what he thought of her.

"Which is why I doubt ye truly intend to dance naked under the moon tonight." He sounded pitifully disappointed, even pushing his lower lip out. "Truth be told, I was holding out hope for that one to be true.

I do nae suppose ye might consider being generous toward me opinion of ye?"

Brenda snorted and propped her hands on her hips but couldn't help but admit to being amused by his humor. Not that she intended to allow him to know it.

"Bothan Gunn." He opened his arms and offered her a low courtesy, but he winked as he rose back to his full height.

"Far from home, aren't ye?"

He shrugged. "I was summoned to court on account of a relative of mine behaving poorly."

"I'd worry more about what the Earl of Sutherland has to say about the matter, considering that relative was killed inside his hall."

Bothan's expression tightened. "Ye can be certain I agree with ye."

She knew him now. She had known the name of the successor of the Gunn chiefdom, but now she had a face to go with it. The Gunns lived very far north, and the hardened man standing before her was a prime example of the strength needed to survive in the extreme Highlands. It was admirable, and he was impressive, but there was no way she was going to allow him to know she thought so.

"Excuse me." Brenda stepped around him.

"Something pressing to attend to, mistress?"

She couldn't resist the urge to look back over her shoulder. "I'm sure the good wives will be happy to tell ye what I am about."

"Perhaps I'd rather hear it from yer own lips." His gaze lowered to them as he stepped closer.

Her insides tightened—he aroused her. She was tempted to linger in the moment, allow the sensation to tease her flesh and remind her what joy there could be between lovers.

If she was willing to trust. Which she wasn't.

"Goodbye, Chief Gunn." Brenda raised her voice enough so the Grant retainers trailing her heard. They stiffened, stepping toward her.

Bothan's eyes narrowed. "An interesting response, lass."

She didn't care for the fact that he'd called it a response. However true, it needled her, making her bite back the retort that sprang to her lips.

Rising to his bait would only confirm his words. So she moved past him, but not before she caught the look he sent her way. There was a promise there, one that sent a shiver down her back.

"Until next we meet."

❧

Someone laughed.

Jane woke with a start, blinking in confusion as she tried to remember where she was. Her memory came back with a brilliant flash of precise recollection of just how she came to be lying on top of Diocail with her bodice open in the afternoon sunlight.

He grunted and sat up as she did. His gaze lowered to her unbound breasts, and his expression became one of male enjoyment before she hastily grabbed the edge of her chemise and tugged it up, fighting to find the ends of the string that would pull the neckline tight.

"What on earth…" She was fumbling to make

sense of her thoughts and, it would seem, her balance as well.

"I should have Muir's balls," Diocail mumbled as he rolled over and pulled at the length of wool that made up his kilt. He began to pleat it but looked up at her with an arrogant grin. "Except I'm too honest no' to admit I benefited from his actions."

"What actions?" She was threading the lace through the eyelets to close her bodice. The lace was long, making the process slow.

Diocail was making good progress at forming all of the wool into what would become his kilt. He reached over and retrieved his belt from where it lay discarded in the grass and threaded it beneath the pleats before he lay down and buckled it. He was turning over and standing, working to tuck in the front flaps of the kilt, before he answered her.

Of course he was. Diocail Gordon wasn't a man to be caught unawares.

He buckled a second belt over his waist to finish the process. "The cider was spiced with a very generous amount of whisky."

Jane tugged the lace hard, and the front of her bodice closed tightly as his words sunk in. She tied a firm knot before adjusting her cleavage and standing.

"Do nae look at me like that, Jane."

"Am I expected to be pleased to know my trust was taken advantage of?" she demanded before looking around for Muir. The urge to take him to task was strong. Diocail reached out and caught her arm, pulling her back to face him.

"It was nae enough to intoxicate ye."

"And yet," she sputtered. "I am…here…"

"With yer husband," he answered firmly. "Naught is amiss, madam. Muir would never have allowed ye to be at risk. No one faults ye for being distrustful of our union. Ye've cause enough for it, but Muir knows I will nae treat ye poorly. He meant to put ye at ease so we might get past what is distressing ye."

His meaning was as clear as a church bell ringing in the morning.

"I do not want this marriage," she exclaimed as she pulled free. One look at his face made it clear he didn't care for the insult. "And neither did you. So, you have no right to be angry that I am trying not to trap you into keeping me. Many a man would thank me for not making him keep an unwanted bride, especially one who came with no dowry and who is not pure."

His expression had become hard, his body tense, but she didn't back away. Jane stared straight at him.

"I did nae want it at the time." He held up a finger to quiet her so she might let him finish his thought. "For ye are no' the only one who understands kindness."

It wasn't what she'd expected to hear. "I don't understand."

"Yer reasons are valid. For all that ye are English and I am Scottish, we were both raised to see wedding as a way to gain wealth. Kindness was only an afterthought."

She nodded, longing for the world to be something it would never be.

"I would have something different between us. Everything else in me life is a duty. What I crave from ye is a wife who chooses me." He moved closer and lowered his voice. "If that were not so, I'd have

claimed ye just now and made very sure there was a witness or two to the consummation, for ye are a prize worth keeping."

It would not have been hard.

The horror of it nearly made her retch. But Diocail grabbed her upper arms and held her in place as she started to recoil, proving without a doubt just how strong he truly was. Her weight was nothing to him.

"I didn't do that, Jane."

She'd looked away, but the tone of his voice pulled her attention back. She locked gazes with him, witnessing the determination blazing there.

"Instead, I proved me worth to ye."

Her cheeks burned with the memory, and his lips twitched. "Did yer last husband ever please ye?"

She gasped at the bluntness of the question. "You shouldn't ask such a thing."

Diocail pulled her closer so she was against his body. His scent teased her senses once more, awakening the yearnings she'd thought well satisfied.

"Answer the question, lass," Diocail's tone was a husky whisper. For certain, it must have been the same raspy tone Lucifer used to lure Eve into sinfulness.

"Did he ever move ye to ecstasy?"

"No." The admission crossed her lips like the darkest confession. "I don't know why it happened."

He grunted. "It happened because I am no' a selfish swine who uses a woman for his own pleasure and hides behind the scriptures that tell him a wife is his property, which makes it permissible to ignore her pleasure." He slid one arm around her waist, boldly cupping one side of her bottom and bringing her into

contact with his lower body. The hard presence of his cock was impossible to miss.

"I wanted to claim ye." In his eyes was the bright glitter of unsatisfied need. "And if ye expect me to understand why ye ended up on a gallows about to be hung, well then, I'll have ye hearing what I am telling ye now."

He released her, and she stumbled back.

"I will have a wife who wants me, Jane." His tone was edged with determination. "Me life has ever been one filled with responsibilities and expectations, but in this matter, I will have something that is me own."

"And I have offered to give you your freedom," she replied.

"In turn, I give ye a choice in whom ye are wed to," he countered.

His offer was tempting.

She felt as though everything she knew were being shredded to reveal things she had never known were lurking deep down inside her. It was a revelation to be sure, one that made her feel as if the entire world were shifting beneath her feet.

"Aye, ye think on that."

"How did ye know—"

He offered her a nod. "Because I am drawn to ye. I notice things about ye that I have nae done before in a woman."

"You want this marriage?" she boldly asked. "I come with naught."

He grunted. "There is a reason me men are so eager to take ye home. Me house is in a state of disorder. They see ye as a solution to it and a way to escape a

long winter of poor fare on the tables. Ye come with the ability to right the situation. No' a single one of them can do so. A comfortable home, that is something me men value."

"As if your people will be willing to follow the direction of an Englishwoman."

He lifted his shoulder in a shrug. "I would no' have thought ye so timid as to be crying quarter before ye even set eyes on them or tried yer hand at directing them."

She rolled her eyes. "That is an underhanded method of gaining my compliance."

He grinned, unrepentant. "I'm Scottish. It's me duty to dupe ye."

She scoffed at him. It earned her a grin that might have been cheeky if he wasn't so imposing, and yet the tension seemed to ease between them.

He opened one of his hands. "What have ye to return to? Truthfully. Ye mentioned a stepmother who seems no' to want ye under her roof."

"That is true." Jane worried her lower lip. "Yet I am not sure I wish ever to be a wife again."

His eyes glittered with understanding. "Ye enjoyed me touch."

And he wasn't going to let her shy away from that fact.

"Yes," she admitted softly, recalling the moment of pleasure and feeling her cheeks heat with the memory. "But…marriage…binds me so very completely to your will…"

"And ye do nae trust me," he finished for her.

"I do not mean it…unkindly. The truth is I knew

Henry more than I know you, and he was quite the disappointment."

There would be no escaping a tower in the Highlands while winter raged around them. That was a fact she'd best get a firm grip on before she landed in dire circumstances. Alicia might not want her, but there would be a place for her in her father's home if she returned.

He grunted but nodded. "Yer husband sold ye."

Diocail's tone was hard as he spoke, and she felt something rising from inside her. A wound still raw and demanding justice. "It is not you."

"Nay, lass, it was no' me." He moved closer, reaching out to brush the side of her face with his hand. She shifted, unwilling to release her uncertainty. But he slipped his hand around her face to cup her nape and hold her in place as he closed the gap completely between them.

"But it will be me pleasure to crush his memory so completely ye will never think of him again."

Oh, so very tempting…

Just like the kiss he pressed onto her lips. Resisting was impossible. She rose on her toes to meet him, slipping so very easily into the moment and letting it clear all her thoughts away while sweet pleasure flowed through her.

Diocail lifted his head, and she caught the shimmer of victory in his eyes. "So I am taking ye home with me."

And that was his final word. She felt her temper rise but also a stirring of anticipation.

"Better hope you don't live to regret it."

He chuckled at her brazen retort before he released her nape and captured her wrist. The light had died while they spoke. Diocail led her back toward his men and the safety they represented. No matter her reservations, she was still warmed by the smiles aimed her way. His men looked toward her for a better life.

Damned if it didn't feel good to be something useful. But they wouldn't be the ones becoming chattel. No, that was the lot of a wife. She climbed into the wagon, settling into the bed as her thoughts churned. Diocail wanted a wife that he'd chosen, and he had been bent into submission to take her.

The answer was really very simple. If she took his house in hand, she'd have a place as his Head of House. By the end of winter, his craving for her would be over. Men changed their minds when it came to bed sport, which was something she knew very well. How many of her friends had been courted so sweetly only to suffer their husbands taking mistresses once their bellies began to swell and the season passed into memory?

It was the nature of love though.

Flights of fancy. Tunes of whimsy. Both solid reasons why marriage was best conducted like a business. Yet that had yielded such an unsatisfying union. At least on her end.

Jane opened her eyes and found Diocail in the dark. *He hadn't taken her.*

Looking at him, she noted all the details of his rugged life that made her own kin label him a savage, and yet he'd shown more mercy and honor than the groom her father had willingly wed her to.

Her thoughts were a jumble as he turned to look at her. The darkness seemed to bring out her cravings, making her lament the distance between them.

Well, you are married to him...

True. She closed her eyes as she contemplated the fact that she had a choice. Did she follow Brenda's lead and cast her fortune on the feelings churning inside her or follow the teachings of her childhood?

She fell asleep before she decided, the warm bed and knowledge that the Gordon retainers would protect her lulling her into slumber.

Five

THE GORDON STRONGHOLD WAS DARK.

Jane had seen other castles with stone the same color, but there was something ominous about the twin towers Diocail took her toward. The feeling might have been partly caused by the dark clouds swirling around behind the castle too; she simply didn't know. The combination hit her like a blow to the midsection.

At last someone started to ring a bell. It was a lone sound in the afternoon and brought swift attention to the arriving party. People began to come out of the buildings, climbing onto the steps that led into the larger keep to get a better view as they rode closer.

What sent a shiver down her back was the way only some of them smiled in welcome.

Diocail's words from the day of their wedding rose from her memory.

"The clan will split, and there will be fighting over who is to take the lairdship. After me, there are at least five men with claims equal to one another. Blood will flow in the spring until one faction takes enough lives to silence the others."

His position was not secure. It was evident in the way many of his people watched them arrive. The dark, brooding stares sent a shiver down her spine. The wagon came to a stop, and she couldn't help but be relieved to know she was going to climb out of it for the last time.

Niven was quick to make sure he offered her his hand. Curious looks were cast her way as she alighted.

"Mistress," Niven spoke clearly.

A man arrived wearing a bonnet with one feather sticking straight up. Another captain then. He reached up and tugged on the corner of his bonnet before Diocail offered him a hand. They clasped each other's forearms.

"We've been busy whilst ye were away," the man began. "Have the kitchen weathertight now, and the hearth's in good order."

He might have been talking to Diocail, but the man was looking past his laird at Jane.

Diocail turned and held out his hand to her. "May I present me wife."

The announcement drew gasps and more than one narrow look. All eyes were on them. Jane placed her hand into Diocail's and held her chin steady. She'd not shame him.

"Me captain, Sorley."

Jane nodded to the man before Diocail took her up the stairs into the larger keep. She was only two steps inside before she caught the stench. It was the scent of urine, no mistake, making her narrow her own eyes as she looked around at the men who were clearly too lazy to make their way to the jakes.

But what made her pause was the accumulation of animal skins on the walls. There didn't appear to be an inch to spare. The entire great hall was draped in hides, most of them covered in thick layers of dust. It was a barbaric display of hunting skills and a wasteful one because those hides could have been put to much better use. Now time had rendered them dry and wasted.

"As ye see, Jane," Diocail said, tugging her gently forward because she'd stopped. "The lads do have a fair amount of reason to act the way they do about keeping ye."

"Indeed," she managed to say as they moved down the aisle toward where the high ground was at the end of the hall. The laird's table was sitting on a raised platform.

It was late enough in the day that supper was being served. Two maids were hurrying to lay out plates for the laird. Niven pulled out a huge chair for her before pushing it back in with a soft grunt because of how heavy it was. She was rather certain the design dated to the Middle Ages at least. The thick coating of dust and grime suggested it was indeed that old.

Everything in the hall was just as ancient and dripping with filth. The candleholders had huge puddles of wax beneath them and more hanging from the holders like icicles. Most of it had been there so long it was dark with grime. Jane shuddered as she contemplated what the shadows hid.

Tomorrow was going to be a long day indeed, if the stench was anything to judge by.

Supper service resumed. The Gordon retainers hurried to fill the long benches as maids brought food

in from the kitchen. Fighting broke out among the men. Several of them pulled the trays from the maids, claiming them before they might be served. Instead they placed the dishes on the table and clustered over the food with a few close friends, gorging on the fare as though they were facing starvation, and it was the end of winter instead of harvest time.

"Have the crops been lean?" she asked.

Diocail shook his head. "The last laird was a miser. I ordered the amount of food increased, but it would appear needs are still no' being met."

The lack of plenty was not going to be present on their table though. A huge platter arrived and was set down with two others to feed Diocail and herself. It was a gross amount of food. Whole chickens with other game meats as well. Three giant rounds of bread and butter surrounded by cheese and fruits. There were two more platters for just the five captains sitting at the high table.

"Holy mother of Christ," she mumbled under her breath as men at the tables looked at the generous fare with loathing in their eyes. "Are we expected to feast while others go hungry?"

Diocail looked as disgusted as she felt. In an odd way, it settled her. She felt that sense of companionship with him once more.

"Colum, may his soul roast in hell, thought it a fine way of enforcing his position as laird," Diocail explained dryly. "Making sure his men knew he ruled them however he saw fit and the fact that those men had pledged themselves to him meant they were bound to him."

Jane shared a horrified glance with Diocail before she realized the men they had ridden with were only just making their way into the hall. Young Bari wore a bright smile of anticipation; however, the rest of the men didn't. They came in with low expectations and settled down at an empty section of the table. Jane glanced toward the passageway where the maids had entered, but no one was there. By the look of the men in the hall, she'd have fled too.

"Kory." She wasn't sure why she simply took charge, only that Bari's seeking eyes over the edge of the table were unbearable. "Take that tray for you and your comrades."

Kory was in motion the moment she called his name. It took a moment for him to realize what she'd said, his face brightening as he looked at the food. He was tugging on the edge of his bonnet as he came to get the large platter.

But the rest of the hall was in a state of shock. Mouths were hanging open as expressions became dark.

"English…"

"She's bloody *English*…"

"He wed an English bitch…"

The Gordons didn't bother to whisper either. They expressed their displeasure to one another in full-bodied voices, and more than one spit on the floor before sending her a scathing glare.

Diocail slammed his mug against the tabletop. "Aye!" he announced in a hard tone. "Jane is me wife. And…" He glared at a man who spat on the floor in response. "As ye can see, she is no' selfish but

a mistress to bring order to this keep and see to the needs of those who serve it."

The Gordons had no idea what to make of their new laird's words. It was clear they wanted to hate Jane, but many watched as Kory and the others began to enjoy the food she had sent from her own table to theirs. Hence, the Gordon were torn between hatred of her blood and the hunger in their bellies.

"Excuse me." Jane tried to push her chair back, but it was too heavy. A retainer standing behind her reached forward and pulled her away from the table.

"Where are ye going, Jane?"

"Clearly to the kitchen." His captains frowned at how sharp her tone was. Jane lowered herself quickly. "Forgive me for being tart. I am distressed to see how little there is for supper. It shames your name."

The captains nodded approvingly at her before she turned and walked behind them. Three steps led up to the high ground, and she was down them in a moment before going through the passageway where she'd seen the maids enter.

Which led her straight into hell.

❧

"I knew ye were bold," Sorley muttered the moment Jane was gone. He was smacking his lips and wiped them on his sleeve before continuing. "But an English wife?"

"Are ye going to tell me offers have been arriving while I've been gone?" Diocail demanded.

Sorley grinned and shook his head. "No' a single one."

Diocail grunted and bit into the bread, only to snort because the grain used to make it was only partially

ground. Pain snaked through his jaw as he clamped
down on a hard kennel.

"Aye, the fare is dry now, but no better for it."
Sorley cast a look toward the passageway where Jane
had disappeared. "Thinking on it a bit longer, I do nae
care if ye found her confessing her dealings with Satan,
so long as she brings order to this house."

"It was no' too far from that," Muir announced as
he took his place at the high table and began to fill his
plate. "Had to cut her down from the gallows, and
none too soon either."

❧

"I do nae need instruction from an Englishwoman."

The Gordon female in front of her was hardly the
first to announce such an opinion. Jane looked straight
back at her. The kitchen staff was united in their stand to
leave instead of accepting her as their mistress. Replacing
them might be possible, but not before the dawn and
the need to have another meal on the tables in the hall.

Of course, the women knew it too. They were
smirking at her, their eyes glittering with the enjoyment
of knowing they had the leverage to make her bend.

Well, there was another thing to be thankful to
Alicia for. When it came to making the best of circumstances, Jane knew that path very well indeed.

"You have all clearly persevered when your burdens
were overly heavy." Jane spoke softly and slowly. "It is
plain you were asked to do things that lacked honor."

A few of the smirks faded. She'd touched on a
chord within some of them. A need to be understood
and acknowledged for their efforts.

"When my father remarried, my stepmother dismissed every servant in the house because she wanted only those whom she had selected," Jane continued. "It was her right, and yet I privately thought it overly harsh to those who had served so diligently."

The tension was mounting in the kitchen. Several of the Gordon retainers had come in to hear what she was saying to the staff, and the hard set of their jaws confirmed that the women were dear to them.

"Since you have all managed to suffer the lack of proper help here, it would seem to me that you should share in the future success of this kitchen." She spoke clearly but firmly. "Your laird has assured me I may do what is needed to set things right here. Proper wages. Adequate staff. Yes, I was born in England; however, when it comes to turning bread, I do not think it matters so much what country one was born in. A wise woman knows how much to set out in the morning so the supper table is not bare and how much effort it takes to see the meal produced."

Some of them were bending. Or at least softening.

"Does that mean ye'll be listening to us in matters of how much to serve?"

Jane turned to look at the woman who had spoken. "I would be foolish not to. This is my first time in Scotland."

The woman's lips parted in a grin. "Ye're in the Highlands."

There was a soft round of laughter in response. Jane took the ribbing with grace, offering a nod of acceptance.

"I am Dolina," the woman announced. "I have served in this kitchen since I was five winters." She

pointed to two girls. "Those are me daughters, and the young scamp over by the hearth is me youngest son. He's not earned a single penny for all the time he's been turning the meat."

The young boy was only tall enough to work the handle that turned the splint in the hearth. He was dripping sweat from working so close to the fire.

Now that Dolina had begun, the others were quick to get into line to air their grievances.

"First, let us see to the matter of the morning meal." Jane raised her voice because the women were converging on her. "Dolina, what is served?"

Dolina was pleased to be asked. She lifted her chin and stepped in front of her comrades to begin explaining the kitchen to Jane. Her young son was sleeping in the corner by the time his mother finished.

Jane was ready to join him. It was overwhelming, the amount of work to be done, but she found herself smiling as she took her leave, even knowing she needed to be back at first light. Dolina wasn't the only one who craved knowing she had a place.

Jane longed for it too. The Gordon towers were a bride's nightmare, but she was willing to try to soften the edges.

"Mistress."

Jane jumped as Niven straightened up from where he'd been leaning against the wall outside the kitchen. He blinked, clearly having dozed off.

"I'm sorry," Jane exclaimed. Just beyond them, the hall was full of sleeping men. Several had been startled out of their rest. They'd jumped right onto their feet and watched her from low crouching positions as they

took in the situation. They sent her disapproving looks before lying back down.

Niven gestured for her to follow him. He plucked a candle from where it was stuck on a spike in the mortar of the wall. She noted another need as they began to climb the stairs with only that lone flame to guide them.

Candles. The tower was nearly pitch-black, and it was drafty, the wind howling through the stairwell. Jane and Niven passed windows and arrow slits that were open to the weather with no shutters to keep out the night's chill.

But at least it carried the stench away.

"The laird thought ye'd like to sleep tonight." Niven opened a door to a chamber. There was a welcoming flicker from a candle left inside.

"Thank you," she muttered. "I am sorry to keep you waiting for me."

Niven tugged on his bonnet before turning and disappearing down the stairs.

The chamber was a small one because the stairs continued and took up part of the width of the tower. She didn't mind. It had a door, which she closed, and then she ventured further, to where a bed waited with the promise of sleep.

Niven's words echoed in her mind as she opened her bodice and laid it aside, stripping down to her smock before hurrying into the bed to escape the night's chill.

Sleep tonight…

The retainer had said what was on everyone's minds, of course. With Diocail proclaiming her his

wife in the great hall, she'd be expected to visit his chamber.

And soon.

⁂

"He's made his mistake now," Keefe informed his friends and allies. "An English bitch is no fit mistress for Gordon land."

"Aye." Sheehan spat on the floor.

"We'll need more support if we're to rid ourselves of Diocail as laird." Phelan offered the hard facts. "Ye share yer link to the bloodline with others, Keefe. There will be more than a few who decide it a better path simply to let Diocail keep the lairdship and breed that new wife to ensure his line because of the bloodshed it will save."

"In that case," Keefe spoke ominously, "we'd best get rid of her before she whelps us a half-English heir."

"Ye'd do a woman harm?" Phelan asked.

Keefe drew himself up straight. "I will remove anyone standing between me and being laird of the Gordons," Keefe declared. "I thought ye were with me in no' wanting an outsider, even one with a blood tie, as laird. Unlike Diocail, ye know well who I am. We've trained together, fought at each other's backs."

"I agreed with ye, Keefe, and I've said clearly enough that I support yer claim to the lairdship," Phelan answered back. "Diocail may have been Colum's sister's child, but he was no' raised up a Gordon. He's as likely devoted to Sutherland as Gordons."

"Aye," Keefe nodded. "We have no way of

knowing who Diocail truly calls his master, and now he's brought home an English bride."

"That's no' a good thing," Sheehan agreed. "She's related to a baron, no less."

"Aye," Keefe growled. "Allow her to have a son, and it's likely Diocail will be dead in his bed so she can have her relatives here while her son is too young to rule. James Stuart is only Elizabeth Tudor's puppet king."

"For all we know, Diocail was nae raised in the north."

"He might well be an imposter," Sheehan agreed. "Better to have ye, Keefe, as laird. I know ye're Gordon."

Keefe nodded. "I am, and I will deal with the English bitch meself."

⌘

The first meal of the day was met with double the number of men who had been in the great hall the night before. They filled the tables, their kilts draping over the edges of the benches as Jane contemplated dropping in a dead faint where she stood.

His home needed taking in hand? Now there was the understatement of the century.

"Well now," Dolina muttered next to her. "It seems ye've caused a sensation, mistress. They've all come to get a look at ye."

The meal the kitchen staff delivered still fell short of the need. Jane felt her cheeks heating as she watched it being consumed and felt looks being cast her way that made it plain she was found lacking.

Her temper sizzled.

"Do nae be so hard on yerself," Dolina offered. "It's

more than those tables have seen in years. The men have been avoiding coming to the hall because of it."

"And now, they will carry away confirmation of my failure to provide enough bread."

"There is enough bread for now," Dolina said. "But we've served all we turned this morning. Without the mill, there will be little for supper."

"I know," Jane agreed. The maids were reduced to turning hand cranks to mill the grain into flour. It was a slow process and made the hands ache.

Grain there was plenty of. The lack of bread came from the fact that the mill was not grinding and hadn't in several years.

Jane took off her apron. "It's time I took a look at the mill."

She needed flour. Otherwise, all the new help in the kitchen would change nothing.

"Are ye no' going to join the laird at the high table?"

Jane scoffed at Dolina. "And allow one and all to see me sitting idle while the needs of my house are not met? I believe there is already plenty being said about me that is not kind."

Dolina smiled, but there was approval in her eyes. "This way then."

Scotland had plenty of water.

Gordon land was no exception. Jane followed Dolina down to where a river roared, even in autumn. A mill was built near it with a huge water-wheel. It sat there, not turning, the giant stone inside the millhouse dusty from not being used. Inside the house were sacks of grain that had been there so long

mice and rats had chewed holes in them and begun carrying away the contents.

The waste sickened her.

With the number of retainers sitting down in the great hall, there was no excuse for the mill to be in disrepair.

They were too lazy or too dim-witted to realize bread would be forever in short supply if the mill wasn't repaired.

Well, she wasn't going to stand idly by. She went into the millhouse, venturing over to the edge where the floor was open to allow one to see the rushing water.

"It is deep enough for the wheel," Jane began.

Dolina joined her, leaning over to peer at the bottom of the wheel. "It looks as if there is a log wedged in there... Go raise the gate to let more water in."

Jane leaned over further as Dolina moved around the side of the mill, and in the next moment, pain split her skull. It was blinding, but she didn't have time to worry about it because she plunged into the river, and it dragged her beneath the wheel. She was pinned against the logs jammed underneath. The rushing water kept her there as she struggled to break free. But the slats of the waterwheel in reach were slick with moss, and her fingers slipped right off them as her lungs began to burn.

Her legs became tangled in the wood jammed under the wheel. She reached up and dug her nails into the waterwheel, kicking at the wood, frantic to reach the surface before she drowned. For a moment, she was straining, using every last bit of strength she had as she felt herself losing consciousness. It seemed to last forever, that moment filled with the pain of

struggling to shove the wood free and her lungs burning for a breath of air.

Agony and more pain filled her last few seconds of life. She jerked and kicked, and suddenly, she was slipping further beneath the wheel. The power of the current swept her under it and up into the sunlight. Jane gasped, filling her lungs with soothing air before she tumbled beneath the surface again like a dried leaf.

That single breath restored her wits. She strained and struggled to swim toward the surface. Her skirts hampered her efforts, weighted down by the water and sticking to her legs.

Like a shroud...

But she fought and filled her lungs again. This time she kept her head above water long enough to hear screaming. It was in the distance, but it gave her hope that she might escape. She tugged and pulled, reaching out, straining toward the shore.

Her reward was a hard impact of rock against her hand. Jane held tight in spite of the pain, using her grip to drag herself from the hold of the current. She emerged onto the bank, fighting to crawl because her strength felt drained. Her hands were still in the mud when someone lifted her off her hands and knees.

"Sweet Christ, Jane." Diocail carried her to the shore, laying her down as carefully as he might an egg. "What are ye doing, woman?"

At that precise moment, she was fighting to remain conscious. The demand in his voice drew her attention. She gasped and coughed as she tried to clear her

lungs. Diocail sat her up, pounding on her back as she hacked with all the grace of a newly netted fish.

But when she was finished, she looked up the bank and saw the waterwheel turning easily in the morning light. Satisfaction filled her with a sense of victory she fully intended to claim.

"I was…" She coughed again and sat up straight. "I was fixing the mill so there would be ample bread!"

⁓

Jane marched past more than a hundred of his men like a Valkyrie.

She was soaked to the bone, the bottom of her skirts becoming a muddy mess as she yanked up the front of them and went straight by the retainers who had answered the screams from Dolina. Diocail's little English wife had her chin held high and a damned stiff spine that looked ridiculous when coupled with dead leaves and slime in her hair, but she refused to be coddled on the riverbank.

Damned if he wasn't impressed.

"Fool woman can't stay out of peril for one day…"

"All we need is an English lady here to look after…"

"Doesn't have the sense of a child…"

Diocail froze. He'd been set to follow his wife, but he turned on the group of his men. They didn't have much concern for the fact that he'd heard them talking ill of Jane. But it was the sight of the freely turning waterwheel that infuriated him the most.

"The next man to speak out against me bride gets the backside of me temper," he warned.

His men bristled. Diocail looked to where Dolina was being helped up from the riverbank. "How long has the mill been in disrepair?"

She was surprised to have him speak so directly to her in front of his men. Diocail watched her draw in a deep breath before answering.

"All season, Laird, and the one before. We've been making do with hand grinding."

"Sorley?"

His captain was quick to step forward.

"How many men have ye been working on the repairs?"

"Close to a hundred," Sorley answered.

"So," Diocail addressed them all. "There are no more than fifty of ye set to the walls and stables. And *yet…*" He gripped his belt as he struggled to control his temper. "I counted more than two hundred of ye thinking to fill yer bellies in the hall, and ye dare to label me wife a lackwit for acting to make sure her duties were fulfilled? What have the rest of ye been doing with the daylight?"

Those who had been so proud of their insults shuffled their feet, losing their confidence. They weren't sorry, but it was a start. The Gordons needed beginnings tenfold because all around them were the ruins of a once-proud clan. It was time they started building a future that was bright with achievement.

"The proper word to describe yer mistress is determined," Diocail announced in a tone that made it clear he wasn't in the mood to be tested. "A trait I recommend ye all adopt right quickly because this clan will only be strong when the lot of ye are strong. Colum was a bastard for letting ye run idle like lads. There is a

high price to be paid for laziness. Riding out to raid the neighbors for the sake of yer pride while yer home is falling to ruin. Well now, I will nae be impressed by the things ye've stolen under moonlight. True men make certain their home is fit for their families."

Diocail drew in a deep breath. "Muir, gather up some of these men and do yer best to see that mill working. It's the kitchen staff's duty to turn the bread, no' to grind the grain."

Muir tugged on the corner of his bonnet before pointing at those nearest to him and heading down to the millhouse. Diocail spared a moment to make sure a fair number of men followed before he turned and headed toward the hall.

Jane's path was marked by a trail of water and mud. She'd pushed her hair back from her face and stood halfway up the steps to the high ground as she surveyed the tables and the efforts under way to clean them. She caught Diocail watching her, their gazes locking for a moment. He felt the connection as much as he saw it. For a moment, he was certain he would have killed any man who thought to get between them. The impulse rose instantly and left behind a twinge to make sure Diocail recalled it.

He wanted her.

More precisely, he wanted her to choose him. Seducing a woman with less experience wasn't very difficult. He'd already have claimed her if that was what he wanted.

No, he craved something different from her. Something very personal.

Nothing less would satisfy him.

❦

"Ye did nae hit her hard enough."

Keefe snarled. "Ye think I do nae know that?"

Phelan shrugged. "Now, ye've gone and helped her earn respect."

"It will be a cold day in hell before I respect any English," Sheehan growled.

"The men will find it easier to forget her blood when their bellies are full," Phelan said. "And no one is going to be so trusting of another accident."

Keefe grunted and drained his mug. "I'll find a way."

❦

Someone was pleased with her.

Jane found a mug of mulled wine next to her bed when she finally sought out sleep. The scent of cloves lifted the corners of her mouth as she sipped at the liquid. It warmed her insides, promising to ease some of the aches from her day. She was so tired she would have fallen asleep anyway.

The day replayed in her dreams as she struggled to avoid thinking about her brush with death. But once in the hold of slumber, the memory rose up, claiming her full attention with a vivid replaying. She felt the crisp temperature of the water as she plunged into it, experienced once again the way the river seemed to be folding her inside its grip. The need to fight its grasp was overwhelming. She was straining to break free, feeling panic well up inside her as it held her in a viselike grip.

"Jane."

Diocail shook her free of the nightmare. Jane opened her eyes with a startled yelp as she tried to shove him away from her. He made a low sound in the back of his throat as her hand smacked into his jaw.

"Oh…" She was breathing hard, her heart pounding as she blinked and tried to banish the nightmare completely. "I'm sorry, Diocail."

His eyes narrowed, but his expression became pleased. "I think that's the first time ye have called me by me name."

He was sitting in her bed with her, and her cheeks suddenly heated as she recalled exactly what he'd done to her the last time they were alone. Her damned clitoris began to throb.

Her body really did have a terrible sense of timing. "I spoke it at our wedding."

"Aye, ye did."

His voice had deepened, becoming raspy as he continued to grin. He reached out, smoothing the hair away from her face.

"Ye took a dangerous risk today, Jane. I've no wish to shame ye in front of others, but I admit I came close to reprimanding ye right there in the hall."

She sat up and scooted to sit against the headboard. "The entire reason I am here is because this house needs to be taken in hand. Did you not like the bread at supper? There was plenty, and your teeth weren't in danger of being chipped."

He grinned, earning a snort from her. "You are the strangest man, Diocail Gordon. Smiling when I show you my temper."

"Admit ye enjoy it," he encouraged her softly, as if

was attempting to lure her away from everything she'd been taught was correct.

"Oh Christ." She aimed a playful kick at him. "I swear, you are worse than Lucifer whispering to Eve. And the church preaches that women are the ones to worry about sowing decency and leading men to sin's door because we are descended from Eve."

Henry might have slapped her for such a comparison. Diocail tossed his head back and laughed. He rolled onto his back, across the foot of her bed, chuckling like a little boy, with the exception of the fact that he was a huge man.

She grabbed her pillow and swung it at him. The impact was less than satisfying because the pillow was thin and old. All it really did was collapse on him and alert him to her attack. The bed rocked as he surged up and captured her, rolling her back as he landed on top of her.

It was all accomplished in a moment, yet it left her gasping, and not because of outrage. No, there was a flush on her cheeks and a twist of excitement moving through her belly. Diocail didn't miss it either. She watched his eyes narrow as she absorbed how good his weight felt on top of her. It was a deep, maybe even a dark admission that took her by surprise because she'd never enjoyed Henry being on top of her.

Diocail's lips curved a bit as he read the emotion on her face. Everything she felt seemed so very transparent to him. It was so exposing and yet intensely exciting. As though he might be the single person in the world to keep her sheltered from loneliness.

But he rolled off her and sat next to her on the bed.

Jane ended up biting her lip to contain the disappointment that assaulted her as a result. He waited for her to sit up.

"I do enjoy it," he offered as she settled across from him. "Yer nature."

"You shouldn't."

He scoffed at her, his grin becoming wider. "Plenty of people told me I shouldn't be laird, and yet here I am."

It was her turn to grin. "Indeed. Shall I say…congratulations? Or promise you I will pray for the Lord to send you strength every night?"

He closed his eyes and offered her a soft groan before opening his eyes again and revealing a glitter of amusement.

"Swear ye will nae leave me to this mess on me own," he implored her passionately.

"I've a lump the size of an egg on my head from seeing to the mill."

His eyes narrowed, and he reached for her, but Jane slapped his hand away. "I wasn't complaining."

Diocail settled back, giving her enough time to realize they were in fact talking in her bed. He made a soft, male sort of sound in the back of his throat.

"The look on yer face tells me yer husband… whatever his name was…did nae take the time to have many conversations with ye while in yer bedchamber."

"I am not certain it matters." She looked away and then returned her attention to his face because she felt like a coward.

Diocail pointed at her. "It matters because the bastard is who ye compare me to."

"Well…" she stammered, trying to decide what she was feeling. He had a valid point; she simply didn't know what to make of it.

"Look at me, Jane." There was a firm note of authority in his tone. Obedience in the bedchamber was something she was accustomed to giving.

"Ye were raised to think of my kind as savages." He leveled a knowing look at her. "Admit it."

She offered him a shrug. "As you were raised to believe all English women are delicate and unable to face challenges."

He enjoyed her comeback, offering her a nod. "And yet I tell ye I enjoy yer passion, and I've proved it by no' raising me hand to ye."

She nodded. "I do not understand the point of this conversation…" She suddenly felt as though sitting still was beyond her ability. "And why are we talking in bed?"

She started to slide off, but he moved faster, catching a handful of her smock and pulling her back onto the bed. "Christ, you have the strength of Hercules."

He deposited her in the middle of the bed and stretched out beside her, propping his elbow on the mattress next to her head.

"We're talking…" He stressed the last word. "Because I'm working very, *very* hard at making sure ye are accustomed to me before we get to know each other as man and wife."

And he didn't have to do it. That hard truth felt like a knife stuck through her chest, reminding her exactly why she didn't care to ever have another husband.

"Christ." He gave her a glimpse of frustration in his

eyes. "I meant that as an offering of me sincerity. Why do ye look at me so wounded?"

"Because I wish to annul this marriage, and you are refusing my plea." He was being more than patient with her. It was a fact that shamed her, and yet his determination only strengthened her resolve to not be bound to any man for the rest of her days.

"That's a truth," he admitted.

He reached out and stroked her cheek. The contact was so pleasing that she fought off the urge to let her eyes slip shut so that she might just immerse herself in the sensation.

"I believe we might be well suited in spite of the circumstances that brought us together," he stated firmly.

"I simply do not care for marriage." There, she'd said it. He deserved to hear the truth of the matter. "The duties of a wife, they…leave me…cold. Widowhood suits me very well. I might stay and serve as your Head of House, and you can contract a wife who is Scottish."

"Ye do nae wish to have children, lass?"

Disappointment moved through her. "I suppose… well…"

His fingers were still in contact with her, trailing across her chin and down her neck. Somehow, she'd never realized how sensitive the skin of her neck was. Diocail followed with a line of soft kisses. He slipped his hand beneath her nape, cupping it and giving her a taste of his strength as he continued to tease her with delicate kisses.

"Diocail…"

He smothered her comment with a kiss that stole

her breath. It was hard enough to part her lips, but controlled in a way that made her intensely aware of how much discipline he maintained over his strength. It aroused her like nothing else ever had, the fact that he was so conscious of her comfort while seeking his own satisfaction.

She reached for him, unable to quell the urge. He didn't disappoint her, moving over her and kissing her harder. It set fire to her passion, making even the fabric of her smock feel too confining. A moment later, he rose above her, sitting back on his hunches before he dug his fingers into the thin fabric of her garment and drew it up and over her head.

She crossed her arms over her breasts as she felt the brush of the night air on her bare skin.

"Ye're a fine-looking woman, Jane. It's going to be me pleasure to teach ye to enjoy being a wife."

She opened her mouth to ask him what he meant, but Diocail was finished with conversation. He pressed her back, folding her into his embrace. The wool of his kilt scratched her legs, but it gave her some manner of assurance that he wasn't going to press himself onto her.

That bit of knowledge allowed her to simply stop thinking. It was much better to feel anyway.

Every inch of Diocail was hard, but he kissed her with sweetness. Taking a long time to linger over her lips, he cradled the side of her head, using his elbows to support himself.

She sighed, opening her mouth and shivering as he teased her lower lip with his tongue. He made a soft sound in the back of his throat that struck her as a more honest compliment than any spoken words.

If that meant she was succumbing to lust, so be it. All that mattered was the bliss their motions seemed to create.

She was kissing him back, pushing her hands into his hair, holding him in place as she took the taste of him she desired. She felt his grip in her hair tightened. A tiny bit of pain went across her scalp, but she let out a breathless little sound of pure enjoyment that Diocail didn't miss. He lifted his head just enough so he might open his eyes and watch her expression. He tightened his fingers again, watching the effect.

She shuddered with something so deeply rooted inside her body it left her feeling nearly desperate to allow it to be seen.

By him.

Only him.

"Ye like me strength." It wasn't a question but an observation. One he followed by allowing more of his weight to settle onto her. He watched her as he did it, gauging her response.

A shiver crossed her skin as her nipples drew into hard points. His lips twitched. She might have labeled it a grin, but it was nothing so civilized. No, it was primal, just as he was. And her clitoris began to throb in response.

"As soon as ye learn to trust me more, I am going to give ye all the strength ye crave." His tone was hard, edged with determination.

"What do you mean?"

He offered her a dark chuckle before slipping down her body. She felt awkward, but he was completely confident in the situation. Drawing his hands along

her sides, he delighted her as he pressed her thighs wide and settled his shoulders between them.

She was mortified, but he looked up at her without a shred of shame that he was hovering over her spread sex. "Trust is earned, Jane. Only a swine demands it from a woman because she has wed him at the command of her father."

He believed what he said. She was transfixed by the sincerity in his tone and the hard glitter of determination in his eyes.

"What are…you…going to do…down *there*?" She scarcely believed she was asking such a question, but Diocail responded with a very arrogant grin.

He teased the curls that crowned her mons. She recoiled. Not because of any pain—it felt incredibly good—but he flattened his hand on her belly, pinning her to the bed.

"I am going to show ye why I would be a very good husband, lass."

Her eyes widened.

Diocail answered her with another husky chuckle. "So ye have heard of it…"

Her face felt as if it had caught fire. Diocail enjoyed it immensely, his fingers dipping down to stroke the folds of her sex. Just the outer edge, but she felt it so keenly, she jerked and sucked in a gasp.

"You cannot be serious," she argued. "No one really does…*that*."

"A man who is interested in being a good lover does." Diocail stroked her again, watching the way she drew in her breath and let it out in a little sigh. "I want to be yer lover, Jane."

"That's a sin."

"Between man and wife? God would no' be so cruel." He sent her a confident look before he lowered his attention to her spread sex.

It was mortifying or, at least, it should have struck her as such.

And yet she felt the first brush of his breath against the folds of her body and shuddered with the deepest pleasure she'd ever felt. Anticipation was like a living force inside her, the skin covering her sex far more sensitive than she ever imagined.

And Diocail seemed to know it too. He teased her with the lightest licks, drawing the tip of his tongue along the outer folds of her sex before using his fingers to spread her open. The air itself felt as though it set off a ripple of delight, but it was nothing compared to the feeling of his mouth when it connected with her flesh.

She gasped and then forgot to breathe altogether as he sucked on her most tender parts, applying the tip of his tongue to her clitoris in a motion that destroyed her attempts to make sense of it all. The ability to think fell away like a handful of dry sand. No matter how hard she tried to squeeze her fingers around it, only a few grains remained, and they were all centered on the feeling he created with his mouth.

She moaned.

It was a wanton sound that stunned her with how deeply sexual it was. But it wasn't enough. She was twisting, lifting her hips toward him as he applied more pressure. She understood now. Knew that the tightening was going to end in a shower of bliss, and she craved it more than ever. The night air was no

longer cold. Her heart was beating fast; perspiration coated her skin. Her hands curled into claws on the bedding as she cried out in desperation.

Diocail didn't disappoint her.

He sucked harder, pressing her to the surface of the bed as he pushed her over the edge into the swirling vortex of ecstasy. It wrung her body out, dropping her onto the bed in a spent heap as she struggled to pull in enough air. For long moments she didn't even care. There was such a warm glow of satisfaction encompassing her body that nothing mattered at all.

She only came back to her senses as Diocail moved. He rose up, the muscles on his arms defined as he crawled up her body. He was hot and hard, and she truly didn't care if he took her. It seemed the natural conclusion to the moment.

Instead he stroked her cheek, easing her hair back from where it was stuck to her wet skin. She reached for him, following her impulses. He cupped her nape, coming to settle over her. He gave her just enough of his weight to make her realize she wanted more. Satisfaction was warming her, and yet there was a need deeper inside her that was still unsated.

So she curled her fingers around his shoulder and tried to draw him closer. His lips curved in victory, but in his eyes, she witnessed something else.

"No." His tone was gruff and edged with hunger. He stroked her face, his eyes narrowing and his jaw tightening before he pushed away from her.

It felt as if something had been ripped from her. Leaving behind a sting to ensure she noticed that she'd lost something.

Diocail was stiff, bracing himself at the foot of the bed as he watched her. She was sure all of her longing was clear on her face. The truth was every defense she had was nothing compared to the raw need churning inside her.

"I will nae have yer compliance in this manner."

He seemed to be telling himself that more than her. He shook his head and rubbed a hand over his face before pointing at her. "No'…like this."

"I don't understand…" And she was fairly certain she didn't want to. The darkness lent itself to the moment, making it seem so very right to welcome him back into her embrace. Jane curled up until she was sitting in the middle of the bed, still feeling more rejected than she'd ever thought possible. "I thought…you wanted…this…"

His stern expression cracked, his lips curling up. "Aye. More than I care to admit." For a long moment, he stared at her, and she witnessed the flare of hunger in his eyes. It sent a ripple of awareness through her, unlike anything she'd ever experienced. It was the sort of look bards sang of when they spoke of heated passion, and it left her astonished to have it aimed her way.

"But I will have ye choose me." He bit out each word. "Freely. Clearly. In full knowledge that ye are doing it."

The determination in his voice was a tangible thing. She felt it as much as heard it and realized how deeply important it was to him. Once again, she felt a kinship. As though they shared a secret with one another, a deep, dark, personal one.

She gathered the bedding around herself. "The sun," she began in a husky whisper, "will not rise for several hours, so…" She sent him what she hoped was just as a determined look. "The door is behind you."

She would not beg him to stay. No.

Jane bit her lip as he nodded, looking for a long time as though he was going to step over the line he'd just drawn between them. His jaw was so tight she caught a glimpse of the corded muscles going down his neck.

And then he was turning, his kilt swirling out to flash his thighs at her because he moved so quickly. Jane tasted blood from biting her lip so hard. The pain mingled with the distress of watching him leave her. The combination left her sitting in the middle of the bed, her fingers digging into the bedding like talons as she felt the chill of the night nipping at her to emphasize just how alone she was.

Another first. Something else she'd learned at his hand, to realize how alone she was and how wanton she truly was at her core.

❧

Shadows had plenty of space to hide in.

Keefe watched Diocail leave and smiled. Anticipation was warming his blood, and his conscience didn't raise anything more than a brief argument against what he'd decided needed doing.

No Englishwoman was going to be Lady of the Gordons. Not after all the Scottish blood the English had spilled.

He'd do the job quickly. Smother her beneath her pillow and let it be said she died from her tumble into the river.

She was an Englishwoman, after all, too weak to survive the Highlands. Diocail's steps grew fainter and fainter until the sound of the night breeze covered them completely. Keefe lifted his foot and started to walk toward the door of the chamber.

But he pulled back as one of the shadows shifted, forming into a man who stood for a long moment in the passageway. He was too close, and Keefe eased back until the darkness made it impossible for him to be seen.

Frustration ate at him, but he'd never gain enough votes to take the lairdship with a murder pinned on his name. Suspicion that he'd taken care of matters was one thing; in fact, plenty of men would support him because they'd trust that he would not allow the English to have even a clod of dirt that belonged to the Gordons. But murder that was proven? Well, that was another matter.

Until a better time then.

It would come. He'd make sure of it.

❧

"Why did ye call us here?" Aylin had never been an early riser. He rubbed his eyes and sent Muir a disgruntled look. "It's no' even first light."

"Close enough." Muir offered him no sympathy. "And the matter is an important one."

"Well, let's have it," Kory asked.

Muir looked around first, making sure they were

alone. "The laird needs a wee bit of help with his bride." He stressed the word *bride*.

Niven scoffed. "The last time we tried to get him someone to offer him advice on pleasing women, he nearly broke our necks."

"No' that sort of help," Muir amended as he cleared his throat. "Anyhow, as to that part of it…the laird has matters in good hand."

"Ye are no' making sense," Aylin groused. "If ye were only going to waste me time with useless prattle, it might have waited until the dawn broke."

Muir reached out and cuffed Aylin on the side of the head. "Ye were sleeping so well on account of the fact that ye had yer first decent supper."

They all shrugged and nodded. "If the mistress managed that in one day, just think what she'll get done by the end of the month."

They all grinned with anticipation.

"So, what is yer worry?" Kory asked.

"The laird, he fancies having a woman who chooses him," Muir explained.

"They're wed," Aylin answered. "It's done."

"And yet," Muir said, leaning in. "It is no'…completely finished."

They all grasped his meaning, bewilderment raising their eyebrows.

"It can nae be," Kory spoke up. "I saw them going off at the festival…heard…well…I *heard them*."

"That's why I woke ye," Muir exclaimed. "Last night *I heard them too*, only I was close enough to listen in on what was said after the moment passed. The laird did nae…ah…take his own pleasure. Told the mistress

he will nae trap her in the union, that he's waiting on her to come to his bed."

They all stared at him for a long moment. "We've got to do something about it," he exclaimed.

"Aye," Aylin agreed. "She'll be seeking an annulment now that she's seen the mess her house is in."

"Well…what can we do about such a thing?" Niven honestly asked.

"If I knew," Muir exclaimed. "I'd no' be here talking, I'd be doing it."

His companions nodded.

"Well, it seems…" Kory was thinking out loud. "The two of them being in separate bedchambers, well, now, that is no' helping matters."

"Aye!" Muir agreed. "The laird said he was waiting for her to come up to his chamber."

"So how do we get her to do that?" Niven asked.

Aylin shoved him in the shoulder. "We needs make up excuses, maybe tell her he called for her."

"He'll only ask her straightaway if she came there because she wanted to," Muir said.

Aylin opened his hands up wide. "Well then, we'll just have to…damage the sheets or do something a good mistress would see to setting right herself."

Muir was nodding. "Aye, the way she went down to the mill, she's no' one to be leaving matters to others."

They shared grins with one another. "So, between us, let's be keeping a watch on her, without her knowing what we're about."

"And any man who sees the opportunity, make sure ye do nae allow it to slip from yer grasp," Aylin added.

"Is nae this deception?" Niven asked. A moment later, he raised his forearm to protect his head as his companions swatted at him.

"It's for a good purpose," Muir informed him. "Do ye want our little mistress to be going back to a father who will wed her to a man such as her first husband?"

Niven peeked at them before lowering his arm. "I did nae think about it quite like that."

"Best for her to be staying right here," Aylin added. "She'll settle in. With a bit of time."

They all nodded agreement before looking around and moving off. Muir enjoyed the sense of relief that went through him. Send her back to England in the spring? Over his dead body.

Six

SNOW FLURRIES BEGAN TO SWIRL BY THE NEXT afternoon. Their arrival sent the men into action as the last of the harvest was pulled in before it froze and was lost. Jane welcomed the frenzy of activity. It kept everyone busy for the better part of the week. No one fell into their beds until well after sundown, and they were up at first light in an effort to collect every plant that might be used to sustain them through the long months of winter. The kitchen staff didn't have time to question her authority. Jane caught them casting her grudging looks of approval as the days passed, and she neither deserted them because the labor was hard, nor made a muck of things because she didn't know the first thing about filling the cellars for winter.

Necessity made strange bedfellows.

At the moment, they were women. The steady sound of men toiling on the roofs and walls gave them confidence they'd all survive to see spring.

Jane caught only glimpses of Diocail as he labored with his men to patch the worst of the holes in the roof. They worked so hard they stripped down to

their shirts in spite of the snow floating in the air. She herself didn't have much time to spare either. Shepherd boys were coming in from the pastures, driving their sheep and cattle toward the protection of the castle walls. The animals had thick coats, grown with the help of grazing all summer long, but when the wind began to wail, they would benefit from having something to huddle near.

The retainers brought their families in too. Many of them didn't have more than homes built of the roughest stone and thatch. Jane struggled to find room for them all.

Which led her to the towers. There were two, with stairs that rose up more than three stories. She looked up one and tried to decide what might be on the floors above. Considering the condition of the rest of the fortification, they were probably in disrepair.

She contemplated the stairs for a long moment, but the wailing of an infant made her lift her foot and begin climbing upward in an effort to see if there was more space available. At least the steps were stone, which gave her peace of mind as she climbed higher. The chill increased too, hinting that it had been a long time since a fire had been lit in any of the chambers.

Jane lifted her hand and looked at the dust coating her fingers from the handrail. She realized why a moment later as a pair of chamber doors came into sight. There was a thick chain looped through the handles with a large lock.

Locks were expensive. And hard to come by as well.

She stared at it, wondering what could be so

important. Looking up, she decided to climb further into the tower. The next floor showed her the same thing. Another lock and chain and even more dust. Here the chain was rusted because of a broken set of window shutters. The wind was howling through the hole, blowing thick feathers of snow against the doors. The flakes slipped down to form a puddle against a huge rotted section of the door, clearly damaged from last winter when snow had drifted against the wood unchecked.

It infuriated her to no end to see such disregard for the tower when the number of people clustered in the hall made it plain there were ample hands to see to the task of making sure the tower was secure. And yet something had kept them all belowstairs.

She made her way to the last floor and stopped, facing another locked door. There was an inch of dust on the floor, proving no one had set foot on the landing in years. Reaching down, Jane took the ring of keys off her belt. Dolina had happily given them to her with a look of relief in her eyes. Unlike at her father's home, this ring was full of keys that were tarnished from lack of use. She moved toward the lock, leaving tracks in the dust and stirring it up so it tickled her nose.

It was a slow process, fitting the keys into the lock and trying them. The lock held each time, making her suspect time had frozen it.

But she kept at it and let out a little sound of victory when one key finally turned. The action was far from smooth. Jane doubled her effort, earning the reward of a grinding noise before the lock gave way and opened. It was a huge, heavy thing. She wasn't expecting the

weight, and it fell from her fingers as it slipped from the chain. The sound of it hitting the floor echoed inside the stairway.

She didn't squander any concern on what the Gordons might think of her actions. Clearly none had ventured up the stairs in years, so they were not in a position to chastise her. She was taking the house in hand, and that meant doing what had been neglected. There was a thick bar over the doors as well. She struggled to lift it, kicking up a cloud of dust with the hem of her skirt as she twisted and tried to get beneath it so she might lift it. She ended up wiping her forehead when she succeeded, wrinkling her nose at the feeling of dirt being rubbed against her skin from where it had collected on her sleeve.

Well, there was no one to see her at present.

The hinges on the doors squealed and groaned as she struggled to pull one open. Beyond it, the chamber was cast in gloom, the shutters closed tight with leather nailed into them to keep the weather out.

That was a relief to see.

She ventured in, stopping by the door to strike a flint stone into a small pile of thatch left there. It caught with a flash of bright light. Jane held a candle to it, waiting until the wick caught before she placed the candle into a holder and used it to light her way into the chamber.

She held the candle up and blinked at what the flickering light showed her.

"Sweet mother of Christ."

All around her were chests and bundles, stacked as high as a man might reach. There wasn't any

furniture in the room, at least not any that was assembled. Off near the wall, she spied a headboard that must go with a magnificent bed. She could see the elaborate carvings. Thick layers of dust covered almost everything, but she could see patterns to the accumulation, showing the seasons as new stacks had been added.

"Colum was a miser."

Jane shrieked. The candle went flying as she swung it at her unannounced company. There was a bone-jarring impact as she struck her target and the candle sputtered out, dropping darkness around them.

"Jane!"

She froze, Diocail's growl familiar. Her fear died in a sizzle of temper. "You scared me near unto death!"

Her hand landed on his jaw before she ever managed to think her actions through. The loud pop bounced off the wall as he reached out and clamped his arms around her.

That quickly she was bound tightly against him. From head to knee, they were pressed together.

"You might have announced your arrival," she hissed after fighting to raise her chin. One of the buttons on his doublet scratched her nose because her face was pressed so hard against his chest.

"I've never known ye to be so skittish before, woman," he snarled. "And ye are supposed to slap a man with an open hand, no' a closed fist."

"My brothers taught me how to fight. Slapping does naught except anger your opponent."

That earned her a grunt, but a moment later, the door slammed shut. Diocail let out a frustrated sound.

"Something always likes to interrupt us…" he muttered as he released her, turning toward the door.

Jane felt her eyes widen at the unmistakable sound of the bar being lowered into place. Diocail cursed, and she heard him running toward the doors, heard him collide with them, and then another growl as he tried to force them open.

"Muir!" He pounded on the door as Jane lowered herself to her knees and felt around on the floor for the candle. The stacks of goods made it so the candle hadn't traveled very far. She found it as Diocail slammed his fist into the door again.

"Curse and rot ye!" he bellowed, but his voice only echoed inside the chamber.

"I doubt anyone below can hear you." Jane made sure he heard her before she ventured closer. There were only the faintest traces of light coming through the edges of the leather-covered windows. She scuffed her feet against the floor to make certain he knew she was approaching.

"Damned fiend has locked us in," he muttered in disgust.

"Why ever would he do such a thing?"

Diocail found the flint and struck it. The sparks illuminated his face. She heard him pull something dry from somewhere, and a moment later, he was dropping sparks into the tinder bowl. Whatever he'd found caught fire. Jane lowered the candle so that the wick caught.

A warm bubble of light enveloped them. It showed her a very disgruntled man with a red spot on his jaw.

"Oohh…" She let out a little sound of distress.

Diocail offered her a snort. "Aye. Yer brothers taught ye right."

"Well," she sputtered. "You walk so silently."

"Ye've said as much before."

He gestured her to follow him. He was intent on one of the windows, and she followed, carrying their single source of light along with her. The stacks of bundles made an eerie setting as Diocail pulled a knife from where it was tucked into the top of his boot and started to slice away at the leather.

"Who would lock us in?" she asked as he worked to pull the leather from the window.

"Me men." Diocail reached in and twisted the lock on the window shutters so he might open them. There was a cascade of dirt off the ceiling when he opened them, and the night wind blew in.

"But…*why?*"

The candle flame flickered dangerously. Jane turned her back on the window to shield the light from the wind.

Diocail offered her a grunt in response.

"If I am expected to understand that," she groused, "I assure you, Diocail Gordon, I do not."

He'd stuck his face out of the window, leaning out as fat flakes of snow flew in. It was bitterly cold now, the clouds thick and swirling around the treetops.

"You're going to catch your death," she warned him.

He grunted and pulled his head back. His hair was wet from snow along with the front of his doublet. "Muir planned this well." There was a crunch and groan as he closed the shutters and twisted the lock into place.

"Planned…to lock us in here?" She realized she was repeating herself, but it defied rational thought. "I still don't understand why they would even think to do such a thing."

Diocail faced her, the expression on his face one of rueful enjoyment. "Clearly…" he began, as amused as he was furious. "They still believe keeping ye is a wise thing to do."

"I am here."

Diocail grunted and started to prowl the confines of the chamber. It wasn't an easy task with all the bundles. He pushed at some and went around others, seeking an escape. Jane followed with the candle, suddenly more grateful than she cared to admit for his company. He made the rounds twice before stopping in the center of the chamber and glaring at the walls in contempt.

"We're stuck good," he said in frustration. "No one in the yard with the snow falling thickly now. It will be morning before we can shout down to someone." He looked back toward the main chamber doors. "At least he provided supper."

"What?"

Her question was answered when she looked near the chamber doors. Sure enough, there was a basket with a cloth covering it.

"So this was…*planned*?"

Diocail offered her an incredulous look. "Have I no' been saying that, lass?"

"Yes, but it still makes no bloody sense." Her tone betrayed her rising frustration.

"I believe they are intent on taking the French

method to celebrating our union." Diocail lifted the basket and pulled out a bottle. "Honey mead."

"So they have locked us in here…"

"So we can nae get away from one another," Diocail finished for her. "And nature can take its course."

Jane stepped back. In fact, she was several paces away before he grunted and narrowed his eyes at her.

"Do nae retreat from me as though ye do nae trust me."

"Maybe I don't trust myself."

Oh, she truly should have learned to hold her tongue! He closed his eyes. "Do nae test me, Jane."

Part of her enjoyed that he sounded as frustrated as she was. In fact, she choked back a giggle, and then another, until she was choking like a daft woman.

Tears filled her eyes, and she heard him chuckling along with her. "Aye, it's sure to be a fine story to tell one day…" he said as he looked around the chamber. "Best we keep our minds on that as we try to make a suitable bed in this place."

"What is all of this?" At least it was a safe topic. One that didn't allow her to think about how many times she'd dreamed about him.

He retrieved the candleholder and picked some bundles up from where they were sitting on a crate. She set the candle in the box, giving it a good push to make sure their only light source was well seated. There was a scratching sound from behind her, and she turned to see Diocail putting more straw into the tinder bowl. He'd pulled another candle from a box and placed it into a second holder on the small table by the tinder bowl.

"It's Colum's tribute," he answered at last.

Her eyes rounded with horror. "And the chambers below?"

Diocail nodded. "He suffered from the sin of greed sure enough. The table empty and the roof leaking, but all of this…stacked and shared with none."

"Shameful." She pulled one of the bundles from a stack and began to unwrap it. Diocail was watching her, and she froze. "I'm sorry. I suppose I shouldn't—"

"Open it," he urged her, his gaze strangely intent. "That is, if ye are planning to continue putting this house to rights."

"I only came up here because the hall is so full of people seeking shelter."

He crossed his arms over his chest. Understanding flashed through his eyes. "I wondered what drew ye here."

"Why are you here?" She'd forgotten all about the bundle, far more interested in him.

God, I've missed him.

The week was suddenly flashing before her eyes, all of the hours when she hadn't seen him, hadn't heard his voice.

Hadn't been tempted by him…

Diocail gave a grunt. "Muir came running to tell me ye'd came this way and there was a crash…"

"I dropped the lock down the stairs," she defended herself. "Any fool could see exactly what made the sound."

"Muir is no fool." Diocail looked around again. "Just a damned crafty bastard. He sent Bari running out to tell me ye were in trouble instead of checking

on ye himself. Diocail offered her a shrug. "I should have questioned it, but I came running."

And she wasn't fool enough to miss the fact that Muir knew full well what he was about. There was something between her and Diocail. An attraction that defied logic. Perhaps it was lust that might be labeled passion since they'd taken a blessing from the church, but in the end, it was carnal. She felt it tugging on her insides, powerless to ignore it.

You are more aware of him than any other man.

It was strangely hypnotic. Like a fae creature whispering in her ear while she slept.

"So I ran up here—" He stopped with his hands on his hips as he shook his head. "And Muir is likely sitting down in the hall laughing until he pisses himself over how simple it was."

"It is rather…amusing." She tried to keep her lips straight but failed.

Diocail offered her a smile in return, one that was menacing. "Aye. Amusing it is. I do hope ye laugh when we're trying to sleep on the hard floor in naught but me kilt."

Which meant he'd have to take it off.

And share it with her.

Her cheeks heated. "There must be something in here to use to keep us warm."

She finished pulling the wrapping off the bundle in her hands and found a length of shirt linen, complete with a wooden spindle of thread provided for sewing it.

"That won't keep us warm, but it might be good if I can find some pelts."

He was moving off toward the darker areas of the

room. Jane picked up one of the candles and followed. For it seemed they were going to spend the night together.

❧

"I did nae think it would work." Aylin shook his head and grinned. He pointed at Muir. "Ye're a crafty one, to be sure."

Muir lifted a mug to his lips and smacked them when he was finished. "The mistress knows how to set the fare on the supper table."

There were nods all around as they enjoyed the few moments of relaxation before they all sought their beds.

"But at what cost?"

Muir tilted his head and looked over to the man who had spoken. "Sheehan, man, do nae go starting with yer complaining about her being English."

"She is English," Sheehan insisted. "It's a fact, no' a complaint."

"No' the way ye say it," Kory answered back. "Ye should be ashamed, sitting there with a full belly and thinking ill of the woman who made sure there was bread on the supper table for ye."

"A Scottish mistress could do as well," Keefe argued.

"Doesn't matter where she came from." Muir thumped the table with his mug to make sure his words were heard. "She's ours now. Good Scottish bellies she's making sure are filled."

"Aye," Aylin agreed. "And it's done."

"Ye said it was not so," young Bari lifted his face to stare at his elders. "That's why ye locked them in together."

"Hush now, lad." Niven pulled the boy close and shushed him.

"But…when ye tell lies…ye get locked in the stocks, me mother always told me so."

"Aye," Niven spoke quickly to try to keep the child silent. "Yer mother told ye right. It's just not exactly a lie. Ye'll understand when ye're grown."

"What does *consummated* mean?"

"Time for the lad to be sleeping," Muir announced.

Niven swung his legs over the bench he was sharing with Aylin and led Bari away. Muir lifted his mug to his lips again but sent Keefe and Sheehan a stern look over its rim. They bristled and turned back toward one another, giving Muir their backs.

Muir took the opportunity to share a glance with Aylin. It was full of accomplishment as well as a healthy respect for the fact that sometimes even the best plans didn't turn out as well as one liked.

Well, if that were to happen, he'd just have to do some more planning.

❧

"The marriage is unconsummated."

Keefe was pleased, to say the least. Sheehan hurried to close the door, and it wasn't because of the snow blowing over the threshold. The small cottage was bitterly cold, and both men went toward the hearth to warm themselves. It was a peat fire and smoldered heavily, filling the top of the cottage with thick smoke.

Keefe sat down on a log to escape the fumes. "All we needs do is get rid of her now before the laird has a chance to sample a ride." He rubbed his hands together

in anticipation. "Tomorrow ye'll bring up yer uncle's cart. We'll load her into it and take her away."

"What makes ye think the laird will no' ride out after her?" Sheehan asked. "With the snow, our tracks will be clear."

"We'll stick to the road, where it will be a muddy mess because the ground has no' yet frozen."

Sheehan didn't answer but stared into the fire. Keefe reached out and hit him on the shoulder. "Ye're either for me cause or no'."

"Aye," Sheehan answered. "I am yer man, and ye know it well."

"So, we're agreed?" Keefe pressed.

"So long as ye'll promise me one thing."

Keefe's eyes narrowed. "What might that be?"

"That we'll no' kill her unless we have to."

Keefe's eyes narrowed, but Sheehan refused to shirk in the face of his displeasure. "She's just a woman."

"Maybe she does no' want to be here," Sheehan argued. "The English do nae care for us any more than we like them."

"They like taking what is ours," Keefe answered. "She's a fourth daughter. Her father can nae get her a better match."

Sheehan shrugged. "Maybe ye're right, but we can give her the chance."

"One," Keefe said grudgingly. "If she hesitates, I'm going to slit her throat."

෴

"A bed fit for a Viking," Jane said.

Diocail looked at her from the other side of the

mound of furs he'd laid out on the ground. The length of shirt linen was resting on top of it all. The chamber was so full it wasn't a very big bed, but with the chill in the air, she'd likely come to appreciate having Diocail close during the long hours of the night.

His belly rumbled, and she laughed, turning around and retrieving their dinner basket. The cleanest spot was on their makeshift bed, so she stepped onto it and settled down. Diocail joined her, watching what she pulled from the basket.

"At least he made sure to provide well," Diocail remarked as he pulled the dagger from his boot top once more and used it to slice into a large piece of meat. "I'm famished."

He stabbed a chunk of the meat with the tip of his knife and lifted it to his mouth. A smaller knife was resting in the bottom of the basket, and Jane used it to slice a chunk of cheese into small cubes. Diocail happily claimed one and then another piece of meat.

"Are ye nae hungry, lass?"

Jane flashed him a smile. "I was working in the kitchen most of the day."

"Ah…tasting, were ye?"

Jane tore a round of bread apart and offered him some. "There is no other way to ensure what is placed on the table is good. I may just turn into the large, round woman I advised you to find."

"Would that be such a terrible fate?"

"You're the one who left my room the other night." Clearly she hadn't learned to hold her tongue yet. Jane fluttered her eyelashes as she looked down on their meal and felt his gaze on her.

"It was no' meant as an insult."

She lifted her chin and locked gazes with him. "I know. That was harsh of me."

He washed his meal down with a long swig of water from a jug Muir had included. She reached for it and enjoyed some as well.

"I will say this for Scotland," she said when she lowered the jug. "The water is the finest I've ever tasted."

"Aye, well, ye're a long way from where the muck of the city is being added to the rivers. I understand the English think it savage to drink it though."

"My father allowed us to buy clean water for the table."

Diocail raised his eyebrows. "I've heard of that at court and such. Can't say I could ever see meself parting with good coin for something that is flowing across the land."

He was making steady progress through their supper. Soon it was gone, and there was a satisfied grin on his lips.

"Ye've barely touched yer share." He plucked a chunk of cheese from where it was sitting on the cloth that had covered the basket and held it to her lips. "How can ye be expected to survive a night in me company without sustenance?"

"Consider yourself to be taxing?" she inquired after swallowing the cheese. He'd opened the honey mead, and she took a taste.

Diocail pointed at her. "I am a Highlander... Ye are an English lass... There are expectations."

There was something about the moment that touched off a spark inside her. Right there, they were

hidden from the world. Whatever they did was going to be a secret between them. At least Jane hoped so. Highlanders didn't seem to show much modesty, especially with regard to their laird's marriage bed.

"Perhaps I am going to be the one to tell you what I expect." No, she wasn't holding her tongue, and for that moment at least, she was very content with her lack of restraint. It was a freedom she'd never thought to experience.

Diocail's expression tightened, but not in the way she'd seen before. This was a different sort of frustration. There was a glitter of eagerness in his eyes as he tightened his fingers on the linen. He was poised, ready to spring at her, and part of her very much enjoyed knowing she'd dared him to do exactly that.

"Ye might try him and see if he is to yer liking…"

Brenda's words rose from her memory, tempting her. He had already proven his ability to please her, and yet she wondered what it might be like to lie with him completely.

You mean you wonder if you will ever get another chance at discovering what it's like to have a lover…

"Jane…"

Diocail's tone was strained. He was drawn tight, waiting on her to commit herself fully. Just as he'd said when he'd left her.

She pushed back and rose. Diocail set the bottle of honey mead aside as she dipped her fingers into the valley between her breasts to find the end of the tie that laced her bodice closed. Dolina had found her garments more suited to the Highland climate and easier to dress herself in.

Now, Jane discovered just how simple it was to tug on that lace and feel the loosened ends of the tie slither through the eyelets that closed the bodice as the weight of her breasts pressed on the front of the garment.

Diocail wasn't slow in responding. He was there, cupping her face and tilting his head so he might press a kiss against her lips.

It was just as good as she recalled.

Better, even. Her dreams were a poor substitute for the way he felt. Or smelled.

She drew in a deep breath, enjoying the way her senses reeled. He cupped her nape, making her his captive as he moved his mouth against hers, letting her feel his hunger.

She kissed him back.

Reaching for him, fighting at the buttons that kept his doublet closed because they prevented her from touching him.

Just him. That was what she craved.

And she wanted the same in return.

So she wiggled free, catching sight of a dark frown on his face before he noticed her fighting to pull the last of the tie from her bodice. His lips curled up, wolfish and pleased by her efforts.

"Christ…" he muttered as she succeeded, and the front of her high-necked smock parted to grant him a glimpse of her bare breasts.

"Ye're a siren for certain, lass…" He reached out and stroked each nipple. "I'd follow these to me death without a complaint."

She sucked in a harsh gasp, the feeling of his fingers

on her breasts stunning her. "I'd follow anywhere you lead, so long as you touch me…"

Her voice was husky and wanton and struck her as perfectly suited to the moment. Diocail's hands cupped her breasts, gently taking their weight before he squeezed them lightly. The sensation was beyond compare, for she'd never once thought her breasts might be the source of so much pleasure.

Wicked?

She bloody well didn't care. What mattered was that they were both there and his touch didn't make her feel the horrible awkwardness that Henry's had. But she did wonder if she might give as much as she received.

She reached for him, slipping her hands into the open front of his doublet and shirt. "Aye…" he ground out as her hands flattened on his skin. She'd barely had time to stroke his neck and breast before he was stepping back.

She let out a little frustrated sound that drew an answering grunt from him. "I need out of these clothes…"

Oh yes. She agreed wholeheartedly.

It should have struck her as an absurd moment. The way they both fought to strip down as though they were too hot. Instead, she tugged and loosened laces until her bodice was laying on the floor behind her and her skirts puddled around her ankles.

Diocail was faster. He opened his belt the moment he shrugged his doublet off, and his kilt went slumping to the floor. His shirt didn't last any longer as he ripped it up and over his head. When the fabric cleared his face, his eyes glittered with hard purpose.

It sent a bolt of anticipation through her, making

her breath catch in her throat. Jane froze, her fingers suddenly trembling so badly she couldn't work the button on the cuff of her shirt. All she seemed able to accomplish was to stare, absorbing the hard strength etched into his flesh. From head to toe, he was savage.

And she craved him even more for it.

He'd come forward on those silent steps of his, moving slowly, apparently worried she might bolt. "Do nae fear me…"

"I don't." Jane didn't think she'd ever spoken truer words. "I just…can't seem to stop…so silly of me… really. I'm not a virgin."

He caught her hand, brushing her fingers away as he pushed the button through its hole to free the cuff. It fell open as he raised her hand and kissed the delicate skin on the underside of her wrist. She shivered, her eyes slipping closed as she let the sheer intensity of the moment engulf her.

"I'm glad ye are no'."

Jane opened her eyes and locked gazes with him. Need flickered in his eyes. It was hard and, somehow, utterly male. She'd witnessed a man looking at her who thought he owned her before. This was different. Diocail wanted to possess her.

"Take me." She wasn't thinking. "Exactly the way I see that you want to."

His eyes narrowed, his lips thinning to show her a glimpse of his teeth. He was menacing and hard, and it fanned the flames licking at her insides. Her clitoris was throbbing, her breasts aching to be against him again, but most of all, she knew she wanted more than the satisfaction he'd delivered with his fingers and tongue.

She wanted him to claim her.

"No more teasing," she continued. "I want to know…you."

Her statement pleased him. She saw the flash of enjoyment light his eyes before he was scooping her up, swinging her against his body as he turned and lowered her onto their makeshift bed. The fur compressed under her weight as he placed her in the middle, the linen soft against her skin. It suited him. And what she craved from him.

Jane reached for him, pulling him down, gasping when his body connected with hers. He was cupping her knees and spreading them as he pushed them up so her center was open. He sat back on his haunches, her own thighs on top of his as his cock stuck out over the spread folds of her sex.

"Ye're me wife, Jane."

He bit out each word as he teased her little clitoris with his thumb. She heard the sound of her wet flesh as need became a desperate thing inside her. She might have begged in that moment for him to take her; there was nothing she cared about except having him claim her.

Reckless…

Savage…

And she felt more alive than she ever had before in her life. As though this was her purpose, her gender no longer less than his but a complement.

"I am, and I demand your favors…husband."

He grunted in response but shifted, setting the head of his cock against her open body. She shuddered, her passage feeling empty. He didn't let her suffer for

long, pressing forward, splitting her open as his length stretched her.

"Christ…" he growled as he fought to stay still for a moment. "I want to ravage ye…"

Her lips were dry in anticipation. Diocail pulled free, his cock wet, and pressed back into her as she lifted her hips.

Control vanished for them both. He covered her, his elbows braced on either side of her head as she clamped her thighs tight around his hips. He rocked her with a motion that built the need churning inside her, fanning it, growing it while they labored toward a common goal. Part of her wanted to savor the ride, but control had slipped from her grasp, leaving her nothing but impulses. She craved him and lifted to take every thrust he drove toward her. He was hard, and she writhed in enjoyment as his strength fed her cravings. They were rushing toward something, and when they reached it, they tumbled over the edge into a swirling storm of sensation. Pleasure gripped her so tightly that she was powerless to do anything except cling to Diocail while she cried out.

He was trapped as well, cupping his hands over her head as he plunged into her, going rigid as he ground out a word in Gaelic. She felt his seed release inside her, a hot flood that triggered another spasm deep inside her. For a time, nothing mattered except holding him as tightly as she might. When she finally released him, her limbs quivered, her skin was coated with perspiration, and he rolled off her as they both gasped as though they had nearly drowned.

It didn't matter.

Nothing mattered but the glow of satisfaction warming her. Nothing at all.

✎

Diocail woke with a start.

He blinked as he tried to recall where he was. It was harder than it should have been, but he caught sight of Jane lying next to him and realized he was still caught in the throes of passion.

It was stronger than he'd ever experienced. His body felt heavy, and the effort of rolling toward his partner was almost more than he could muster. But he needed to be near her. He pulled his kilt over them, tugging a corner of one of the furs along with it to keep the chill of the night away. Jane muttered in her sleep, and he smoothed his fingers along her cheek, easing her close.

The need to slip back into slumber was strong, but he fought it for a moment, looking down at the way Jane was nestled along his side. Her scent was in his nostrils, her pink nipples bare for him to see. She was so perfect in that moment, beyond beautiful. He curved his body around hers, cradling her head in his hand before locking the other on her hip.

His.

Perfect.

Two different words and yet very much the same to his way of thinking.

✎

The hard, long days of labor had taken their toll on both of them. Jane slept deeply, blinking her eyes as she

tried to wake and identify what had disturbed her. She discovered she was peeking over the edge of whatever was covering her, just able to see past it into the morning light. It made her blink as she became accustomed to it, her vision sharpening after a moment.

"Holy Christ!" she swore as she recognized Muir and Niven.

Blinking didn't make them dissipate either. She was back to wishing she knew how to curse.

"Ye've had yer fun." Jane let out a squeak as Diocail spoke beside her. She recoiled, earning a snort from him as he clamped his arms around her.

"Now get out so the lass can dress," he barked at his men. "She's no' wearing a stitch." Diocail's tone warmed with amusement that made her strain against his hold. All that gained her was a rumble from his chest as he held her steady.

There was a bark of laughter from one of the men looking down on them. Jane was frozen with horror as she realized Aylin and Kory were also there. They had the audacity to tug on the corner of their bonnets when they saw her staring at them before they made slow progress toward the door.

"Lord grant me the strength no' to lay the lot of them low," Diocail muttered into her hair.

The moment the door closed he released her. She rolled out of the bedding and sucked in her breath at the chill. Diocail had cast off their makeshift bedding and sat eyeing her.

"I do nae believe I've ever looked forward to spring so much, because I know I can keep ye bare in our chambers when the weather warms."

She intended to make some reply after retrieving her high-necked smock and pushing her arms into the sleeves. But he was watching her, and it made her suddenly shy as memory rushed back to remind her of just how brazen she'd been.

"What troubles ye, Jane?"

He rose, and she realized he'd slept in his boots. In fact, she still wore her stockings, her shoes caught in the puddle of her skirts. She heard him pulling his shirt on as she found her hip roll and tied it in place.

"I'm just cold."

She lifted her skirts high over her head and dropped them down her body. The waistband caught around her waist because of the hip roll as Diocail hooked her with one powerful arm and pulled her against him.

"Perhaps ye need a wee reminder of just how much ye enjoy being mine."

She didn't. Not that Diocail gave her the chance to say so. He pressed a kiss against her mouth as he cupped her nape to hold her steady for the assault. It wasn't a hard kiss, but it cut her to the core. Even in the bright light of day she craved him, reaching up to stroke his neck because she just didn't seem to be close enough.

"Aye, that's the way," he muttered as lifted his head and aimed a determined look into her eyes. "We'll stay right here if that is the way ye need it to be."

Part of her liked that idea very much. But there was bright light coming through the edges of the closed window shutters, and she knew she'd be foolish indeed to squander the fine weather. "The snow will return soon enough."

Diocail lifted his head from where he'd been

nuzzling her neck. "Perhaps winter is a fine season as well. I have the feeling I am going to learn a new application for the long, cold nights."

He pressed another kiss against her lips when she tried to wiggle from his embrace. "I suppose I should be understanding of yer shyness," he said as he released her.

Jane felt him watching her as she grasped the open sides of her waistband. Her thoughts were in a tangle, and he seemed the most solid thing in the chamber, so she ended up looking at him. His brown eyes were steady but filled with questions. But she pleased him by looking at him, and he let out a soft sound.

"Aye, I will be patient."

He turned and somehow found the tie for her skirts. He held it out as she reached for it with fingers that at least didn't shame her by trembling.

For a moment, the chamber was filled with the sound of clothing being donned. Diocail pleated his kilt and lay down to buckle his belt in place. "Help me with me buttons, Jane."

His tone was tempered, but she heard the authority in it. Jane was already working the bottom ones through their holes before she thought to question his command.

"You don't need help dressing." But she continued to work her way toward his collar.

"Nay," he admitted. "It's an excuse to get ye near me, and I am no' ashamed to say so." He reached down and lifted her chin so their gazes locked. "Are ye ashamed? Last night, ye were—"

"I know." She stepped away and smoothed her hair.

"It distresses ye now?" He wasn't going to allow the matter to remain unspoken.

"Truly," she began. "I have no idea what to think." She stopped with her hand on her forehead. "Never have I behaved in such a manner. You bring out something in me that has my thoughts all…tangled."

He flashed her a grin. A wolfish, smug expression that made it clear he enjoyed her admission. "Well now, that's fine praise."

Jane offered him a frustrated look that earned her a mock reverence from him.

"Just remember, I didn't pray for patience with your men," she advised him. "Best get on your way and make certain I don't catch them in the stairwell."

"I'm planning on being at the bottom to see which one is fool enough to let ye close enough to kick him in the arse."

He reached up and tugged on the corner of his bonnet before he disappeared through the chamber doors. It left her with a moment of privacy to reflect. Jane turned and looked at their bed of pelts.

You enjoyed it…

She had, and part of her wasn't sorry one bit. No. Instead, she felt the flutter of something inside her, something that felt a whole lot like she was finished being ashamed of who she was. Or perhaps she was admitting her true nature at last.

Whatever it was, she decided she liked it.

So did Diocail…

She turned and left the chamber with a blush staining her cheeks, but not because of what she'd done. No, the heat stemmed from the thoughts she was

entertaining about what to do with him once the sun set that night.

❧

"Mistress."

Jane turned around and found a man standing near the door of the cellar. She waved the woman she was working with on, earning a nod. Both of them were hauling bundles of late-season vegetables to the lower rooms where they would stay fresh with the help of the chill.

"Yes?" Jane asked.

Whoever he was, he looked a bit uncertain. He'd taken to looking around instead of at her. A tingle touched her nape, but he looked back at her.

"The mill." He spoke low and gruff. "Dolina said ye were needed."

Dolina was proving to be indispensable. Jane trusted her judgment and dusted her hands on her apron. "Thank you for coming to fetch me."

He looked at the floor again but cleared out of the doorway.

It would take time.

She repeated those words as she made her way away from the towers with the man following her. Honestly, she could not begrudge him or any of his clan for having reservations about her, since she herself had needed to be locked in a chamber with Diocail to face her own feelings.

She was content in that choice now.

She felt herself smiling, had worn a silly expression of joy for most of the day because it felt as if there was

a bubble of happiness stuck in her chest. She hoped it never worked its way free.

The truth was she'd honestly never believed she might be so happy. Never suspected she might be filled with it so fully she wanted to twirl around in a circle and then stop and say a quick prayer of thanks because of how grateful she was.

So she would smile at the man trudging along with her, thank him kindly for his time, and let him see she meant to make his life as comfortable as she might.

"Thank you for fetching me—"

Something slammed into the back of her head. Jane stared at the man's tight expression as she felt the pain rushing through her head, and then darkness claimed her like a raptor snatching a mouse from the ground.

Quick, silent, and deadly.

❧

"I should lay ye low."

Muir wasn't concerned. In fact, he offered Diocail a smirk as they worked on the stable roof. "Ye should be thanking me," Muir responded.

"Aye," Aylin added. "Ye are nae so easy to sneak up on. Thought we were going to have to use the club to knock ye senseless to keep ye in that chamber."

Diocail shot them a look that sent both Aylin and Muir into a fit of snickers.

"Well, now, it would have served to get the lass to cradle ye sure enough!" Muir exclaimed with malicious glee.

"Aye," Diocail agreed. "And it would have gotten ye a very well-deserved arse kicking."

Muir opened his arms wide. "I'm wounded. I witnessed with me own eyes the pair of ye snuggled against each other, the mistress's hair all tousled and her bare—"

"Enough," Diocail interrupted with a mock look of reprimand. "She is yer mistress…save yer colorful talk for others."

Muir lifted his hands in mock surrender, but he was still grinning as he leaned over to resume working. It was hard toil, dark clouds appearing on the horizon to encourage them to move faster. Soft noises came from the horses below them, as though the beasts were thanking them for making the roof secure again.

He was besotted.

There was no other reason for him to be so pleased. Even his men's jesting made him happy because it was true, Jane had been his. *Was* his.

He'd craved it but never thought to enjoy something so very much. Taking the lairdship hadn't filled him with the same sense of contentment, even though his mother had spent her life telling him it would.

Having Jane choose him, well, that had given him a whole new perspective on just what true happiness was. Retiring to bed early was far more attractive than he'd ever considered it to be because he knew she'd be there too. He glanced over his shoulder at the sun, willing it to sink.

Instead he spied a woman's head at the top of the ladder they'd used to climb onto the roof. It was one of the women from the kitchen, a mature woman who he'd noticed stepping up to help Jane take charge.

She looked straight at Diocail. "I can nae find the mistress."

❧

Whatever she was lying on jerked and rolled.

Jane let out a groan as she tumbled and felt the bruises from other impacts. The pain was enough to have her fighting to clear her thoughts and wake completely. She had been tossed into a cart, was now lying on her back as the thing made its way down a rutted road. The scent of mud and horse manure came up from beneath it, and she could see the mud through the rough planks that made up the bottom of the cart. She was sitting at an angle, which meant it had two wheels.

Her wrists were bound. She strained against the rope and felt it tearing her skin. The binding held, keeping her hands locked behind her. All she could do was fight to press her feet against the bottom of the cart in an effort to stop herself from being flung about.

Diocail.

He would come for her.

Jane latched onto that thought and tried to let it be the only thing in her mind. She didn't dare allow herself to feel the bite of the rope on her wrists or notice the way the cart was covered in thick leather to make sure no one saw inside it.

No.

She must not think of anything except Diocail. He didn't know how to fail, didn't have weakness in him. He would come for her. And she would not disgrace him by being afraid.

❧

"I should have put some of the lads on her." Muir shook his head. "Until she was more settled. I did nae think she'd bolt."

Diocail knew without a doubt that his temper had never been so tested. "Better to know." He growled at his captain. "Better that I understand she wants naught to do with me."

"She's just no'…settled yet." Muir attempted to soothe him.

Diocail reached out and grabbed the man by the front of his jerkin. "I defended Colum against Tyree even though I felt the world would be better off without him. I took that woman to church because it was best for all of us, but I will no' have a wife who runs away from me."

He was snarling by the time he finished. Diocail watched acceptance wash over Muir's face. "Aye, we do nae need to be begging her to like us. If she's so keen to be on her way back to England, good riddance."

Muir spat on the ground to make it clear that he stood with Diocail on the matter. Aylin slowly nodded.

"Ungrateful bitch," Aylin muttered.

Diocail quelled the urge to defend Jane's name. News was spreading fast through the castle that she'd run from him. Women were clustered in the doorways, leaning their heads toward each other as they whispered.

"How long does it take to saddle a damned horse?" he bellowed.

"Leave her," Kory advised. "Ye can gain an annulment on grounds of abandonment."

"I brought her here," Diocail bit out. "And it has

nae changed that we do nae need a dead Englishwoman on our land."

"Aye," Kory groaned as the stable hands began to pull horses into sight. "We'd better go get her. Even if I am no' looking forward to sharing a roof with her through the winter."

"She'd better stay out of me path," Muir declared, raising his voice so it could not be missed. "We've things we could be attending to. Tasks that need doing, and now we're setting off to waste our time."

❧

There was grumbling aplenty as the men mounted and rode out. Dolina stood and watched, a troubled look on her face.

"That's what becomes of an Englishwoman being brought here," Eachna remarked.

Dolina turned to contemplate her.

"What is that look for?" Eachna demanded to know. "I am no' the one who has caused trouble."

"We do nae know for certain the mistress left of her own free will."

Eachna made a scoffing sound. "Of course she did." The maid looked both ways before she leaned in and lowered her voice. "He was raised in the north. Lord knows what happened in that chamber last night, but I know that the mistress is a woman with a firm spine. She'll no' settle for being rutted on. The truth is I admire her for no' submitting."

"I suppose it might be as ye say," Dolina muttered. "Still, she did no' appear to be displeased this morning."

"Of course not," Eachna said. "Muir and his friends

would have locked her away again so the laird could have time to breed her and force her to stay. No father would have her back with a Scots babe in her belly."

Dolina had to admit it was a reasonable explanation.

Still, she hated to think Jane would run. She wanted to believe that the sparkle she'd glimpsed in Jane's eyes that morning had been one of happiness.

Well, it had been. Only the reason behind it was different than Dolina had thought.

Jane had clearly been anticipating her escape. It was going to be sad indeed to see her brought back.

❧

"I say we slit her throat."

Jane felt her heart accelerate. She applied all her strength to keeping her eyes from widening but knew she failed when the man in front of her smiled.

"Aye," he informed her gleefully. "There is a nice place…just over there where I can leave ye for the wolves to enjoy."

"That was no' the plan, Keefe."

The man in front of her turned on his companion. "The hell it was no', Sheehan."

Sheehan was older but by no means feeble. There was gray in his beard, hinting at wisdom. He stepped closer to Keefe as Jane struggled not to draw attention to herself.

Her life was being debated.

"Ye agreed to allow her the option to leave Scotland," Sheehan stated slowly.

Keefe gestured at the dark mass above them. "It's set to storming. I do nae care to spend me time on the

road, freezing because of her. Best to tend to the business now. We can return to the tower and be warm."

"Go up to the tavern," Sheehan advised him. "I'll watch her."

They had stopped just outside a village. The sun was beginning to set, but she could only tell because the light was fading. The clouds were too thick.

"Ye'll come with me," Keefe declared. "Phelan will take the first watch."

Phelan didn't appear very pleased, but he grabbed the back of his kilt and raised it up to cover his head and neck. Keefe nodded at him before he shot Jane a look full of promise.

Evil promise.

❦

"Wake up now."

Jane didn't have much trouble obeying. She had no idea how she'd managed to fall asleep in the first place. Sheehan was leaning over her. She caught a flash of moonlight off the blade of his knife as he slipped it between her hands and jerked it upward to cut the rope binding her.

"Keefe is young and passionate," he said with regret. "He'll slit yer throat, make no mistake."

She didn't doubt it. Jane bit her lip, waiting to see what this man had planned for her. She rubbed her wrists, absorbing the fact that he'd freed her, and tried to draw hope from that action.

"Take this." He dropped a leather pouch into her hand. "And hide yerself somewhere in the village. Once we're gone, hire yerself someone to take ye

south. Show yer face on Gordon land, and I'll have to silence ye meself."

Jane bit back the polite word she started to mutter. He didn't deserve gratitude, for he had helped to take her away when he might have raised the alarm, and yet, as she jumped down from the cart and felt the ground beneath her feet, she couldn't deny that she was thankful.

"Get moving." He made a motion with his hand. "Keefe is fond of drinking, but he'll notice I'm gone before long."

He didn't need to tell her twice. Jane turned and ran. It wasn't hard, not a bit.

For she was running for her life.

⁂

Fear played with the mind.

Jane discovered her senses keener, details more pronounced. She heard the men in the tavern, detecting Keefe's laugh in spite of how many men were with him.

The scent of fresh snow was crisper as she trudged through it and then realized her tracks were plain. With a gasp, she hurried down a street that had other tracks in the fresh snow and then around a corner, pressing her back against the wall even though she smelled the scent of piss on the stone.

Ahead of her, she watched as two men relieved themselves before wandering down the road toward their homes. She shuddered in distaste but didn't dare show herself. The best she might do was focus on the fact that she was free.

But how will you survive?

She was already shivering. The coin purse was tucked into her bodice, but she didn't dare go into the tavern for a room.

The wind whipped up, bringing a new scent. She turned, blinking as she found herself staring at a man. He was facing her. As though he could see her in the darkness.

Keefe? Had he noted her escape?

"Jane."

Diocail's voice washed over her like warm water. She let out a gasp, needed the wall for a moment to support her because her knees had become weak.

"Thank Christ." Jane reached for Diocail as he clasped her close. He was hard, but there was something else, a stiffness that had her withdrawing from him. He gave a snort and pulled her back into the main road, where light made its way out of the businesses there.

The look on his face confirmed what she'd felt.

"Ye're a damned fool, Jane," he rasped out. "And lucky I came after ye. Yer pride will nae protect ye from the winter cold."

"Do you think I left on my own?" He did. She could see it in his eyes. Fury flickered there, and if she had any doubts, all she had to do was look past him at his men.

Niven, Muir, Kory, Aylin, and the others sent her glares that made it plain they felt she should hang her head in shame.

"Well, I did not," she informed him with a rise of wounded pride. "I was taken by your clansmen."

"We needs get back to the tower."

Diocail wasn't interested in debating the issue or listening to her. He'd condemned her, his judgment cutting her so deeply that she let him lift her up and onto the back of a horse without another word.

It was a cold trip back, but not because of the snow. Her heart was draining of every bit of warmth. Her elation at seeing him come for her had been the last, cruel twist of the knife, it seemed. A last taste of perfection before Fate ripped happiness from her grasp. The only kindness shown her was the fact that no one seemed to want to look her way.

It was a silent trip back to the castle. Jane slid from the back of the horse as the men ignored her. But she wasn't willing to let injustice settle on her so easily.

"I did not run away." She tempered her tone, making a solid attempt at discussing the matter.

Diocail turned to face her, Muir shadowing his laird. His expression was tight.

"How can you believe I did?" she asked him.

"I do nae want to." Diocail's temper broke. "For all that it's true me men employed a fair bit of trickery to see us brought together, the union was a pleasing one. I asked only one thing of ye, Jane, to choose me freely." He stopped and shook his head. "Aye, well, ye've made yer choice clear, and I will no' ignore it. But ye will have to wait until spring to leave."

Her eyes grew round as she witnessed the flash of pain in his eyes. Never had she expected to see any weakness in him or to think she could touch such a spot within him.

He was wounded.

Deeply so.

And she was as well. Pain was welling up inside her, threatening to drown her. "You don't trust my word."

"Trust?" he bit out. "Ye were given the run of me house! I set ye above every other woman here and told them they'd respect ye or answer to me."

And he thought she'd rejected him in front of his clan.

"Well, ye can have what ye wish," he informed her through gritted teeth. "In the spring, I'll have ye taken south."

"I did not leave," she informed him with just as much heat. "Damn you for a fool for thinking I did."

"It isn't the first time," Diocail cut back. "And I'd be a fool to ignore it a second time."

His men stood watching and listening with expressions that condemned her. Diocail turned and left, and his men went with him without a single word.

She could go after them—name the culprits and force the issue—but she realized that she had yet another thing in common with Diocail.

She wanted him to choose her.

Trust her.

Take her word and never question it.

Set her above the rest of the women? No, he'd tossed her into the fray to see if she would survive.

Well, what did she expect?

Happiness?

Marriage never led to that sort of thing.

Not for her anyway.

This was the reason she had to return to England. More than one noble marriage proved it was impossible to rise above the bad blood between nations.

There might be short periods when contentment prevailed, but in the end, the distrust was too strongly rooted in them all. Best to return to her own nation.

Best?

Well, perhaps most fitting was a better way to phrase it.

Seven

THE UPPER CHAMBERS WERE A TREASURE TROVE.

Jane might have been reeling from the shock of having Diocail turn his back on her, but she couldn't completely ignore the beauty of what she found in the bundles. Of course, the reason she was working in the chamber was that no one wanted to see her face. It was harsh, but she enjoyed having the privacy to deal with her own feelings.

Only her mother's death had ever affected her so deeply.

You haven't known Diocail long enough to suffer heartache…

And yet when had Fate ever been kind to her? Unfairness was something she should expect. It wasn't the first time Fate had turned her morning milk sour.

"I thought better of ye."

Jane blinked, wondering if her sanity had finally broken, and she was hearing voices.

"Staying up here, as though ye do nae expect stubbornness from that man ye're wed to." Dolina stepped into the chamber Jane had claimed as her own and

looked about. "Ye've been in here for a fortnight. Even if ye have made good progress, I know it for what it is. Ye are hiding."

Dolina had clearly come to take issue with her. Jane fought back a smile because no one bothered with someone they'd dismissed as beneath them.

"The staff made it clear I was not welcome in the kitchen." Jane took a moment to admire the chamber. "And the men do not care to suffer me in the hall."

Two weeks later, she was still unable to grasp how completely Diocail and his men had turned from her.

Well, she could treat them with the same disdain, by Christ.

Her temper was poor company though.

Dolina was watching her. "Ye are well suited to him."

Jane snorted, unable to control the response. Dolina's lips twitched in victory. "It's a solid truth, seen it with me own eyes. There is passion between ye."

"I suggest you keep that opinion to yourself, Dolina," Jane muttered. "For your *laird* will not thank you if he hears it."

Dolina settled her hand on her hip and offered Jane a look full of confidence. "He is certainly no' the first man displeased by me opinion or by me voicing it. I assure ye, that fact will no' silence me. Foolishness turns me stomach. It's one of the finer things about living in the Highlands, being able to tell men when they are being pig-headed."

Jane smothered a little giggle behind her hand.

"Feels good?" Dolina asked. "To laugh?"

Jane let out a sigh. "Yes. And I do thank you for trying to be kind to me."

Dolina lifted an eyebrow. "Kind? Have ye forgotten the state of this house? There is naught kind about me coming up here to ask ye to come below. I need the help. Eachna is back to thinking she should run things, and ye know well she can nae make a decision and stick to it. Chaos has taken over as every maid tries her best to do the least for her pay. For all that Eachna likes the idea of leading, even she will welcome ye back if ye get that unruly lot under control."

Jane let out another giggle.

"No one wanted ye there before, but ye proved yer worth," Dolina continued. "The women are nae so blind as the men, and I've wagered a good silver penny against ye taking in hand those who are bold enough to try ye."

"A penny, is it?"

Dolina nodded.

"Well, I would not want you to lose that," Jane answered. She reached over and replaced the rope stopper in the top of the ink well. "And...Dolina. I appreciate you taking me to task over hiding."

Dolina bestowed a different sort of smile. Jane decided it was the kind of smile that her own mother might have given her when she had made her proud, had her own mother lived long enough.

⁂

"Try me, sir, and you shall regret it."

Diocail looked up as Jane appeared in the back of the hall. The sight hit him like a blow to his unprotected gut. Her voice set off a jolt of excitement despite how deeply she'd wounded him.

It didn't seem to matter. No, he still felt something shift inside him at the sight of her, reminding him how hard he'd struggle not to cross paths with her. He couldn't trust himself not to bend.

As though she was indispensable to his ability to draw breath.

"All of you will heed my rules," she warned them. "I shall bring this house to order."

His men weren't backing down. Two of them spat on the floor right at her feet. Plenty of his people turned to watch, waiting to see what their little English foundling was going to do.

Jane wasn't daunted. She lifted her hands, and a moment later she'd tossed the contents of a pitcher at the retainer.

"Ye damned bitch!" he roared as he fell back a step in surprise. "That was cold!"

The retainer lifted his hand, intending to slap her.

"Hold." Diocail's command echoed down the hall.

His man turned an incredulous look on him. "Did ye see what she did to me? This English strumpet?"

Diocail made it to where Jane was standing firmly in the face of his man's temper.

"And it will be the least I do to you if I catch you pissing inside the passageway again," Jane informed the retainer. "This tower reeks because you all treat it like a swine pen." She shifted her attention to Diocail. "Food is carried through that passageway, and I will not have our skirts stinking because your men are somehow ignorant of where they should relieve themselves."

Diocail felt his eyebrows rise. Jane nodded once before she turned and went marching back toward the

kitchen like a Valkyrie. His tongue stuck to the roof of his mouth as he noted several of the women from the kitchen falling into place behind her.

His man started to follow. Diocail blocked him with his arm.

"She is not a strumpet," Diocail informed his man softly but with the clear ring of warning.

His men didn't care for him defending her. They glowered at him.

"And she's correct." Diocail turned to face them. "This tower reeks."

"She labeled me a swine. Before all," his retainer protested. "She needs to be bridled and taught to mind her sharp tongue."

It was a harsh suggestion. The bridle was a metal cage that locked around a woman's head, with a tongue plate set into her mouth. A new emotion moved through him, and he realized it was shame because his argument with Jane had granted his men permission to treat her harshly.

A leader needed to be more conscious of what his actions unleashed.

"She spoke the truth, and if ye do nae care for the sound of it, do yer pissing elsewhere," he informed his men. Muir and Kory were among those listening, and Diocail shot them a hard look. "Ye wanted this place taken in hand. She's doing it, so ye will mind her when it comes to matters of the housekeeping."

His comment wasn't popular. His men shifted and narrowed their eyes before they left. Muir remained and more than one of the retainers looked to him to reason with Diocail over the matter.

"Ye said ye were finished with her."

"I know what I said," Diocail snapped back.

However, his words were like a yoke around his neck, dragging him down with their weight, though he wished for nothing more than to be free of them. His pride was a different matter though; it wasn't yet willing to bend.

Muir offered him a slight shrug. "Aye, well, since she is here, best for her to be of use. At least until ye can send her back to England."

"Don't test me."

Muir offered him an expression of innocence.

"And do nae try that with me either," Diocail exclaimed. "Ye're playing again. Meddling in me personal life."

Muir shook his head. "Ye're laird. The day ye took that position, the matter of yer marriage became more than a personal one. Ye have position but no' privacy."

Diocail bristled, but Muir only sent him a self-assured look before he left.

He'd have a say in who his wife was. And damn it all, he'd have a woman who chose him.

Jane had.

The memory surged up from where he'd locked it away. Diocail watched it flash through his mind, leaving a sting from how hot the need to have her still was inside him. Just one glimpse of her had been enough to rekindle the flame.

Well, that and the way she'd stood there, unwavering, as a man who topped her by several inches threatened to strike her.

Not while he was laird.

The thought flashed through his mind and ignited his temper. Damn the passion between them, and curse her for a fool because she'd left him.

He needed to banish her from his mind. But it seemed that was not the need in which his body was interested. He was being drawn back to the flame, and he didn't want to resist the pull between them.

⤙⤚

"Good night, mistress."

Jane froze. She turned and blinked, but it was Eachna who had spoken. More than one of the other maids turned to face her and nodded.

"We'll get to scrubbing the passageway tomorrow," Jane said to test them.

"It will be a relief for the senses, to be sure," Dolina added.

"Aye," Eachna agreed. "Now that the men are no' going to be ruining our efforts."

"Me sons will be learning the error of their ways if they do nae heed the mistress's rules," Dolina announced. "We've enough to do without cleaning up after them as if they were babes still in skirts."

There were nods all around and mutters of agreement. Jane was grateful for the dark of night because she felt the unmistakable sting of tears in her eyes.

Acceptance.

Hard-won and worth it because nothing given could ever touch her so deeply.

"Until sunrise," she said softly before venturing into the passageway. A chill went down her spine, driving away the moment of joy.

She didn't care to walk alone.

The dark shadows might hold Keefe or another man who wanted her dead, yet the women behind her gave her hope that it would not be so simple for someone to discard her now. The dagger tucked into her belt helped as well.

Jane smiled ruefully as she made her way to the stairs of the tower with all the chambers filled with Colum's tribute.

"Why are ye going that way, Jane?"

She shrieked and turned to face her company. Diocail cursed as he jumped away from the blade of the dagger. He'd made a miscalculation though, and a thin line of blood appeared on his forearm.

"Christ almighty, woman!" He looked from his forearm to the dagger she held in front of her. "What do ye think ye're doing turning on me with weapon in hand?"

"I didn't know it was you." Her voice betrayed how frightened she was. Her heart was thumping in hard, frantic beats that felt as though they shook her entire body. "It might have been Keefe again."

Diocail had gone still. She'd seen him stand steady, but this was different. It was a tightening of his body, and she could feel his rage.

"Don't you dare become angry at me now."

Jane stuffed the dagger back into its sheath and forced herself to draw in a deep breath because her damned voice was cracking. She would not allow him to hear her break.

He stepped closer. "Ye never uttered that name before."

He was towering over her, and the darkness of his expression pleased her because at last he was angry on her behalf. Which only infuriated her because she shouldn't be weak enough to need his protection.

"You dismissed my explanation and never allowed me to give you details," she replied, fighting to make her tone even.

But she couldn't stay still. It felt as if she were coming apart at her very seams. Tears were gathering in her eyes, but she was angry!

And she refused to be anything else.

Jane turned and ran up the stairs. She hoisted her skirts out of the way so she might take the steps two at as time. She made it into her chamber and stopped as she drew in breath, certain her heart was going to burst and hoping it would hurry because she wanted to escape the churning emotions welling up inside her that threatened to reduce her to tears.

Diocail caught her by the upper arm and whirled her around to face him. "Ye have no trouble taking me men to task in the hall, woman."

"And you"—she jabbed her finger into the center of his chest—"have no difficulty telling me I am a liar in front of your men!"

The chamber echoed with the sound of their breathing. It was harsh and raspy as they faced off with one another, teeth bared. He was so powerful, his presence reaching across the space between them as she struggled to think.

Her mind refused, letting go of her desire to think in favor of feeding her need to reach for him. They collided, meeting in the space between them as

though some command had moved them both toward each other.

It was an explosive connection, control shattering as she touched him once again. Diocail growled against her mouth as he gripped her nape and claimed her as his possession.

But she kissed him back, rising onto her toes so she could meet him halfway. She wasn't going to be taken, oh no. Jane sent her own tongue into his mouth to stroke his before she pulled away from him and boldly reached for his belt buckle.

"I am not going to be yours, Diocail Gordon," she declared as his kilt fell to the floor.

"Ye sure as hell are." He kicked the fabric across the floor and jerked his doublet off. His cock was already hard, pushing out the front of his shirt.

"No," she informed him slowly. "You are…going to be…mine."

She wrapped her fingers around his member before she finished speaking. Her head was tipped back so she could watch his face. He bared his teeth at her, and it filled her with a white-hot confidence.

In that moment, they were evenly matched, and she was eager to reduce him to the rubble he'd left her in. So she slipped to her knees and worked her hand along his length. The skin was satin soft and warm. It delighted her, the sensation of petting him.

The truth was she hadn't really looked at it the last time. Now she took a long look at his cock, from the crown to the base where his seed sac hung. She teased his staff, stroking him with her fingertips and then closing her hand around its girth to pump her hand up and down it.

"Sweet Christ…" he growled at her. "Where did ye learn that from, woman?"

Satisfaction filled her at the way his voice rasped through his teeth. She'd done that to him. The same way he'd reduced her to a withering mass of uncontrolled need.

Well, not quite in the same manner.

"I learned it from you…" she muttered as an idea formed in her mind.

"Holy Christ!" he exclaimed as she licked his cockhead.

Diocail recoiled from her but backed into the wall. Jane was quick to follow, renewing her grip on his member and closing her mouth around it once more.

He caught a handful of her hair, but she felt him quivering. She teased the ridge that ran around his cockhead with her tongue and heard him curse. But the grip on her hair became one of encouragement. She took it to heart, licking and sucking on his member. There was a slit running along the top of it, and a salty fluid appeared there as she labored. She licked it away and pressed herself forward so that more of his member thrust into her mouth.

Diocail's hips pressed toward her.

His motions matched her memory of the way she'd bucked beneath his mouth. The way he gasped told her he was in the midst of passion too. She wanted to drive him over the edge while she was the one in command.

She felt the moment approaching, could feel his member hardening to the breaking point. He was driving it toward her, holding her head in place as he neared climax. The room echoed with his growl as his

seed spurted into her mouth. It was hot and thick, and she sucked on him harder as she drew it from him.

She left him leaning against the wall, his knees slightly bent as he gasped and shuddered. Jane sat back, watching him. She might well have been on her knees, but he was the one who was conquered. He'd tipped his head back, giving her a look at the corded muscles that ran down his neck.

Exposed. Just as she'd been for him.

They were like two side of a coin, incomplete without the other side. And yet unable to see one another clearly.

"Proud of yerself…"

It wasn't really a question. Jane absorbed his words as his gaze seemed to pin her in place.

"As much as you were…when…" The look in his eyes made her too breathless to complete her statement.

"When I did the same to ye," he finished.

Anticipation was flaring inside her, twisting her until she felt as if she might snap, and all the while, she recalled how much she'd enjoyed it when he did take her to that point.

And beyond.

"I enjoyed it."

He was opening his cuffs, the motion of him pushing the buttons through their holes so very slow. She was almost certain she could feel the time between each of her heartbeats in that moment.

When he finished, she realized her mouth had gone dry. She was mesmerized by the way he straightened up and reached for the hem of his shirt. He found the

edge of the garment while keeping his gaze locked with hers and pulled it up and over his head in a powerful motion of arm and shoulders. The shirt fluttered to the floor, off to the side as she drank in the sight of him.

Bare.

Hard.

His member hadn't slacked. It stood at the ready, as though she'd dreamed draining it.

"Oh aye, I'm right thankful indeed, lass…" He lowered himself to his knees, but there was nothing submissive about it.

She stiffened, feeling as though he were closing in on her, and the glitter in his eyes proved that she wasn't wrong. He flattened his hand on the floor and crawled toward her as she leaned back.

"Very thankful…" His brogue intensified with his emotions. "Because now…*now*…I am going to last a very long time between yer thighs."

It was blunt.

Raw.

And exactly what she craved.

He hooked her thighs and tugged her legs out from beneath her. A cry escaped from her lips as she landed on her backside, the fabric of her skirt and bum roll cushioning the impact as he pulled her legs out straight and slid up between her thighs. But her hip roll pushed her bottom into the air, her spread sex facing the ceiling.

Diocail grinned as he teased her folds with his fingertips. "Do ye want that, Jane?"

She was spread wide, her skirts flipped back as he flashed her a grin of victory. He held her thighs, keeping

her pulled against him so his member lay straight across her open sex. She gasped, the sensation ripping through her. The anticipation was going to kill her.

"Do ye want me to ride ye?"

He found her clitoris and rubbed it gently, wringing a cry from her. "Yes!"

Need was threatening to consume her. It was a twisting mass inside her, and she wanted to be flung into its center. "Unless you're too spent."

His eyes narrowed at her brazenness. "No' by half, lass, no' by half…"

He was leaning over her, his cock delving into her open body. He stretched her, and the feeling was perfect. She didn't want him gentle. Didn't want to be submissive.

He plunged into her all the way to the hilt, and she was surging upward, wrapping her arms and thighs around him as she shoved them over. He clasped her against him as he rolled and landed on his back.

"Well, I am not in the mood to be ridden," she snarled at him from on top. She lifted herself up and plunged back down onto his member with a harsh breath.

"Let us see if ye can stay in the saddle." He reached up and popped open her bodice. "For I am no gelding."

He wasn't. His cock was hard inside her. She lifted herself off him and plunged back down as he tore at the front of her bodice until her breasts were free. They bounced as she moved until he cupped them, brushing her nipples with his thumbs while she controlled their pace.

He shoved at her clothing, rising up to push it down her arms and bare her. His growl mixed with

the cry that escaped her, and all the while she rode him, feeling the need to move faster, to come down on him harder.

He found the tie that held her skirts together at her waist and ripped it open, dragging them up and over her head before he was turning them and pressing her down onto her back. Her hip roll lasted only a moment before he was pressing her flat, clasping her wrists above her head as he growled.

"Ye're mine, Jane…mine, and I am going to have ye…take ye…make ye cry out."

She didn't want to escape, but she twisted against his hold. It was some instinct, rooted in the fibers of her being, to rise up against him, somehow proving she was strong enough to be his match, not just his choice.

He enjoyed it.

She witnessed the flash of savage pleasure in his eyes as he moved against her harder. They were both panting, driving one another at a frantic pace. Her heart was near to bursting again as Diocail held her down. She bared her teeth and decided she had never felt more alive.

She did cry out.

The sound echoed around the chamber as she arched and pleasure tore away everything except her husband. Diocail was there with her, pushing her to the very limit her flesh might tolerate as she heard him lose his battle to hold off his own release. He jerked with it, burying himself to the hilt while his seed spilled inside her. There seemed no end to the madness, and she happily surrendered to it. Some things could not be understood. They simply were.

At that moment, she was simply his, and to argue was to deny her own nature. So she didn't. They collapsed against each other, the night wrapping them in darkness to cradle them.

∝

He hadn't slept well since bringing her back.

Diocail opened his eyes and stared at the ceiling as that bit of truth hit him. He was tired, bone weary, but he struggled to fend off sleep because it would deny him the chance to pull Jane close. He needed that much more than rest.

Her breathing was soft against his shoulder now. Both their bodies relaxing, although collapsing was perhaps a truer description. He was spent. And he'd never been more willing to admit it.

He gathered the strength to sit up. There was no bed in the chamber. He spotted the bundle of bedding Jane had clearly been using, and it shamed him.

Still, part of him recognized the spirit she had. She wouldn't put the staff to the trouble of ensuring her comfort when there was so much to do. She shifted, pulling her knees up as the night air chilled her bare skin. He reached for the bedding, shaking it out before lying it down and gathering her close. He rolled them onto the furs, keeping her close as he covered them.

She opened her eyes, blinking as he settled onto his back. "Go to sleep, Jane. Tomorrow will be time enough for talking."

She held herself stiff for a moment before the warmth from his body eased her back into sleep. She relaxed against him, her hand resting on his chest.

For the moment, it was everything he'd hoped for.

Of course, in the morning, he was going to have to deal with matters.

⤜

"Mistress… Mistress… Mistress!"

Bari came up the stairs like a hound on the trail of a fox. Someone had made him bathe, and his clothing was clean, but his hair was a wild mass of untamed curls as he skidded to a halt and blinked at the sight of his laird standing with sword in hand and nothing else on.

"Is yer manroot frozen from being naked, Laird? Is that why it is a sin to be unclothed?"

Diocail let out a word that made Jane smack him on the side of his leg from where she was hiding beneath the bedding. He looked down at her. "Ye do nae understand Gaelic."

"Bari does," she reprimanded him. "And that needed no translation—your tone was quite telling."

Bari was grinning and showing off his two missing front teeth. "He said—"

"I know what I said, lad, but the lady does nae, and she is a lady." Diocail found his shirt and pulled it on. "What has ye coming up here in such a hurry?"

Bari's expression changed instantly. "The men are…" He looked at Jane and froze, his eyes large and round in his young face.

"Doing what?" Diocail demanded as he pulled his boots on.

"They are…lifting their kilts…doing what the mistress told them no' to do, and the women in the

kitchen are threatening to cut off their…manroots… and…and…oh please, get dressed, mistress!"

Bari looked around the room and found her clothing. He dragged it over to where Jane was peeking at him. "Ye're too hot under there, mistress," he exclaimed. "Yer face is all red…"

Diocail choked on his amusement a second before he scooped Bari up and headed for the door. He deposited the boy at the opening and pointed him down the stairs. His kilt was still draped over his arm as he looked back at Jane.

"I'll deal with the men."

"I can do very well on my own, thank you."

Diocail didn't heed her. No, he closed the door behind him and left.

Well, she'd be a liar if she didn't admit it was a relief to have something to keep them from being alone now that the sun had risen.

Curse Fate.

Bari's words rose from her memory, and she threw the covers back. Her temper sizzled as she fought to get into her dress. By the time she found both of her shoes, she was in a full fit. Of course, the Gordon retainers wanted just that.

Jane stopped in the stairwell, contemplating her next move. She drew in a deep breath before descending the last steps as though she didn't have a care in the world.

Diocail lifted an eyebrow, but his men sent her looks that made it clear they expected no better of her.

"English noble…"

"Sleeping late while others do the work…"

Dolina let out a little growl, and many women standing in the hall nodded agreement.

"The mistress"—Eachna stressed the last word—"works as hard as any of us."

"The lot of ye should be ashamed," another woman said.

The scent of fresh urine was strong. Jane lifted her nose and sniffed long and hard. When she finished, Diocail was looking at her with one eyebrow raised, waiting to see what she was going to do.

Part of him was actually looking forward to it.

"It would seem," she said as she faced the kitchen staff, "that the men…" Jane fluttered her eyelashes. "Our lords and masters…" There was grumbling as she made the statement. "Prefer filth to hot meals on the tables."

Understanding began to dawn on the women. The men had been puffed up with pride, intent on their course of action. A few began to follow her thinking, and they didn't care for the conclusion they arrived at.

"To carry food through filth would be very careless of us…" Jane smiled at the men.

"Aye," Dolina stepped up. "Someone could take ill."

"Be a terrible thing for us to be responsible for," another woman added.

"So," Jane stopped in front of Diocail and lowered herself. "We will not bother any of your men with our efforts to make this a fine home. For you all…" She sent a glance around the clustered group. "Have made it very clear that you prefer…rough conditions."

She straightened and shot the men a firm look before turning and disappearing into the kitchen. The women followed her.

Valkyrie.

Diocail stood and watched Jane go, enjoying the way she held her chin steady.

"What is that supposed to mean?" one of the men demanded.

"It means," Kory bellowed at the man who'd spoken, "we're no' getting anything to eat on account of yer behavior."

The men broke into curses and complaints. One of them pointed at Diocail.

"Take yer wife in hand."

The boldness of that demand sent silence through the men as Diocail turned to face the perpetrator. His retainers waited to see if the insubordination would be tolerated.

"Was this yer idea?" he asked softly. "This display of yer…what exactly is it, man? Truth be told, I can nae imagine why any of ye thought pissing inside yer own hall in the dead of winter was a grand idea."

"She was disrespectful yesterday." The man nodded. "Needed a lesson." He sniffed. "Like the one ye gave her, showing her who her master is." He made a vulgar motion with his hips.

Diocail felt his temper heating, but Kory snorted and pointed at the men. "Ye need to learn that it is always wise to keep the cook happy!"

Muir let out a chuckle. "Aye. We'll all be learning how important that one is now. The tables are going to be bare until the women are happy, make no mistake about it."

"But…they have to cook." The man still wasn't ready to admit defeat. "I'll get the priest on them."

Diocail grunted. "Shut yer jaw, man. Keep on like that, and ye'll be sorry when they serve up something that will tear yer insides up. I am no' so great a fool as to turn a blind eye to the improvements me wife has brought to this hall."

"She ran from ye."

Diocail slowly smiled. "That's part of the fun."

Damned if he didn't enjoy the sound of that a bit too much as Muir sent him a questioning look. Diocail took a moment to sweep his men with a hard glance. "I suggest ye all get to scrubbing that passageway. I doubt ye'll be eating another hot meal until it's clean and as sweet-smelling as a spring meadow."

Narrow-eyed looks were cast at the ringleaders. It became clear who they were as the main body of the men broke away, moving off to begin cleaning the passageway.

"Part of the fun?" Muir questioned Diocail softly.

Diocail sent his captain a hard look. "Bring Kory, Aylin, and Niven."

His men were quick to join him in the room that served as his private study. The room was off to the back of the hall and still filled with Colum's things. Only the long table that served as a desk had been cleared off as Diocail began the process of bringing the contracts and books to order. There was a pile of messages stacked in one corner large enough to knock him flat if it fell. He suspected some of the letters might be older than he was himself. But there were more pressing matters.

"Jane named Keefe as the man who abducted her."

There was a stiffening of his men. The others who had claims to the lairdship were well known because

Diocail was no fool. He'd keep his friends near and his enemies closer still.

"Are ye saying ye believe the lass now?" Aylin asked.

Diocail felt the sting of guilt burning a hole in his gut as he nodded. "I am no' certain of anything except there is no reason for her to know that name or to think he might have reason to harm her. Preventing me from having an heir would be something Keefe would be very interested in doing if he still had his eye set on me position."

"Unless she's been getting the women in the kitchen to talk," Muir countered. "Now that they've accepted her, she might well have learned who the other bloodline relatives are."

"Aye," Diocail replied. "I thought of that as well." He held up his forearm. "She turned on me with a drawn dagger when she did nae know it was me in the dark."

His men looked from the thin line of dried blood back to his face.

"So," he continued. "I think I'd be a fool to dismiss the fact that she might have been telling the truth. It is no' in Jane's nature to strike out like that, and she was frightened. I saw it clearly, and it shamed me to know she feels that way inside this tower."

That made them shift. Guilt was making the rounds through them all, for none had spoken a kind word to her since they'd returned.

"If ye take a moment to think it through," Muir began, "that business at the mill was suspicious."

Diocail grunted. "Aye, she said she had a goose egg on the back of her head."

"And ye dismissed that?" Niven asked incuriously.

Kory elbowed him. "Ye didn't think to ask how she ended in the water either."

"None of us did," Aylin admitted disgustedly. "To my shame, it never crossed me mind to question the incident."

"Which would make this two matters, and if we take the lass at her word, that means we've been negligent," Muir said.

Diocail nodded. "She needs looking after, but we still need to know what is truth and what is nae." He locked gazes with Muir. "Keep it quiet. If Keefe is trying to get rid of her, I need to catch him with the evidence to make it plain to the rest of the clan. For her sake more than me own."

His men nodded and tugged on the corner of their caps. Their support brought him a measure of relief, but the tension between his shoulders persisted.

The reason was simple.

He wanted her.

Uncertainty was smoldering inside him, and the problem was he wasn't sure if it was going to die out or erupt into flames. He wanted it to die. Wanted to be able to move past his injured feelings and go forward, but he didn't think he would ever banish her from his mind.

Or his heart.

⁓

Her bedding was missing when she made it to her chamber that night.

Jane blinked once she finished barring the chamber door and took in the bed set up in place of the spot

where she'd been sleeping. It was quite the sight for sore eyes. No gold-and-gem bit of finery would have pleased her more.

She smiled as she moved toward it, reaching out slowly to stroke the thick bedding spread out over soft sheeting. A pair of plump pillows waited for her head as the scent of rosemary assured her it was clean.

"I am glad to see it pleases ye."

She wasn't as startled by Diocail as she'd been the night before. The truth was he'd been in her thoughts for most of the day, so it was simply fitting to have his voice come out of the darkness. He moved away from one of the far walls.

"Ye might have directed the staff to see to the matter before now," he said.

Jane looked back at the bed, feeling a blush stain her cheeks. She had felt as if the steps leading up to her chamber were almost impossible to mount because of how tired she was, but now her body was warming at his appearance.

"Say what ye are thinking, lass."

This was the side of his nature she had no defense against: the man who had moved his men away so she might bathe and spoken so frankly about why they had to wed. She shifted away from him.

He let out a soft grunt. "I see I have made a grave tactical error in no' directing the staff to put this bed against a wall."

Understanding dawned on Jane, making her giggle softly. He raised an eyebrow as he sent her a look across the bed. "So it amuses ye to think of me chasing ye around the bed?"

"You would be disappointed if I simply flopped down in the middle of it and assumed a submissive position to perform my wifely duties."

So very brazen…and it pleased her to the core to know she didn't have any intention of simpering with him.

Diocail's eyes flashed with enjoyment. Hard, male enjoyment.

"Let's not be hasty now." He braced his hands on the side of the bed. "Ye have no' ever tried… flopping down on a bed…perhaps we might give it a go-round—"

"It would serve you right if I did exactly that." She was being tart once more, but he could leave if she displeased him.

Instead, his lips twitched, forming that grin that she seemed to enjoy so very much. It was only a fleeting moment though before his expression hardened. "Are ye barring that door against me?"

"No," she snapped.

The flare of temper disgusted her, and she shook her head. "Please go. I do not want to argue with you."

He offered her a soft grunt. He'd straightened up and crossed his arms over his chest while considering her across the expanse of the bed.

"Perhaps we might settle this matter," he began.

"I'm not certain what you are talking about."

He came around the bed. Standing in place took more discipline than it should have, but it seemed she forgot just how large he was. Sensation rippled across her skin. He stopped only a pace from her, and her heart started to accelerate.

"We wed under difficult circumstances," he began. Jane nodded.

Her response pleased him. She found it touched her deeply to see it flash through his eyes. Brown eyes.

Warm, secure, strong. She didn't understand why she lamented the fact that she hadn't been able to stare into his eyes lately; all she knew was that she had missed doing so.

"So." He reached out and stroked her face. "Last night…"

She quivered, the connection of their skin setting off a reaction he felt as well. He paused, his eyes narrowing while he teased the surface of her lips with the tip of his finger.

Delicious…

His touch was simply more pleasing than any sensation she had ever experienced in life.

"Last night," he repeated, clearly intent on finishing what he wanted to say. "Well…it proved we've a fine foundation for this union. More than most couples discover once the vows are spoken and the sheets turned back."

Her cheeks were stinging, and she fluttered her eyelashes, but she was also smiling, reveling in the truth of his words. Oh, how she knew that truth!

"Trust is more important than passion," she muttered, hating the way the words sounded because she knew they were so very true.

His expression tightened. But he fought to temper it.

"I can forgive ye, Jane." These were difficult words for him to say. She watched the way his jaw was clenched as he forced them out. "Ye have been raised to fear me."

He was offering excuses…and she didn't want them.

"I did not lie."

His expression darkened with disapproval.

She stiffened, withdrawing a step so his hand wasn't in contact with her face. She needed that space so that she might think clearly. But he came after her.

"Do not," she warned him. The hand she lifted between them was not going to stop him if he decided to press the matter. "I cannot think when you touch me."

His lips twitched.

So arrogant. And yet it sent a jolt of excitement through her.

"Ye tempt me to forget everything in favor of putting me hands back on ye."

It was an admission that echoed the same need she was trying so hard to clamp down inside of herself. "Well, we've never shared a bed before."

And maybe it would be a terrible thing to waste the moment. Brenda Grant's words rose once more from her memory to tease her with the opportunity at hand. What made Jane reach for the tie holding her cleavage was the fact that she very much feared those words could also haunt her.

Diocail's eyes narrowed as her fingers dipped into the valley of her cleavage. She popped open the knot and slowly began to tug the loosened lace through the eyelets running down the front of her bodice. The plain clothing suited her perfectly right then because she was certain no fancy dress could have put quite the same look on Diocail's face.

At that moment, he was mesmerized. By her.

Which made her breathless and giddy and stoked something deeper inside her. It was that same part of her personality he seemed to unleash. There was so much left unsettled between them, and yet, at that moment, the only thing she cared about was the glow brightening his eyes.

The night air brushed her breasts through the open front of her partlet shift. It opened down the front like a shirt. The edges gapped with her motions, exposing a strip of bare flesh.

"Christ almighty, if this is bewitchment, I will do yer bidding gladly."

His tone was husky, and it sent heat surging through her body. Opening her waistband was a necessity because her clothing felt too tight.

And warm.

She let out a little contented sound as her skirts and hip roll slid down her legs to puddle around her ankles. She was left in her shift, exposed to his keen gaze. Diocail took a long moment to sweep her from head to toe.

"Now watch me…"

His tone was commanding but edged with need. She obeyed willingly, without a care for how submissive it might seem. She craved the sight of him. Watching him bare his body for her fanned the flames of her desire. His kilt was easily shed, and his shirt didn't take much more attention. She drank in the sight of him, boldly staring at his cock.

"No' just yet."

She lifted her attention to his face. It was drawn tight, demand flickering in his eyes.

"Turn around, Jane."

She didn't want to comply. He knew it, reaching out to cup her far shoulder and turn her. The shift of power between them left her neck tight.

"Last night…ye took me…" His breath teased her ear, and then he was kissing the side of her neck.

She shuddered, a soft, breathless sound filling the chamber.

"You enjoyed it."

He chuckled in response. "I did, but tonight ye'll wait for me…" He stroked the other side of her neck with one fingertip. "And enjoy knowing that I am contemplating where to touch ye next."

She shuddered, drawing a chuckle from him that was very male and arrogant enough to have her turning to face him. He clasped his arms around her, binding her against his body instead.

"Diocail."

"I admitted enjoying ye taking me." He leaned down and bit her softly on the side of her neck. "Tonight ye are going to admit ye like it very much when I claim ye."

She wiggled against his hold, not because she truly desired freedom but because she simply had to touch him. Her craving for him was too sharp, too insistent. Desperation was clawing at her insides, and nothing mattered except gaining satisfaction.

"Get on with it," she growled.

He let out a sound very close to a snarl. "With pleasure." He turned her toward the bed.

He pressed her hands down onto the soft bedding as he gripped her hips. The head of his cock teased the folds of her sex from behind as he thrust forward.

It was a hard possession. The bed shook as Diocail rode her from behind with deep thrusts. She was leaning over the bed, her weight braced on her hands as she lifted her bottom for each new plunge. It was what she craved, and it took over her mind, shattering her thoughts as instinct and need controlled her completely.

But she peaked too quickly. Her cry was long and thin, a combination of pleasure and lamentation for how easily they both were spent.

"More…" He rasped next to her ear. "That was nae enough…"

He scooped her up and deposited her in the bed. Still reeling, Jane rolled over, sighing as the bed ropes took her weight and she settled onto the soft surface. She heard him unlacing his boots. Recognized the sound in some part of her brain that wasn't still absorbed by the glow of satisfaction.

"I want…so much more…"

The bed rocked as he crawled onto it and pushed the bedding aside to cradle her. He was searching through her hair, seeking the pins that held her locks to the back of her head. Somehow, it was more intimate than anything else they had done.

More like the secret things she thought lovers might do in the dark hours of the night.

Those things you've never experienced…

And now, nothing was going to stop her from experiencing intimacy. Not logic, not reality.

Jane sat up, her back to him as he worked to free her hair. The single candle she'd brought with her was burning on the stand next to the door, its golden light just reaching them.

"I wanted to touch this…the night I carried ye to the fire to dry it." He combed his fingers through her newly freed tresses, sending a deep ripple of enjoyment through her. "I believe I was as close to acting the savage ye English believe me to be as I ever have been that night."

"You jest." She arched her neck back as he grabbed a handful of her hair.

He tightened his grip, giving her a taste of his strength as he bound her to him with a solid arm around her waist. "No. Ye test me in ways I do nae care to admit."

Leaning back against him, she noticed all the details that were different between their bodies. His chest was covered in crisp hair that tickled her back, and he was wider than she, making it so comfortable to lean against him. He'd settled onto his haunches again, his knees on either side of her as he cupped her breasts, and she watched while he teased her nipples into tight peaks.

"I hear the king has a wall of mirrors in his palace…"

Diocail slid his hand across her belly and lower, to where curls decorated her mons. "I'd like to have a mirror…right in front of us…tonight…"

She drew in a ragged breath as she imagined what it would be like to see themselves as they were. "I'm sure that would be…sinful."

"Are we no' made in the image of our creator?"

She choked on a round of snickers. "Oh Christ, Diocail!" She couldn't stop laughing and ended up doubled over as she chuckled.

"You, sir…" She struggled to not sound breathless. "Are going to land us both in the stocks."

"It would be worth it." He muttered against her ear as he sent his fingers into the folds of her sex. She was still wet from their coupling. His movement should have made her shift away, but he found her little pearl, and she gasped. "I want to watch ye…as I build yer passion…"

His was rekindling as well. Between them, she could feel the length of his member hardening. It was a promise he'd satisfy the need he was stroking with his fingers. Her heart accelerated as her breathing became little gasps.

"We're no' going to rush this time…" He held her still, all the while teasing and worrying her little clitoris. She was so wet she could hear it while he fingered her. He was driving her toward a peak. She felt it twisting inside her belly, the throbbing intensifying.

"I want to ride you, Diocail!" She was torn between demand and begging, struggling against his hold as he released her and she turned to face him.

He cupped the back of her head, kissing her as hard and deeply as she craved. And the other thing she needed was there too, all she needed to do was claim him.

He cupped her hips as she climbed onto him, her thighs opening to spread around his lean hips while he held her weight and settled her onto his length. It completed the moment. She kissed him back, teasing his tongue with her own before she began to lift and plunge back down.

There wasn't a hurry.

No, they were exactly where they both needed to be. This time, she rode him long and at a steady pace

while he gripped her hair, and she watched the need flickering in his eyes. It might have lasted for hours; Jane had no idea. She'd never been so close to someone. It defied definition and thought.

It simply was, and when the wave crested over them, she collapsed into the glow of satisfaction with complete submission.

❧

"What does yer sister write?" Phelan demanded.

Keefe sent him a hard look. "I can nae read any more than ye can. Me sister was taught by one of the nuns, and the woman did nae allow boys into the convent."

They both looked across the tavern common room at Sheehan as he made his way about asking for someone willing to read. Keefe toyed with the edge of the letter as he watched his man. Luck finally favored them. Sheehan held up a coin, and the man in front of him nodded agreement.

Sheehan kept a firm grip on the money as he led the man back toward them. Keefe held the letter tight. "Ye are far from home, Gunn."

The man settled on a bench and eyed him. "It's barely started to snow. Ye sound soft."

The woman serving the ale came near, reaching out to place a mug in front of the Gunn retainer. He flashed her a grin that earned him an appraising look from the woman.

"But I do like some…soft things," he informed Keefe when he returned his attention to him.

Keefe held out the letter. The man took it and broke the seal.

❧

"What manner of business was that?" Bothan Gunn asked as Maddox returned.

"The sort that would make me mother proud," Maddox answered as he straddled a bench. He held up the coin and flipped it into the air before catching it and tucking it into a pocket on the inside of his jerkin. "And me belly as well, for it will buy me some fine supper on the morrow."

"As if I do nae feed ye well enough," Bothan groused.

Maddox feigned shock. "Well now…me *laird*…I meant no…disrespect!"

Bothan kicked him in the shin, causing Maddox to chuckle. He reached into the center of the table where the remains of their supper lay and selected a section of the broken bread. "Ye see…" He bit off a chunk and chewed it with a good-natured look on his face. "There are appetites ye provide for and then…well, other hungers I like to feed."

Maddox cast a longing look at the tavern wench.

"Ye mean ye have to pay for that?"

It was Maddox's turn to do some kicking. Bothan sent his man a grin. "Sorry to hear of yer lack of luck, me friend. Indeed I am. So ye read to earn yer…tumbles."

The other Gunn retainers gained a good chuckle at Maddox's expense. The captain took the teasing in stride, smirking. "It beats being virgins such as the lot of ye."

The last of the supper was finished off before Bothan spoke again. "What is the news from Gordon land?"

Maddox shrugged, uninterested. At least he was until his fellow retainers leaned forward, looking to him for a bit of entertainment. It was slim pickings in the tavern. An old man with an eye patch was jabbering on about how he'd lost the eye in the vain hope someone would fill his cup. But it was the posted sign against gaming that ensured everyone was going to have a dull evening. The tavern owner was keeping a sharp eye on his customers with a large club hanging from his belt to enforce his rules. Gaming turned ugly too often for his taste, it would appear.

Maddox leaned over the table. "Seems the new mistress of the Gordon clan has returned home."

"Aye, I saw her and Diocail at the festival," Bothan remarked.

"It seems this is a second time she has returned, and in disgrace, no less. The lass ran away, and Diocail had to fetch her so she would nae freeze. He's vowed to send her back to her father in the spring."

That gained a raised eyebrow from Bothan.

Bothan cast a glance toward the Gordon retainers. They were nearly touching noses they were clustered in so tight. The letter was open on the table between them, and a blind man wouldn't have missed how pleased the news written on the parchment made them.

Which made him suspicious. He was going to make sure he rode across Gordon land on his way north.

❦

"She's seen our faces."

Keefe snorted, making it clear he wasn't interested

in Sheehan's warnings. "But the laird does nae believe she was forced to leave."

Sheehan cocked his head to the side. "We ride into the yard, and it's likely to bring the whole matter up for discussion. More than one man will question just where we have been."

"That fool woman has let half the clan into the towers," Keefe declared. "All I have to do is wait until nightfall, and then I'll slit her throat. Even if the laird suspects something, he'll have no way to prove anything."

"That will no' gain ye the lairdship," Phelan pointed out.

"It will keep her English father from ruling us through her son," Keefe declared. "Ye heard what me sister wrote. The laird is seeking her out, even though he called her a liar. She is bewitching him, and let us no' forget that her last husband ended up dead at the hands of a mob. Who's to say she did no' play a part in it? Maybe that is the true reason those same townsfolk tried to hang her."

They were hard facts to ignore. Keefe watched Sheehan and Phelan bend beneath them. They nodded and followed him into the stables.

⁂

"We did nae finish speaking last night."

Jane turned around with the bar in her hands to discover Diocail pulling his shirt on. The man she'd woken up to holding her securely against his body was now stern-faced.

Yes, the morning light was as sharp as always.

She set the bar against the wall and gathered her

courage. "It might be best if we do not raise that topic." Jane looked straight at him.

He'd sat down to pull on his boots. He tightened each one above his knee with the aid of a small buckle before he drew in a deep breath and stood.

"I can forgive, Jane."

They were hard words for him to speak. She recognized the effort, felt the temptation to allow him his way in the interest of keeping the happiness she felt when he was there with her.

"I did not leave you." She forced the words out. "And I will not build a life with you on lies."

He crossed his arms over his chest, gripping the fabric of his shirt as his jaw tightened. "Would ye prefer I simply keep ye? Behave as the savage ye believe Highlanders to be?"

"I never called you such a thing," she defended herself. "You judge me harshly."

"And ye clearly believe I am a fool," he argued. "Ye have been the one demanding an annulment."

She drew in a breath, hoping to calm herself. "I did ask for one."

"More than once."

And he was a proud man.

"I meant no injury to you, Diocail." She opened her hands as she sought the right words. "I judged you by the actions of my last husband. You are nothing like him. I know that now. Our union happened so quickly that I acted in haste. Forgive me for that."

His stern expression softened. She watched the pleasure flash in his eyes. He moved toward her, granting her hope. A resolution might indeed be theirs.

"Aye, I do." He reached out and stroked her cheek. "Promise me ye will nae leave me again."

She stiffened, withdrawing so his hand was no longer in contact with her skin. "So I am to offer you my trust, and you deny me yours?"

His jaw was tight again, confirming she was correct.

"I asked ye for yer word, Jane."

"Because you believe I lied to you," she countered. "I might have asked for an annulment, but I never called you a liar in front of others."

"This is no' about anyone except us," he exclaimed. "When I close me eyes at night and rest beside ye, I will know ye do nae plan to slit me throat."

Jane wanted to argue with him. It would have been a relief to feel her temper rising. Instead, what filled her was a cold certainty that he did not trust her, and that distrust ran so deeply in him there would be no changing it. That unbendable part of him was now the wall separating them.

"I did not leave you," she muttered softly. "And I will not welcome you back to my bed so long as you cannot accept my word. You are not the only one who wishes to close their eyes and trust the one they sleep next to."

Henry would have laughed at her for such words or slapped her for the impertinence. The wife was chattel, the husband her master. She backed away from the horror of knowing Diocail could do as he wished with her.

But what sent tears into her eyes was the fact that she'd tasted something with him that had made her believe happiness might be hers.

No, it was fleeting. Touching her only long enough

to make certain she noticed the lack of it when it departed. She dashed into the stairwell to keep him from seeing her cry.

Ah…Fate.

How could she have forgotten the sharp edges? Today she felt the cut even more deeply because this time her heart was laid bare.

Love truly was the torment so often written about in plays that ended in death. No slice through her flesh would have hurt her as badly, no, not even if her arm were cleaved clean off. Love was the cruelest weapon of all, for it broke her heart in two, but left her drawing breath so she might suffer the agony.

She had the distinct feeling it would indeed last for a lifetime.

⌒

"So, ye love him."

Jane looked up and found Dolina watching her.

"I did not say—"

Dolina waved the towel she was holding in the air between them. "It's written on yer face."

There was a pair of giggles from two maids working at the long table in the kitchen. In fact, Jane made a full turn and realized the only person in the kitchen who looked unaware of what was going on was Dolina's young son, who was turning the meat in the hearth.

The strangest sensation went through her. As though she was relieved. And she realized she was indeed happy to know the matter was out in the open.

"The next thing ye are going to say is that it matters naught," Dolina continued. "I will save ye the breath.

It's written on yer face, and the laird is, well…" There was more laughter, only this time it was a mature sort of amusement. "The laird is smitten with ye."

"He thinks I am a liar."

Dolina pursed her lips. "Men," she began, "have more pride than is healthy."

Eachna snorted.

"I hear yer mother died young," Dolina said.

Jane nodded. "Childbed fever."

Dolina nodded slowly. "Well, if she were here, she'd have taught ye a few things about the nature of a man. Since she is no', it falls to me, for I…we… can nae have ye bending so easily. The men around here already have too many ideas about how much coddling they should receive from us."

Brenda Grant suddenly came to mind as Jane dusted her hands on her apron and discovered several women moving in close with amusement glittering in their eyes.

She was nearly giddy as they leaned in and began giving their advice. It wasn't the fact that they were helping her find a path toward resolving her issues with Diocail that pleased her so much. No, it was the acceptance she'd won all on her own. And she would not be giving that up.

Diocail would be the one to adjust his thinking.

❧

"Did ye have a change of heart, lad?" Sheehan asked.

Keefe grunted and grabbed a round of bread from the center of the table, breaking it before answering. "The door was barred," he grunted as he chewed.

"Why would it be barred?" Phelan asked.

"Simple," Keefe said. He looked around and lowered his voice. "I told ye already, she's bewitching him. Luring him into her bed and doing…"

"Doing what?" Sheehan pressed him for details.

Keefe opened his hands between them. "As if I know anything about dark arts." He stabbed a piece of cheese with his knife and brought it close to his lips. "But I will say this. The door was barred, so she must have wanted to hide something. All the more reason why we need to be rid of her for good. Ye wait and see, next season the crops will fail on account of that English witch."

⁓

"Looks as though Bothan Gunn has gotten caught in the snow."

Diocail looked up as Muir popped his head over the edge of the roof he was working on.

"He's waiting outside the gate."

Diocail followed Muir down the ladder and into the yard. Bothan had let his beard grow and looked a lot like a bear making ready for winter. He was wearing a full sheepskin down his back with the fleece facing up to protect him from the falling snow. There were strips of that fleece wrapped around his horse's legs too.

That made Diocail frown.

Bothan was ready to travel. Something else had prompted the man to stop.

Diocail lifted his hand and waved Bothan forward. "What has ye stopping?"

Bothan tilted his head to one side. "Am I no' welcome? It's snowing."

Diocail sent him a hard look. "And ye are dressed to ride north. Do nae forget, I was raised at Sutherland. This"—he pointed at the fresh covering of white snow—"is no' really deep enough to be called snow. No' by ye anyhow."

Bothan offered him a knowing chuckle. "I knew there was something I liked about ye, Diocail Gordon."

"Come inside," Diocail offered. "Yer gilly looks hungry."

The younger boy assigned to Bothan as his personal gilly bristled under the comment. He was determined to be every bit as tough as the men he rode with. Of course, that was why Diocail chose the lad to make the comment about—his skin wouldn't thicken without a few jabs.

It was the way boys became men.

It was the way of survival.

❧

"Do all witches bar their doors?"

Muir turned around and found young Bari standing near him. "What are ye doing asking a question like that, lad?"

Bari didn't look at the captain but watched Diocail as he and Bothan Gunn walked toward the hall. "Is the laird bewitched because the mistress is English, or is it on account of him going to her bed?" the youngster asked. "Is it sinful to seek out the company of women?"

"Who have ye been listening to?" Muir managed at last, confounded by the child's questions.

"A retainer…I only saw his plaid…he said the mistress barred the door to her chamber so she could practice…dark arts with the laird."

Muir went still, and Kory moved closer. Bari looked between the two men, trying to decide if he'd done something wrong. He lowered his chin and rolled his lower lip in.

Muir was suddenly there on a knee so he was at eye level with Bari. "When did ye hear that being said?"

"Where did this happen?" Kory demanded.

Muir held up a finger to quiet his fellow retainer.

"Ye've done naught wrong." Muir assured Bari. "Telling the truth is no' wrong."

Bari nodded, letting out a sigh of relief. "I was no' spying…at least, I was no' trying to listen in. Me mother always did say that I should no' be hiding inside the house when she and me father were talking about things me ears did nae need to be hearing."

"Yes," Muir agreed. "But tell me again what ye heard."

"Where were ye, lad?" Kory asked.

"In the hall," Bari answered. "One of the hounds has a litter of pups. I was under the table with them, and that is when I heard…one of them asking the first man if he'd had a change of heart."

"About what?" Kory demanded.

Muir shoved him. "Ye're confusing the lad. I'll ask the questions."

"That is all I heard," Bari said in a rush. "They left after that, saying the crops would fail if they did nae

deal with the English witch. Are they going to hurt the mistress?"

"No." Muir stood and rubbed the top of Bari's head. "We'll not be allowing harm to come to her."

"I don't think she looks much like a witch," Bari continued.

"That's because she is no such thing," Kory informed the child.

"Then why is she barring her chamber door?" The child's curiosity wasn't satisfied.

"Because we're a bunch of fools," Muir muttered, shooting Niven a hard look. "Find her and do nae leave her unattended."

Niven nodded, and Bari made to escape from the two men because it seemed as if they were angry.

"Oh, no, lad." Muir grasped him by his small shoulder. "I need ye to come with me."

"Have I chattered?"

Muir smiled at the boy as he started after Diocail. "Ye've done good, lad. Very good indeed."

Bari smiled, but he was soon back to rolling his lower lip in as his laird glared down at him, clearly displeased by what he had to say. Chief Gunn wasn't any more pleased and looked as though he just might reach out and send Bari sprawling with one of his huge hands.

"Well done, lad…"

Bari looked at his laird, baffled by the words of praise compared with the dark look on his face. Perhaps he'd understand when he was older. His mother had said as much many times. He just wished he knew when exactly he would be older.

～

"I've been a fool." Diocail didn't much care who heard him either.

"Ye were no' alone in that," Muir said quietly.

Diocail locked gazes with his captain. "Someone is watching her?"

Muir nodded. "Niven."

"We needs find them." Diocail wasn't comforted by the knowledge. "The lad does nae know the danger he's in."

"I'll go looking for Keefe," Bothan added. "I know what he looks like, and he will nae be keeping an eye out for me."

Diocail nodded, his mind on Jane. A quick glance around the hall confirmed she wasn't anywhere in sight.

He prayed to God he wasn't too late.

～

Dolina stepped back and admired the mirror they had just brought up the stairs. She cut a look over to Jane. "I knew there was a reason I liked ye."

Eachna nodded. "I certainly never thought to see the men scrubbing the passageway."

Jane looked around the chamber where Diocail slept. The laird's personal rooms took up the entire top floor of the second tower. Once inside, you could see every direction from the windows. Which was likely a good thing because the filth inside was astounding, inches thick in places.

Eachna was struggling to remove the canopy covering the master bed.

"Niven, could you please help?" Jane asked.

The retainer was hovering outside the chamber door, likely to make certain she wasn't taking her spite out on Diocail's personal things. Jane looked back to see if he was going to ignore her. Instead he reached up and tugged on the corner of his bonnet.

The respectful gesture stunned her, and she stood frozen for a moment as he went over to look at the canopy. "I'll fetch a few of the lads to help me."

He was gone a moment later, giving Jane a moment to admire the huge mirror they'd brought into the chamber. It was five feet high and mounted in an ornately carved frame. One of the treasures Colum had received at some point and left in the other tower.

Jane smiled at it and the reflection it showed of the bed. Diocail claimed he enjoyed her spirit? Well, she was going to put that to the test.

"Ye are going to make me blush," Dolina exclaimed with a mocking, fanning motion of her hand.

"Doubtful," Jane answered. "Considering you were the one to advise me to stop allowing my husband to think he knows everything."

Husband…

It sounded right, more than right, really.

It seemed almost perfect. Jane was looking forward to making the stubborn Scot apologize to her for thinking her a liar.

He might not do it…

She drew in a stiff breath and refused to listen to the part of her that said he might refuse. Good fortune often came to those who worked hard for it. She fully intended to be rewarded for her tenacity.

Niven returned with Aylin and two others. They tugged on the corners of their caps as they entered. Niven directed them, and within moments they had the entire canopy removed.

"Ye have the right idea, mistress," Aylin remarked as they all got a look at what had accumulated on top of the canopy. Jane shuddered as she caught sight of at least two long-dead mice.

"Best we take that down to the yard…" Dolina muttered.

She and Eachna began to guide the men toward the stairs. They bumped against the walls, the wooden frame making scraping sounds as they made their way down, and Jane laughed.

There was a sense of satisfaction filling her as she realized she was taking charge of the house. Her house.

"I've been looking high and low for ye, Jane."

Diocail was suddenly there, his voice awaking flutters in her belly.

Anticipation.

Doubt.

She decided she was going to hold tight to the first one as he came across the chamber toward her. They had always reacted to each other, and today she enjoyed the sensation, intent on making sure she had years to experience it.

"I am taking the house in hand," she informed him. "If you had seen the top of that canopy, you would be grateful."

Her words confused him for some reason. He seemed to shake out of whatever had sent him looking for her. "I am no' the one who asked for an annulment."

He was exasperated with her, and she decided it was the most welcome sound she'd ever heard. She stuck her finger into the center of his chest as she stepped up close. "I am not the one who doubted your word. But...I can forgive too."

His eyes lit. She watched the elation brighten his face as his hands tightened on her elbows.

"Jane..."

She was intent on his eyes but heard the impact of something on the back of his skull. He staggered toward her, his hands tightening to a painful grip as he fell onto her. She collapsed under his weight, struggling to escape from beneath him before he smothered her. But gaining her freedom didn't bring her any relief.

"Luck is with me today...," Keefe announced in a soft voice. "Ye should have gone back to England, bitch, for I will no' have ye on Gordon land, much less as mistress of this tower."

He'd used the heavy pommel of his dagger to knock Diocail on the back of the head and was now turning the point on her.

She should have been afraid. Instead, she was furious to see Diocail injured, and the need to retaliate rose inside her.

"Do you truly believe no one will question our murder?" She was against the wall, her hands flattened on the stone.

Keefe slowly grinned. "Let them. I will tell one and all that the laird saw ye for what ye are at last and ran ye through."

Jane inched along the wall. Keefe glanced back at

Diocail, and she might have taken that moment to escape, but she couldn't leave Diocail.

"You don't believe he should be laird."

Keefe snapped his attention to her. She slipped another few inches along the wall now that he was focused on her. Anger flickered in his eyes as he stepped toward her.

"He…is no true Gordon." Keefe was following her, intent on making her see his point. "No' that I'd ever expect an Englishwoman to understand the way it is in the Highlands."

"I understand bloodlines." Jane eased further from Diocail's crumpled form. "Is that why you took me away?"

Keefe's lips twisted into a sneer, and he pointed the dagger at her. "Admit ye plan to use yer son to rule this clan."

"I have no son."

"Ye have nae bled since coming to this tower."

Her focus had been solely on gaining as much distance between Diocail and herself, but Keefe's words distracted her. "That does not mean——"

"Everyone knows what it means," Keefe hissed as he rushed her. The tip of the dagger was against her neck, its point slicing into the delicate surface of her skin. "We are nae fools, English! There are those among the laundresses who do nae care for yer plans to rule us any more than I do. They wash yer linens and tell me ye have not bled…" He looked down at where the point of his weapon lodged against her throat, slipping it toward the visible vein on the side of her neck. "I am going to make ye bleed."

She clutched at his wrist, knowing it was a lost cause, but unwilling to surrender her life without a fight. Keefe snickered and then made a strange sound before he was suddenly gone.

Diocail flung the other man away, placing himself between them.

"Thank God," she muttered.

"Stay back, Jane," he warned.

Keefe had regained his balance, tossing the dagger into the air as he began to slowly circle Diocail. Blood was trickling down her neck, but she was more concerned with the rage burning in Keefe's eyes.

"To the door, Jane…now."

Diocail had placed himself between her and Keefe, moving the other man around so the path toward the door was clear.

"But—"

"Go now, woman!" he growled.

Keefe snickered. "Ye see why I am concerned? She is no' biddable."

"She is loyal, something ye know naught about."

Diocail reached down and pulled the dagger from the top of his boot. It was a small one compared to the one Keefe held, but her husband took up a stance between her and the door, clearly intending to defend her escape. The only way she could help him now was to raise the alarm.

She pushed off the wall, propelling herself toward the open chamber door. Keefe lunged after her. She heard Diocail collide with him, the sound of hard flesh meeting making her gasp. It was a horrible thing to know they were intent on killing one another.

Her heart was racing as she took to the stairs. They had not seemed so long before; now she felt as though she couldn't lift her feet fast enough, almost as though they were stuck to the stone. She fought to move faster to somehow stop murder.

"Mistress!"

Niven was around the corner, hooking her about the waist. They both would have tumbled down the last flight if he hadn't taken control of her. He lifted her high, turning with the momentum of her downward flight and placing her on her feet on the step below him.

"What—"

Niven didn't finish his question. His eyes focused on the blood running down her throat, and then Diocail's voice was bouncing through the stairwell.

"Get her out of the way, Niven!"

There was a whirl of motion and a hard grunt as Diocail kicked Keefe in the chest. It sent him tumbling toward her and Niven.

Jane let out a sound of surprise as Niven hoisted her high while moving down the stairs. He'd always struck her as young for a retainer, but he proved just why he'd been allowed to ride with his laird by reacting faster than Jane could manage to think. She was half over his shoulder, bracing her hands so she could remain upright, watching the battle unfolding behind her.

Keefe lunged at Diocail, intent on cutting him in the leg. The light flashed off his blade, her brain noting the detail. A line of blood appeared before Diocail sent Keefe sprawling with a hard blow from his knee to the other man's chin.

And then she was spinning free, Niven releasing her as he let out a shrill whistle. Jane skidded to a stop, her skirts swishing out in front of her. Muir and Kory were running toward her, and her brain felt frozen.

Kory reached her first, locking his hand around a handful of her skirts and jerking her toward him. He moved out of her way, sending her stumbling as he ducked around her and placed himself between her and the fight behind her.

Keefe came tumbling out of the stairwell, cursing and jumping to his feet.

"Ye're no' fit to lead this clan," Diocail informed his opponent. "Sneaking about to do yer dirty work when I offered ye the chance to challenge me fairly before all."

Keefe realized they had an audience. "That was before ye brought an English noble woman here to steal Gordon land."

"Ye're babbling nonsense," Diocail hissed. "A laird is expected to marry for advantage."

Keefe pointed at Jane. "She plans to use her son to take our land after she kills ye!"

Diocail tilted his head to the side. "I want to kill ye for laying me low abovestairs and cutting me wife, but ye sound like a lunatic."

"She has no' bled!" Keefe announced to everyone. He turned in a wide circle. "Ask the laundresses. And she bars her chamber door at night. She is a witch!"

Muir tossed a dagger of the same size as Keefe's toward Diocail. Her husband caught it with an ease that made her shiver.

"No, she's barring her chamber door because I was

too big a fool to listen when she told me someone stole her away." Diocail's tone betrayed his rising rage. "I had faith in me fellow Gordons. Faith that the matter of me being laird was settled and that ye'd be man enough no' to lower yerself to harming a woman."

"It will never be settled so long as ye are laird," Keefe declared.

A dangerous gleam glittered in Diocail's eyes. "Then ye may take up the matter with me, man. Only a coward steals a man's wife or sneaks up behind him. I stood in this very hall and offered ye the chance to challenge me. Man to man. That's the sort of courage I believe the Gordons deserve in a laird, and I will nae have ye wearing me colors."

There was a ripple of agreement from those watching. Keefe didn't care to hear it either. His face darkened as he tightened his grip on his dagger. "I am no' alone in me thinking."

"I'll deal with yer compatriots after I finish ye."

Jane jerked, reading the way Diocail's body drew taunt. The impulse to scream at him to stop was almost too strong to ignore, but she realized that crying out would shame him. Niven was near her, standing half a step in front of her. She dug her hands into her skirts as she quelled the urge to surge forward.

She loved Diocail and had to accept all that he was.

The two men circled, crouching low, gauging each other. They were both hardened and confident. Diocail had no intention of hiding behind his men.

Barbaric.

Savage.

She was quite sure the people in the town where

she'd been raised would have labeled him exactly so. And yet she discovered herself agreeing with Diocail's methods. He did not want to split the clan, so he was risking his own life to ensure that the fight started and ended with him.

She felt a hard grip on her shoulder. Jane only glanced back for a brief moment, but it was enough to see Bothan Gunn.

There was a grunt as Keefe lunged toward Diocail. A sharp sound of metal against metal rang in the air as the two men fought.

Keefe went for the kill. Diocail defended and avoided the plunge of Keefe's blade. Keefe went stumbling past Diocail, making it possible for him to lock the man in a choke hold. Keefe didn't surrender. He thrashed and tossed them both to the ground, the pair grappling in a sweaty mess of muscle and profanity. The daggers were out of reach, but Keefe pulled a smaller knife from his boot, slicing upward and catching Diocail on the side of his arm.

Ruby-red blood spurted onto the floor, the scent of it nauseating her, but what made her want to retch was the fact that it was Diocail's. Bothan's grip tightened on her shoulder, making her press her heels even harder against the floor.

She'd not distract her husband.

Keefe was seething with rage, the need to kill burning in his eyes. By comparison, Diocail looked disgusted as he smashed the man in the back of his knee to cripple him.

"Enough, Keefe!" Diocail growled. "Do nae make me kill ye."

Keefe lifted his head, blood running from his nose. For a moment, he appeared ready to be done with it, his anger spent. Diocail was nodding, the men clustering around them, offering a mutter of approval for the way it all ended.

"It is finished," Diocail announced.

"And witnessed," Bothan Gunn replied.

Diocail looked toward Jane, locking gazes with her. There was a flutter of motion near him as Keefe surged up and off his knees. Her eyes rounded as the light flashed off one of the larger daggers he'd retrieved from the floor.

It was merely a moment, and yet it felt as though it lasted an hour. She watched Diocail read the threat off her face, saw him turning to face the blade. Bothan was pulling her back as Diocail tried to lunge toward Keefe.

Diocail only had time to defend himself, grasping Keefe's hand and turning the blade back on him. The momentum of the attack sent them sprawling onto the floor. There was a dull sound as Keefe landed on the blade. Diocail could only look into the man's eyes as he died.

Jane was certain she would see that moment for the rest of her days. She was horrified, but satisfied too.

She stumbled back as Bothan reached Diocail, pulling Keefe's body off him. Muir and Kory and too many others to name were there as well. Keefe was rolled onto his back, his body flopping onto the floor with a dull sound as his blood seeped around the edges of the blade buried in his chest.

Jane was moving backward, recoiling from the

horror of it all. She lifted her skirts as she turned and climbed the stairs, seeking escape.

⁓

Diocail followed her. The chamber door shut with a soft sound, and Jane turned on him, staring for a moment, soaking up the sight of him as she tried to absorb the fact that he was well and safe.

"It's over, lass…" He came toward her, reaching for her.

She hit him, hammering her fist against his chest. It made a dull sound as tears suddenly flooded her eyes. "How could you take such a chance?"

Jane didn't wait for her demand to be answered. She aimed another blow at Diocail and then a third.

"Jane…" he grunted as she landed her blow, and he wrapped his arms around her, binding her in place.

"Let me…go…" She was straining against his hold, tears streaming down her face as he held firm. "Now."

He turned her loose and jumped back a pace when she lifted her fist. "You should be worried," she informed him. "I want to beat you within an inch of your life for taking such a chance!"

He crossed his arms over his chest and raised an eyebrow at her. "I'm worried ye might do our child harm."

She gasped, shaking, as everything that had just happened seemed to assault her all at once. "I am not with child."

At least she hadn't really thought about it. But she did now, standing still as she considered how long she had been at the towers.

"Jane?"

Absorbed by her thoughts, she jumped and blinked as he asked the question. Diocail took the moment to move close to her, reaching out to stroke her cheek gently. His touch made her tingle, awakening life inside her, as spring did when it drove winter away.

She closed her eyes, savoring the feeling. "You have no right to take issue with me when you are the one who just risked his life."

Diocail's expression tightened, his gaze lowering to her neck as he lifted her chin. "He...drew...yer... blood."

Each word was tight and edged with rage. He stepped closer, his fingers still beneath her chin as he locked gazes with her. "I was a fool no' to believe ye, and I will fight a hundred men if that is what it takes for this clan to understand they will never touch ye." He stroked her cheek. "Ye are mine, Jane."

No words had ever pleased her more. She trembled with joy, feeling it wash through her like a flood.

"Do ye forgive me?"

His tone was stern and guarded, but it was the look in his eyes that sent fresh tears spilling down her cheeks.

Diocail Gordon needed her to forgive him.

She witnessed the truth in his eyes. He suddenly lowered himself to his knee, wrapping his arms around her and pressing his head against her lower body.

"Forgive me, lass...I've too much pride."

She smoothed his hair back, her fingers shaking. "I do...I love you."

He looked up at her, stunning her with the glitter of tears in his eyes. He drew his hands around her

body, gently settling one over her belly. "Are ye carrying, Jane?"

The note of hope in his voice made her wish she might answer him with a yes. "It's really too soon to know...for certain. My courses might simply be late."

His lips curled into a huge grin. He pressed a kiss against her belly before rising. "But ye are late!"

He was suddenly moving across the chamber. He reached for the chamber door and yanked it open. Aylin and Niven stood there, both jumping at the suddenness of the door moving. They regained their poise quickly, tugging on the corner of their caps.

"Ring the bells!" Diocail announced. "We are going to have a child."

"Diocail!" Jane ran after him, clutching at his arm. "Do not. I am not certain."

Niven stopped two steps down, looking back at them. Her husband looped his arm around her waist and pulled her close, turning to nuzzle her neck. "In that case...best we make very, very...certain."

Her face went up in flames as she heard his men chuckle.

"Have you no shame?" she demanded as he scooped her up and walked her back toward his huge bed. She heard the door closing behind them as Diocail settled her.

"With ye? No' a shred." He pressed a kiss against her mouth, one that warmed her to her core and drove the worry from her at last.

"And I like the gift..."

Her thoughts scattered by his kiss, Jane blinked as she tried to decide what he was talking about. Diocail

grinned, a wolfish, arrogant curving of his lips that was joined by a flash of anticipation in his eyes.

"A fine place for it as well."

She gasped and then giggled. The mirror. It stood where she'd had it placed, where it afforded them a fine reflection of themselves on the bed.

"And ye, my English flame…ye have no shame either." He was seeking out the tie that held her bodice closed, his fingers delving between her cleavage.

She reached out and touched him on the chin. "No, husband. What that mirror means is that I was determined to make this union work in spite of your stubbornness."

He popped the knot on the lace, and she felt her breasts push the front of her bodice open. Anticipation filled her, heating her blood with the need to be joined with him.

"I am a Highlander…stubborn is part of me nature…" He reached into her open bodice and cupped her breasts. "But I'll apply meself to demonstrating it in more…pleasing ways, wife."

He brushed her nipples, making her breathless.

"See that you do…husband."

❦

A week later, Diocail got his wish to have the bells rung.

Jane rose from bed and only had time to dash to the garderobe before she was heaving up the contents of her belly. The effort was intense, leaving her sweating in spite of the chill in the air. Every muscle she had was quivering as she emerged to be swept against her husband's hard body.

"Ye're carrying!" he declared in a tone rich with happiness. He turned them around in circles before laying her on their bed. He backed up a step, fixing her with a glance that looked very much like he was attempting to memorize the sight of her there on the bed.

"I love ye."

It was a solemn declaration. For a moment, she didn't feel worthy, and then she realized what she truly felt was complete. The phrase *soul mate* had never really had meaning until that moment.

"As I love you."

He winked at her, turning around to find his shirt before he wrenched open the chamber doors. She let out a little shriek as she dove into the rumpled bedding because she was only wearing her chemise.

"Ring the bells, lad!" he announced to the retainer standing outside the door. "We're going to have a child."

The retainer grinned and set off down the stairs. Diocail turned and curled his finger at her. "Out of bed with ye, Jane."

She slowly smiled. "Yes, it would seem this marriage duty has been seen to."

Diocail's smile faded. "And just what do ye mean by that, woman?" He knew exactly what she was hinting at. He propped his hands on his hips and glowered at her. "Now maybe in England…" He stressed the name of the country. "Maybe in England, couples sleep apart while the wife is with child, but this is Scotland."

She crawled out of bed, walking toward him as the morning sunlight cut through the thin fabric of

her chemise. It really was too lightweight a fabric for the season, but the chill was nothing compared to the thrill she experienced when his lips curved in the sensuous manner that made her quiver.

"Scotland…" She purred, exactly the way Brenda had. "Yes, you do have some very interesting customs here…"

"We do," Diocail responded, joining in her teasing as he settled his hands on her hips. "We like to please our wives…very, very, often. So do nae be thinking to leave me bed."

"Hmmm," she muttered before backing away from him as the bells began to ring. It started with one, and then more of the large brass bells mounted on the walls began to fill the morning air with their sound. The news spread fast, and it wasn't long before the bell in the village church was toiling as well.

Diocail picked up a length of wool and draped it over her shoulders. A few moments later, they had company. The women clustered around her as Muir and his men slapped Diocail on the shoulder.

"Dolina," Jane muttered, raising her voice so that Diocail was sure to hear. "My husband had warned me that Scottish customs are different than English ones."

"It is a fact." Dolina's lips twitched as she fought back a smile because she knew her mistress was making ready to toy with her husband.

"Is it true that the father of the child must wear a dress while his wife is in labor to confuse the demons who might wish to steal the unbaptized child's soul?"

Dolina made a scoffing sound under her breath as she tried to swallow her mirth. "It is very true, and all

of his friends…" She raised her voice to make sure it was heard. "Must appear to be midwives."

"That is no' the custom I was talking about, Jane."

Jane turned and sent her husband a feigned look of innocence that made Muir choke. But Diocail's eyes were glittering with happiness, and she knew without a doubt hers were as well.

❦

Symon Grant used the long winter months to deal with the letters that needed his attention.

"Still at it?" Brenda asked from the doorway of the study.

Symon looked up, his chin shaved clean now, even if there was a lingering sadness in his eyes. His wife was long dead, but she seemed to remain in his heart.

"Only because I have failed to make a choice," Symon confessed as he pressed his hands flat on the desktop and rose from his chair. He was staring down at two letters.

Brenda moved forward, intent on somehow lending comfort as he tried to confront the very distasteful duty of selecting a bride. There were also two miniatures with the letters, each one showing a girl of the right age for marriage.

"For all that I selected Tara in this very manner, it leaves me cold this time," he grumbled before walking away.

Brenda peered at the letters, but they were equally well composed, listing the attributes of each girl. But something else gained her attention. It was a letter

Symon had pushed off to the side with her name clearly written on it.

Symon was stretching his back. It popped, and he rolled his shoulders before he realized what she'd taken off his desk. "That intrigues you."

Brenda jumped, startled because she'd been absorbed in reading the letter. "No' a bit."

Symon's eyes narrowed. "Ye're the one who told me we both needed to start living again, Brenda."

The truth was the Grant castle was a silent place, inhabited by too many ghosts. They were the last of their line, Brenda and Symon.

Brenda's eyes flashed. "I agreed ye needed yer backside kicked. Niul McTavish was here and did exactly that. Ye are laird."

"And ye are me cousin," Symon continued as though she hadn't argued with him. "And we are the last of our line. Niul McTavish made the point that both of us need to start living again."

"I am me own woman, by yer father's decree when he died." Brenda was so passionate the letter crumbled in her grasp. She looked down at it and scowled before tossing it back onto the desk. "Bothan Gunn can find himself another bride. I will no' wed him."

"Ye are yer own woman. I promised me father on his deathbed I would no' force ye to wed." Symon perched himself on the corner of the desk. "Just as I am laird, and no one can force me to wed."

Brenda let out a little sound. "It's yer duty."

"And yet no' yers?" Symon tsked at her. "As the only other member of our line, I argue with ye, Cousin. For I have tried, and still there is no heir."

"Argue as ye like." Brenda moved away from the desk. "It will do ye no good. I have had all of marriage that I ever wish to experience. Ye do nae promise obedience when ye wed. A woman does."

"I saw ye with him."

Brenda stopped halfway to the door of the study. For a moment, it appeared she was going to continue on, but she turned to look back at Symon.

"I saw ye talking to Bothan at the festival." Symon slowly grinned. "Ye blushed."

"It was a warm day," she exclaimed before she turned and left with a snap of her skirt because she took the turn around the doorway so quickly.

Symon reached down and picked up the letter from Bothan Gunn. The man was direct, but the wording of the letter didn't really ask for permission to court Brenda.

Symon slowly grinned. No, Bothan had informed Symon of his intentions. It made Symon chuckle, something he realized he hadn't done enough of since losing his wife.

Four years. The time seemed to vanish, and Niul McTavish had been correct in telling him and Brenda that Grant Castle had become a place of tears and lament.

Symon looked back at the letter from Bothan Gunn and nodded before he reached over and rang a small bell. It took a few minutes for a maid to come into the doorway and lower herself.

"Take this to Mistress Brenda's chambers and leave it on her pillow."

Senga had served in the castle for a long time. She

boldly looked at the letter before she sent him an amused look. "This will warm things up for certain."

Symon flashed her a grin. "Me hope exactly."

She clicked her tongue before lowering herself again. A ring of keys hung from her belt, declaring her high position in the household. "I'll be sure to see there are a few sets of clean sheets waiting for yer bed."

Symon frowned.

"Because I wager yer cousin is going to pour salt in yer bed after finding this on her pillow."

Symon snorted, amused even by the idea of his cousin's spite.

Yes, it was time to have life back in the castle. He sat down and concentrated on the two miniatures with a renewed interest.

~

"Ye are blessed beyond words to be able to birth yer babes in so little time." Dolina shook her head, sending Jane a slightly envious look.

"Me mother was like that," Eachna remarked as she handed the new baby to Jane. "All her babes came just like yers. Quick and fierce."

Jane was leaning back in the birthing chair, sweat on her forehead, but now that her baby was breathing, the pain didn't seem nearly as bad. It was all dissipating in the rush of meeting her son. How he'd arrived wasn't nearly as important as the fact that he was there.

She'd known she was going to have a baby, but she was astonished to gaze on the tiny little miracle her child was. Seeing his little chest expand with breath

filled her with more faith in life than she had ever imagined she'd experience.

There was a cry from down the hall. Dolina went to the chamber doors, opening them only enough to slip through. She came back a few moments later. Her face was turning purple as she held in her amusement long enough to make it across the chamber to where Jane sat with her baby. "They are still down there, every last one of them in skirts, while yer husband is acting as if he is giving birth."

"We should tell them the baby is here," Jane said.

"Do nae ye dare," Eachna reprimanded her. "We have nae had this much entertainment in years."

Jane lost interest in everything else as her son opened his eyes and looked at her. His head was covered in dark hair, and the women had encouraged her to pull her breast free from her partlet so he might lay his cheeks against it. He moved his hand, placing his tiny fingers on her skin, and she was fairly certain nothing had ever felt so perfect in her life.

❧

"Ye're no' doing it right," Muir exclaimed.

Diocail grunted and straightened. "Fine. Show me how since ye seem to know so much."

Someone cleared his throat, and Diocail looked up to see Sorley standing near the door to the hall. Bothan Gunn was there beside the man, his lips slowly curving as he took in Diocail and his men.

"Laird Diocail Gordon?" Bothan questioned.

Diocail grunted as Muir dug out the two bowls he'd stuffed into his jerkin to look like breasts.

"Aye," Diocail replied, offering the man his hand. "I am surprised to see ye."

The man's gaze swept him from head to toe, taking in the makeshift dress Diocail was wearing. "Clearly."

Diocail only shrugged and slapped him on the shoulder. "Ye're in time to raise a toast to me babe."

"Ye do nae say son?" Bothan asked as he walked with Diocail toward the high ground.

Diocail left a trail of discarded costume pieces as he went. "Lad or lass, all that matters is Jane coming through it strong and healthy." Diocail shot him a hard look. "That's the only thing I pray to God for."

One of the maids served them as Diocail kept a watch on the stairwell. Women came and went with baskets of linens and kettles of water, but they didn't stop to look at him. Young Bari was perched on a stool, looking up the stairs as he worried his lower lip.

"What has ye riding south?"

Bothan slowly grinned. "Brenda Grant."

That distracted Diocail from his worry. "From what I hear, the woman enjoys being unbridled, and Symon swore to his dying father he would no' make her wed against her wishes."

Bothan lowered his mug. "So I hear as well."

Diocail's lips curved into a wide grin. "I wish ye luck, man, for I believe ye'll need it."

Bothan raised his mug toward Diocail. "Ye're the first man who has no' tried to talk me into a more biddable female."

"Where is the fun in that?"

"Exactly me thoughts," Bothan replied. "Exactly so."

"Dolina is waving, Laird!" Bari chirped as he took off up the stairs.

Diocail sent his chair back so fast it hit the wall. Bothan watched him go, trying to decide if it wouldn't be wiser to turn around and ride north before he was as smitten as Diocail clearly was.

Bothan stayed where he was because he'd had a long, cold winter and all of the planting season to try to shake Brenda Grant from his thoughts.

She was still there, so he was going to face her and the strange way she affected him.

❧

The chamber was quiet at last.

So many people had been in and out. Jane drew in a deep breath now that only Diocail was there with their son. The scent of amber and rosemary lingered from the herbs the midwives insisted on using to purify the chamber. Everything had been cleared away, including the birthing chair. She was sore but content as she felt Diocail crawl onto the bed next to her.

"I didn't think to see Bothan Gunn here again, much less intent on courting Brenda Grant."

Diocail's tone was hushed as he lay in the bed next to Jane. Their son was falling asleep on her breast, his lips locked around her nipple.

"Or that he'd catch ye wearing a dress?" Jane mocked softly.

Diocail pointed at her. "That was yer doing, madam."

"You think because I'm English I can't jest?"

Her husband grunted and sent her an annoyed look. Jane snickered, sealing her lips so the only sounds

that made it out were half-smothered ones. They both looked down at the baby, but he was well asleep. Diocail gathered him up as gently as he might an egg and settled him in his cradle next to Jane's side of the bed.

The weather was fine and warm now, and when Diocail lay down behind her, pulling her close while they both listened to the sound of their son's breathing, everything was perfect.

Fate could be reasonable after all, it would seem. Love, although very difficult to understand, seemed worth the effort.

Diocail smoothed Jane's hair back, settling his head on top of hers. The strong beat of his heart was against her back, and the warm breath of their son touched her fingers where she had them resting next to his head.

Yes, perfect.

So very, very perfect.

❦

She should have burned it.

Brenda glanced at the letter, wondering once again why it was still in her chamber. Did she want him to come? Was that it?

Would it be so terrible?

She avoided answering that question. She thrust the letter aside in favor of contemplating other tasks. Running the castle was a huge responsibility, and she'd risen to the occasion since Symon had no wife. Of course, now that spring was past and the crops were in the ground, Symon would be attending to the duties of securing himself a wife.

It was expected.

And yet she found herself contemplating how her life would change once he brought a bride home. That did not mean she was contemplating Bothan's offer.

She turned around and looked at the letter once more. It wasn't even an offer. It was a declaration of his intention to court her in the summer.

Well, she had plenty of intentions of her own, and none of them included being claimed by the Gunn chief. She would not wear the shackles of marriage ever again.

Not even for love.

About the Author

Mary Wine is a multi-published author in romantic suspense, fantasy, and Western romance. Her interest in historical reenactment and costuming inspired her to turn her pen to historical romance with her popular Highlander series. She lives with her husband and sons in Southern California, where the whole family enjoys participating in historical reenactment.